Advance praise for April Dá

"An engrossing and original tale of love, betrayal, and extremely large birds, April Dávila's *142 Ostriches* is a novel that blooms like springtime in the California desert. Fiercely independent, brave, and tender, Tallulah Jones is a heroine for our time."
—Seth Greenland, author of *The Hazards of Good Fortune*

"Vividly imagined and deeply felt, *142 Ostriches* is an utterly absorbing tale of an intrepid young woman coming of age in the California desert. I loved Dávila's big-hearted debut about land, family, and the ties that bind. Highly recommended."
—Lindsey Lee Johnson, author of *The Most Dangerous Place on Earth*

"*142 Ostriches* is unlike anything I've read before. Wholly unique, this cinematic novel exposes readers to the relatively unknown industry of ostrich farming. In Dávila's skillful hands, the desert comes alive and the ostriches are as compelling as the human characters. Tallulah herself is a memorable, strong-willed protagonist. Her struggle to negotiate family obligations with her own desires feels both singular and highly relatable. I loved following her through the pages of this fast-paced and lovely novel."
—Amy Meyerson, author of *The Bookshop of Yesterdays*

"April Dávila has made the rare thing: The perfect meeting of plot and character. A hurtling adventure of family intrigue helmed by a heroine for the ages, Dávila's novel will make your heart swell as big as an ostrich egg, and then hatch it."
—Katie Williams, author of *Tell the Machine Goodnight*

Please turn the page for more advance praise!

"Dávila's observant prose conjures the drama of sun-scorched days and the calm of cool painted evenings as it chronicles the struggles and rewards of a rugged life in the vast Mohave. This is a story that envelops you with a sense of place, and uses its setting to reveal how the human heart, like wildflowers after a rampaging storm, can thrive in the harshest conditions. It is a tale as surprising and delightful as a profusion of florid color in the sandy stretches of the California desert."
—Yvonne Puig, author of *A Wife of Nobel Character*

"*142 Ostriches*, April Dávila's utterly unique novel, nails the *Zeitgeist* when she inherits a Death Valley bird ranch she'd hoped to escape. An avian Greek chorus, the birds seem to observe and share her longing *to stand in a place of my own choosing.* With unsentimental acuity, her narrator confronts the intangible covenant foisted upon her, and the reality that the disposal of her flock, from *nature to product,* is by no means a matter just for the birds."
—Rita Williams, author of *If the Creek Don't Rise*

"An unusual ranching tale set in the Mojave Desert, where the herd is a flock of eight-foot-tall birds and their wrangler a young woman raised by her gruff grandmother who dreams of another kind of life. A twisty, warmhearted story of family, community and fate, a thoroughgoing delight."
—Janet Fitch, author of *The Revolution of Marina M* and *Chimes of a Lost Cathedral*

"Compelling and beautifully written—you need to read this book."
—Erin La Rosa, author of *The Big Redhead Book* and *Womanskills*

142 OSTRICHES

April Dávila

KENSINGTON BOOKS
www.kensingtonbooks.com

This book is a work of fiction. Names, characters, places, and incidents either are products of the author's imagination or are used fictitiously. Any resemblance to actual persons, living or dead, events, or locales is entirely coincidental.

KENSINGTON BOOKS are published by

Kensington Publishing Corp.
119 West 40th Street
New York, NY 10018

All Kensington titles, imprints, and distributed lines are available at special quantity discounts for bulk purchases for sales promotion, premiums, fund-raising, and educational or institutional use.

Special book excerpts or customized printings can also be created to fit specific needs. For details, write or phone the office of the Kensington Sales Manager: Kensington Publishing Corp., 119 West 40th Street, New York, NY 10018. Attn. Sales Department. Phone: 1-800-221-2647.

ISBN-13: 978-1-4967-2470-0
ISBN-10: 1-4967-2470-4
First Kensington Trade Paperback Edition: March 2020

ISBN-13: 978-1-4967-2471-7 (ebook)
ISBN-10: 1-4967-2471-2 (ebook)
Kensington Electronic Edition: March 2020

10 9 8 7 6 5 4 3 2 1

Printed in the United States of America

For Daniel

if I were to leave this desert
who would cherish transparent
light who would nurse broken stones
who would mother the cold

—Richard Shelton

ONE

Four days before the ostriches stopped laying eggs, Grandma Helen died in an accident that wasn't really an accident. It was a Sunday, when almost everyone was in church, when the only other trucks on Route 66 were bigger than hers, their immense grilles roaring toward her, then escaping one after another, until a tomato trailer out of Sacramento proved too enticing.

She had nowhere to be, no appointment to keep, no need that would require a drive through the heat of the Mojave in July. She hadn't called up the stairs to ask if I needed anything from town. The last thing I heard of her was the rasp of her keys as she scooped them from the counter, the bang of the screen door as she left. Then nothing until the phone rang hours later.

"Tallulah?" The deep voice on the other end of the line hesitated. "It's Sheriff Morris. I hate to tell you this over the phone," he said, "but I wanted you to hear it from me." And I knew. Just like that. In my mind, I could see Grandma Helen's thick hands urging her pickup over the double yellow lines of the narrow highway. I felt the perfect silence that filled the cab, the way time slowed down in the moments before everything exploded in twisted metal.

"You all right?"

The afternoon light drifted in through faded yellow curtains. The tawny tile of the kitchen countertops gleamed. "Yeah," I said. "I mean . . . no. Thank you for calling." I hung up. The walls of the small kitchen pressed in around me. My chest ached.

I pushed through the front door and sank onto the steps overlooking the rolling expanse of desert. The hot, dry air outside burned my throat and seared my lips. In the corral, the ostriches strolled past one another, their long, meaty legs unfolding with each graceful stride. Our old border collie, Henley, trotted by on his way to his favorite cool spot in the barn. The leaves of the walnut tree whispered in a faint, hot breeze. And still she was gone.

How strange that one phone call from a man I barely knew could all but erase my grandmother from my life. I half expected her to emerge from the barn, rubbing at the crease between her eyebrows with her knuckle and grumbling about mice in the food stores. But she didn't.

The sun crept toward the violet crags of the San Gabriel Mountains in the west. The light tilted and shadows stretched. Eventually, my aunt Christine's minivan came up the half mile of gravel that was our driveway and parked in the shade of the walnut tree.

Eight months pregnant, she slid down from the driver's seat the way honey falls from a spoon. She gripped the frame of the van until she was steady on her feet, then turned to me with her arms wide. "Tallulah, sweetheart." She wore a draping dress with pale pink flowers on it, the fabric stretched taut over her belly.

I let her envelop me in a hug. Tears rolled down my cheeks. She patted my back. "It's okay," she said, though we both knew it wasn't.

She put her arm around my waist and marched me into the kitchen, where she filled the kettle with water. The weather was far too hot for tea, but the chill of the air conditioning indoors seemed to make space for it, and the death of the family matriarch called for chamomile. Aunt Christine moved with utter assuredness, as if the news of Grandma Helen's death had come with a set of instructions.

Sipping our tea at the kitchen table, the two of us could have passed for sisters. She was only six years older than me. A surprise baby, born after Grandma Helen thought her years of childbearing were over. I had been a less welcome surprise, conceived before my mom even finished high school. My hair hung longer than Aunt Christine's, bleached a brighter blond by the sun, and my skin held a deeper tan for the same reason, but the oval shape of our faces, the thin lips, the arching, nearly invisible eyebrows—in those ways we were almost identical.

She pulled the tea bag from her mug and dropped it in the trash, leaning over her belly to see that it landed true. Still moving with that sense of purpose, she rummaged around until she found Grandma Helen's address book, an ancient thing with a row of gold letters on little black tabs. She flipped to the D tab, marked her place with a manicured finger, and dialed.

"Lizzie," she said, "it's Christine, Helen's daughter. I'm afraid I have some sad news. There's been an accident." Her voice cracked a little as she explained, repeating what the sheriff had told me.

I stared at the untouched mug growing cold in my hands and listened as she called a dozen people, explaining over and over about the accident. I grew more skeptical every time I heard the word.

Grandma Helen had convinced me, after I graduated from Victorville High, not to go off to college like my friends. She even gave me a small raise for my work on the ranch, and at first I gloated about making money while my friends all took on debt, but as time went by and I saw online that they were making their way in the world while I continued to do the same shit I'd done for years, I got antsy.

I applied for a job with the Forest Service but didn't say anything about it to Grandma Helen. Not until they asked me to come in for an interview. When I did break the news, she dropped her fork midmeal and left the room. We didn't even argue. I cleaned her plate along with mine and reminded myself that I'd known she would be upset. It would pass.

Her objections ticked up a notch after I passed the physical exam for the job. She stubbornly insisted that she needed me on the ranch. When I argued she could hire someone to do my job—and for less—she grew sullen, hardly speaking to me for days.

It wasn't until my final acceptance letter arrived, telling me I'd been temporarily assigned to a fire prevention handcrew in Montana, that her anger boiled to the surface and we argued about it. And the very next day there I was, sipping tea and listening to my aunt inform everyone of the accident that had taken Grandma Helen's life. Accident my ass. She had wanted me to stay, and when I said no, she put everything in my hands and bailed, knowing I was the only one who could run the ranch in her absence. It was a dirty trick.

Three days passed in a flurry of activity. I kept my head down and my opinions to myself through meetings with the funeral director and with Grandma Helen's lawyer. No one was terribly surprised to learn that she'd left the ranch to me. None of her three children had any interest in it. Still, everything had to be made official. Paperwork had to be signed and local acquaintances needed to know when and where we would be mourning, as if these things followed a schedule.

While Aunt Christine arranged everything, I struggled to keep up with the work on the ranch by myself. The flock could lay dozens of eggs every day in the hot summer months of the peak season. Each egg had to be collected, washed, polished, and stacked in cold storage for eventual shipping out to specialty grocery stores all over the country. Without Grandma Helen, it was difficult to keep up.

It used to be that we had a routine. Grandma Helen would lure a hen off her nest with a handful of grain while I swiped the eggs and loaded them into the wheelbarrow, and then we prepped them for shipping together. Now I had to do it all myself, and it was even harder than I had anticipated.

The third morning after Grandma Helen's supposed accident, I parked the wheelbarrow next to one of the nests and dug some grain from a zippered pouch on my belt. I clicked my tongue the way Grandma Helen always did, and the dust-colored hen lifted her head toward me, her big eyes focused on my cupped hand. She reached with her serpentine neck and I pulled away. Ostrich nests aren't like the nests of smaller birds, with twigs and grass like a finch would build. An ostrich nest is simply a circular indentation in the sand with a ridge pushed up around it to keep the eggs from rolling away.

The hen leaned side to side to get her legs under her and rose up, a feathered balloon, revealing three eggs the size of footballs. Soft dust clung to the creamy white shells. She strode toward me and I retreated. When she cleared the nest, I dropped the grain and rushed to collect the eggs, but I was only able to grab one before the hen returned and snapped at me, giving my arm a sharp pinch before she settled down onto the two remaining eggs. I cursed, shaking my arm against the pain, and began again. It took me eight frustrating hours to do a chore that would have taken two with Grandma Helen.

At the end of the day, I stormed into the house with my arms covered in red welts and flopped into a chair at the kitchen table. It was stupid trying to run the ranch on my own.

Aunt Christine had taken over the kitchen to prepare for the funeral reception that would bring everyone to the house the next day. She set paper napkins in tidy piles on either end of the table and wiped down the counters.

"Don't touch anything," she said. "I'll get you something to eat." She opened the refrigerator a crack and held up both hands to keep the foil trays of lasagna and spaghetti from falling out. Ever since news got out about the accident, people I hardly knew had been showing up on my doorstep with offerings of pastas and casseroles. Aunt Christine's church friends mostly.

She slid a plate across the table to me: linguine in a pine-green pesto sauce. My hunger hadn't registered until I took the first salty bite. My mood lightened a little as the food filled my stomach, but my arms continued to throb where the birds had nipped at me.

While Aunt Christine was pulling mugs from the cupboard and stacking them near the coffeepot, I dragged Grandma Helen's address book across the table and flipped to J. The first entry was for Joe Jared of the JJ Ostrich Operation out of Yuma. I stared down at the name, written in my grandmother's elegant cursive, tall and sloped to the right. Joe Jared had been salivating over the ranch for decades. With our land, he could increase his production by fifty percent while lowering his delivery costs to his primary market in Las Vegas. Every few years he sent a purchase offer that Grandma Helen rejected without even reading. I didn't have to be stuck on the ranch, no matter what Grandma Helen had thought. There was one more card I could play.

But even thinking of selling brought on guilt. If Grandma Helen had wanted the ranch sold off, the money evenly distributed among her children and grandchildren, she would have said so in her will. She'd left it to me because I could do the work. I knew how to manage the birds and was familiar enough with the billing that I could figure it out. She trusted that I would carry on with the business.

Aunt Christine continued to bustle around the kitchen, arranging plastic forks and spoons upright in cups on the counter, little bouquets of disposable flatware.

I let my finger trace down the page of the address book. Below the entry for Joe Jared, the page was a smudged mess dedicated to my mom. The first entry for Laura Jones was logged in ink. The address—some crappy apartment in Hollywood—was scratched out with three efficient blue lines; in the margin was my name, with my birthday written in tiny print underneath.

The next entry was in pencil, erased and rewritten so many times that the page had developed a small hole and my grandmother had been forced to use a third entry for my mother. That one had also been erased and rewritten so many times that it would be worn through soon. I wasn't even sure if the Oakland address we had for my mom was current. Usually, she called to let us know when she moved, but sometimes it took her a while. Over the years, her cell phone number had become the most reliable thing about her.

"You called to tell her about tomorrow, right?" my aunt asked. She had come up behind me without my noticing. I startled and flipped shut the address book.

"Yeah," I said. When I'd called my mom, she had sounded upset but not devastated. Her exact words were "Oh, shit." She dutifully took down the address of the church where the funeral would be held and said she would come. It was the same well-these-things-happen attitude that everyone had, and I wanted to scream at them all. Grandma Helen had had a full life, yes, but it wasn't supposed to be over. She had checked out and abandoned us all. No one understood that but me.

Aunt Christine plucked her oversize purse from the kitchen table and slung the strap over her shoulder. "I'll pick you up at ten. Please be ready."

"Uh-huh," I said absentmindedly, opening the address book

again after Aunt Christine wedged herself out the front door. As soon as I heard her engine cough to life, I dialed Joe Jared's number.

"Helen Jones," he said when he answered, apparently reading off his caller ID. His voice came through with such force that I recoiled from the receiver, a tickle boring deep inside my ear.

"No," I said, bringing the phone closer so I could speak. "It's her granddaughter, Tallulah." We had never met. I felt cold, but my palm was sweating against the receiver. "Are you still interested in buying our ranch?"

I was taking that job in Montana.

TWO

The next morning, I got up early to collect as many eggs as I could before the funeral. Joe Jared had been excited to get my phone call, but until all the details of the sale were worked out, the chores that made up my daily life on the ranch would need to be attended to.

The sky hung heavy with the scent of a coming storm. Rain was a rare and welcome thing in the desert. Soon, the low clouds would open up as if sliced from below with a blade. A deluge would fall for an hour, maybe two, soaking the parched land and setting everything to sparkle. I loved rainy days. Everybody did. Giddy children would dance in the streets with their heads thrown back, and the adults would gather in grateful clusters to agree on how much we needed the water. Nobody owned an umbrella.

Wrestling the wheelbarrow from the barn, I shoved it through the sand to the center of the corral. The metal grate at the base of the elevated grain silo came open with a clunk, and the ostriches all swiveled their heads. The bird feed slid down a metal sluice into the trough below, and the birds gravitated toward their breakfast.

I ducked out of the way, daydreaming about Montana, where I wouldn't spend my days being pecked at by aggressive birds that outweighed me by two hundred pounds. Up and down my arms, the welts they'd given me held every shade of bruise. I planned to collect the eggs while the ostriches were preoccupied with their meal, hoping to avoid as many nips as possible, but as they rose to their feet, I saw that the nests were all empty. All except one, in which a solitary egg rested on its side.

Confused, I scooped it from the nest. It was warm and had a good weight to it. I scanned the floor of the corral for the distinct white curves of the eggs, but there were none except the one in my hand. I cradled the egg in my arm and walked the full length of the corral, taking in one empty nest after another. The sandy rings looked like little blast marks left in the wake of some bloodless battle.

Over at the feed trough, the birds reached past one another with their long necks to poke at the grain below with quick, deliberate jabs, the way my aunt would check the temperature of a pan by tapping at it. Outwardly, everything was as expected.

From the far end of the corral, I watched as the birds finished eating and drifted away from the empty feed trough, dispersing into the corral. The hens loped to their nests and settled their desert-brown bodies precisely as they did every day. There was nothing unusual about the birds. In fact, once the hens sat down, hiding their empty nests, I almost doubted myself, but the weight of that one single egg told me I wasn't imagining things.

My thoughts went immediately to the conversation I'd had with Joe Jared the night before. He had been eager to move ahead with the purchase of the ranch, but I had no doubt he would back out of the deal if something was wrong with the ostriches. Not that he cared about the eggs as product. He ran a meat and leather operation, hatching the eggs and raising the chicks for slaughter. But he needed eggs all the same.

Can't run an ostrich ranch without ostrich eggs.

Still carrying the one egg in the crook of my arm, I took hold of the beak of a nearby female to check for signs of sickness. Her feathers fluffed in protest and she shifted on her nest, but I held firm and she allowed me to pull her face close to inspect for congestion or sticky eyes or anything that might signal a sickness of any kind. There was nothing. I checked one of the males too, but by all outward appearances, they were in perfect health.

I climbed up the feed silo ladder to inspect the grain for rot, thinking maybe the lack of eggs was due to a problem with the birds' food, but there was nothing wrong there. I even took a sip from their water trough, testing for a bitter taste or funny smell. The water was cool and clean. Of course, I knew there were things I wouldn't be able to detect, but subtle toxins would take time to do damage. I couldn't explain the sudden stop of egg production over one night. It didn't make sense. Nothing appeared amiss. Nothing except the lack of eggs.

I was still trying to figure it out when I saw my aunt's minivan approaching. I delivered the lone egg to the cold storage unit and hurried inside to change.

At the beep of Aunt Christine's horn, I emerged in a recently purchased, black cotton sack of a dress that was too tight in the shoulders but mercifully covered the bruises on my arms. I climbed into the passenger seat. Aunt Christine wore an elegant black maternity dress with a satin V-neck. She gave my dirty boots a sideways glance but said nothing.

My cousins sat subdued in the two rows of seats behind me, clad in matching black dresses. The oldest had been a baby when I came to live on the ranch, the center of attention in every room. Then, just as she took her first steps, the second was born, then the third, fourth, and fifth, dividing the family's adoration until they ceased to be individuals and became simply "the girls." Five babies seemed like plenty to me, but then, after a gap of several years, Aunt Christine announced that God had seen fit to bless their family once again. Another girl.

My aunt, burdened with the weight of that sixth pregnancy, leaned into the steering wheel with determination. It was a miracle she could even reach the pedals considering how far she'd put her seat back to accommodate her extended middle. She threw the minivan into gear. "After the service," she said, the van rumbling over the gravel drive, "I need you to collect the photo of your grandma. I had it framed. I'll collect the flowers and the urn." Her energy for funeral planning was impressive, but that was what Aunt Christine did. She took care of things. She was good at it.

I gave a worried backward glance at my birds as we drove away from the property, wondering again at the lack of eggs and nursing a hope that the empty nests were a fluke. In the distance, the tips of the mountains scraped a gray ceiling. The minivan zipped along under the somber sky.

Aunt Christine counted off the people she expected to attend the reception at the ranch, grouping them by family. "That's nine cars," she said. "I told them all to park against the corral fence so we don't block anyone in. Hopefully, this rain will hold off until we get everyone inside." She leaned forward, straining over her belly, to peer up at the sky through the windshield. "I've got coffee set to brew, and a couple of the ladies from the church will make sure folks get enough to eat." She glanced over at me. "All you have to do is smile and be polite."

"I can be polite," I said.

On our left, PFX Cement rose up out of the earth with its five industrial silos and three enormous geodesic domes. A twisted tower of massive tubing climbed twice as tall as the silos, surrounded by scaffolding that never came down but somehow managed to appear temporary. My boyfriend worked for the company but had traded in a vacation day to join me at the funeral.

"Devon coming?" Aunt Christine asked, as if reading my thoughts.

I nodded. Devon brought a welcome balance to Aunt Christine's structured tension. It was comforting to know that he would be at the church.

We came to Sombra and breezed through the only stoplight, continuing on into the expanse of desert surrounding the small town. Eventually the scrappy desert brush and rolling hills gave way to the tract homes and strip malls of Victorville. The sky was holding when we arrived at the High Desert Oasis United Church of Christ, but I could smell water on the wind, feel it on my face and arms.

As we crossed the parking lot toward the massive cement block of a building, I surveyed the collection of cars, wondering if one of them was my mom's. Last I knew, she had a beat-up black Integra, but that had been eleven years ago. I had no idea anymore what kind of car she drove. We passed a Subaru with a bumper sticker from Redwood National Park. I tried to conjure an image of her camping up near Willits or Ukiah. Seemed unlikely, but no more so than her driving the Ford pickup parked next in line, reporting every day to some respectable job and collecting a steady paycheck.

The truth was, I had no idea who my mom was anymore. After eleven years, how could I? Odds were she hadn't changed much. She probably still worked nights at some bar and slept all day. Or maybe she'd finally taken those online classes she always talked about and was working as some kind of administrator in an office building in downtown Oakland. A paralegal maybe. We passed a Mercedes and I tried to picture her driving it, her blond dreadlocks wrapped up in a bun on top of her head, but I couldn't keep a straight face. Then again, none of Grandma Helen's acquaintances drove such a nice car. I sobered and prepared myself for whoever we might find inside the church.

The double doors facing the parking lot hung open despite the threatening weather. Aunt Christine, the girls, and I followed the center aisle and emerged from under a deep balcony. It was an ugly, cavernous church. I had attended each of my cousins' baptisms there, and every time I noted the stoic lack of beauty, the aggressive scent of industrial cleaning products that never seemed to dissipate. The place was covered—floor, walls, and ceiling—in an oatmeal-colored fabric. The only natural light floated in through one large, circular window above a stark metal cross. No stained glass, no structural details. I thought how I would joke later with Grandma Helen about how tacky the place was, but then, just as quickly, realized I wouldn't.

The thirty or so people who had taken the morning off to pay their respects didn't fill the first two rows of pews. The giant stage could fit three hundred people easy, and I could envision a giant choir singing, arms raised, but on that day it was empty except for a small table covered in white lace. On it rested a wooden urn between a vase of lilies and a framed photo of my grandmother.

I hovered beside Aunt Christine as she greeted friends in hushed voices. A round woman with short curly hair and glasses took my hand. "I'm so sorry for your loss," she said. I recognized her but didn't know her name. She had brought a lasagna out to the house, big enough to feed twelve people. "Thank you," I said, grateful when another approaching well-wisher, a middle-aged man with a wiry beard, compelled her to move along, sparing me from any small talk. "I'm sorry for your loss," he said. I looked past him to scan the faces in the room. None were my mom.

I wondered if I would miss any of these people when I was gone. My aunt was sweet but overbearing about the way she wanted things done. As for the rest of the people gathered there, I hardly knew them: acquaintances of my grandmother, friends of my aunt.

Aunt Christine's husband, Todd, strode the side aisle of the church with his cell phone pressed to his ear. His stylish blond hair matched the self-assured smile of a guy who was used to people liking him. He lifted his free hand and waved it, as if dismissing a bad idea, and snippets of a contentious negotiation floated over the pews: *that's unacceptable, you call him.*

My cousins spotted their Sunday school teacher, Mrs. Michaels, and rushed to wrap her lower half in a hug. In the dim light, her fiery red hair reminded me of a chicken's comb. With the girls fluttering around her in their black dresses, she could have been a fat Minorca chicken, an appearance only emphasized by her pointy nose and too-small eyes. She reached to take Aunt Christine's hand in an awkward clasp. "I'm so sorry for your loss."

"Thank you," Aunt Christine said, and she agreed when the girls asked if they could sit in the second pew with the chicken lady.

At the very back of the church, under the enormous overhanging balcony, I could barely make out the shaded figure of my uncle Scott. He looked healthier than he had in recent memory. He was clean-shaven and his shaggy brown hair had been cut short.

Uncle Scott and Aunt Christine were not on speaking terms, so it had fallen to me to break the news to him about his mother's death. When I called, he had told me, unprompted and in a pleading tone, that he had been sober for five months. That was a good run for him—if he wasn't lying.

The guy in the ill-fitting suit next to him was Matt, Uncle Scott's best friend and NA sponsor. His hair was pulled up into a topknot and he was scrolling through something on his phone. The icy glow of the screen lit up his goatee. Matt's hipster affectations were annoying, because really, there was nothing hip about Victorville, but Uncle Scott tended to avoid him when he was high, so the fact that he was there was a good sign.

Aunt Christine stiffened. She had spotted them too.

"Do you think we could—"

"No." She took her seat and folded her hands in her lap.

It didn't feel right to make my uncle sit all the way in the last row like an outcast, but the fact that Aunt Christine hadn't thrown a fit and insisted that he leave was a minor miracle. I decided not to press the issue.

I raised my hand to throw a little wave at my uncle, hoping that Aunt Christine wouldn't notice. He returned my wave, but I couldn't see his face well enough to make out his expression. Aunt Christine glanced up at me expectantly. I took my seat.

Devon appeared at the end of the pew. In the three years we'd been dating, I had never seen him in a suit. The smooth gray fabric emphasized his broad build and hid the slight paunch of his beer belly. He smiled when our eyes met and he scooted into the pew next to me. He kissed my cheek. The soapy smell of shaving cream floated around him. "Sorry I'm late," he said.

"You're not."

He laced his fingers into mine. Devon's hands were rough from his work at the plant and his fingernails always held thin lines of white cement dust no matter how much he scrubbed. They were strong, reassuring hands. "Thank you for coming," I whispered.

"Of course." He lifted my hand to kiss it and my sleeve fell away, displaying the collection of bruises on my arm. He winced.

"Stupid birds." I pulled the fabric back into place.

"You should hire someone to help out," he whispered.

"I know," I said. I had intended to. When I was a kid, still too young to be in the corral, Grandma Helen had a guy who helped out during the summer months. A dark-skinned man with a stern face. I thought his name was Carlos, but when I flipped through Grandma Helen's address book, there was no one by that name listed. I figured I could probably drive into Victorville and talk to the guys who stood on the corners hoping for work. I had even looked up the word for ostrich in Spanish, to augment my intro-level language skills. *Avestruz.* That was before I set things in motion with Joe Jared. He would bring his own guys in. All I had to do was keep things running long enough for the sale to go through.

I hadn't told Devon about selling the ranch. He knew about my job with the Forest Service, of course. It wasn't a secret. He had supported me through the application process despite his reservations about my being gone for months at a time. We had agreed to see how it went, maintaining our relationship long distance. But now, with Grandma Helen gone, I could hardly expect the birds to take care of themselves while I was away. He probably thought, like everyone else did, that I would give up the Forest Service job and stay on at the ranch. With everything that had been going on the past few days, I hadn't had a chance to tell him otherwise.

"Devon, I—"

But before I could say any more, Pastor Phillips took the stage wearing a black suit and a plum-colored tie. A portly man with white hair, he walked slowly to take his place at the front of the church. He invited everyone to take their seats, but the small crowd was already sitting, waiting for him like schoolchildren, faces tilting up from the first few pews.

"I'll tell you later," I whispered.

Pastor Phillips spoke about finding God's grace in hard times. He held out his hand toward the small wooden urn and told us Grandma Helen was in a better place. She would have hated the whole thing. She had never understood Aunt Christine's embrace of religion.

Faith and motherhood were intricately entwined for my aunt. It was as if the nurses, while swaddling her firstborn, had tucked God into that striped hospital blanket right alongside the baby. The Heavenly Father came home with them that day, and religion became a part of their lives as much as sleepless nights and dirty diapers. Over the years, as she brought home each new baby and her collection of striped hospital blankets grew, Aunt Christine became more and more serious about her faith.

It didn't make sense to Grandma Helen. When pressed, she would say that the desert was her church, the perfect rhythms of nature her hymns, the elegant wisdom of the ecosystem her Bible. She put her trust in the shifting sands that surrounded her and said that if there was a God, he resided in the wind and the moon and the unrivaled yellow of a desert marigold.

I planned to spread Grandma Helen's ashes in the desert, after all the religious observances. Grandma Helen had said goodbye to her husband in the same way, many years before. I had never known my grandfather, but it was nice to think of them together again, their remains blowing across the great expanse of the desert in swirling gusts of wind. Pastor Phillips carried on, quoting the good word and expounding on God's love, but my mind returned to the ranch, worrying over that one lone egg.

I shifted in the pew, anxious to be done with the service so I could get home and check for more eggs. Without them, I could forget about selling the ranch. It wouldn't be worth the barren land it was built on.

THREE

When the funeral finally ended, I rode home from the church with Devon in his banged-up SUV. Halfway there, a fat drop of rain, carried ahead of the storm by the wind, burst against the windshield.

Watching in the rearview mirror, I could see the nine cars that followed us in a solemn procession from the church to the ranch. They were spaced evenly behind us on the highway, like a line of ants winding over the pale Mojave Desert.

Another drop exploded on the windshield, then another. I wished it had been raining the week before. If it had been raining, I could have believed that Grandma Helen's death was an accident. The highway might have been slick, her vision obscured or perhaps confused by headlights on the wet roads. But the day of Grandma Helen's death had been clear and sunny from dawn to dusk.

I considered the framed photo of her I held in my lap. I had snapped the shot myself, a few summers ago, after I graduated high school and Grandma Helen began paying me for my work on the ranch.

With my first paycheck, I bought myself a phone. The trip into town took most of the day, and when I returned home to the ranch, Grandma Helen sat reclined in one of the wicker chairs on the front porch, the green glass of her beer bottle wet with condensation, her head resting against the outside wall of the house. I joined her on the porch and pulled my new gadget from its box. I touched the unmarred glass of the screen and left a perfect fingerprint.

Grandma Helen had been skeptical of the utility of a cell phone way out there in the desert. Service was spotty at best, and carrying anything shiny into the corral with the ostriches was akin to filling your pockets with birdseed. They were quick and curious and drawn to any unfamiliar object.

Preoccupied with the device, I experimented with ringtones, sending unnatural trills and toots into the otherwise tranquil evening. To emphasize her opinion of my purchase, Grandma Helen made up her own names for the sounds as I tried them: chicken fart, sinkhole, dying dog. I ignored her, but she kept on, cracking herself up. I snapped a picture of her chuckling at her own jokes. The low light streamed in over the mountains in the west and it caught a glint in her pale blue eyes, the lines around them lifted in an easy smile. That moment, with her arm slung over the back of the chair, her hair loose around her face, that was how I wanted to remember her. It was nice that Aunt Christine had framed the photo for the funeral. It was just the kind of thing I never would have thought to do.

I cracked the car window and lifted my face to breathe in the scent of water in the air. Devon flicked the wipers to clear the drops that had begun falling in earnest. The sign for Wishbone Ranch came into view on our left like a miniature billboard, its tall lettering bold against the whitewashed wooden planks. Devon slowed.

His tires crunched against the gravel as we pulled off the paved road. The driveway marked the corral's southern border, and I strained to see if there were any eggs, but the brown-quilled females were all sitting on their nests, blending into the desert landscape. Again, I questioned what I had seen that morning.

The darker male ostriches milled about the corral, necks stretched high, feathers rustling. Of the 142 ostriches on the ranch, most paid no mind to the comings and goings of cars, but one bird always made it his business to track visitors.

Grandma Helen had called him Theo; I didn't know why. He was about eight feet tall. His black wings were tipped with white, same as his tail. Fine floss coated the ashen skin of his neck. He was a textbook example of a male ostrich and would have blended seamlessly with the flock except that he could not resist the urge to inspect any vehicle coming up our drive.

Within seconds of Devon's car turning off the highway, Theo found his stride beside us, nothing but the thick wires of the corral fence separating us. Normally, he would have escorted us all the way to the walnut tree in front of the house, but his attention was drawn by the car that pulled in after us.

Breaking away, he looped back. I watched in the rearview mirror as he was distracted again and again by each car that exited the main road. Like a nanny in charge of too many children, he ran in circles, trying to be in nine places at once. The rest of the flock watched with blank stares.

By the time we parked, the rain was falling hard. Plump drops coated the windshields faster than the wiper blades could clear them, and at first I didn't notice the Dodge Ram waiting outside the barn on supersize tires, floodlights and gun rack rigged to the cab. Its nose aimed down the driveway toward us. The license plate read OSTRICH. It was Joe Jared.

The rain found my arms and face like a thousand incessant questions as I jumped from Devon's SUV, the photo of Grandma Helen tucked under my arm, and hurried over to Joe's truck.

His giant boots squeaked against the metal rungs of the truck as he climbed down. I marveled at the crude size of him. Built like an ox with a glandular problem, he had broad shoulders that lifted his six-foot-four frame, and where most men either tapered or bulged in the middle, his body melted down into the two gigantic tree trunks that were his legs.

"Tallulah, I'm so sorry for your loss." Joe Jared's voice filled the yard the way an elephant would fill a teacup.

"It's not a good time," I said, crouching under the pelting rain and casting glances over my shoulder at the arriving guests, wishing for some way to hide Joe Jared from view. The timing was terrible. I hadn't told anyone I planned to sell the ranch, and Grandma Helen's funeral was not the time or the place.

The cars that had followed Devon's SUV from the church parked one by one along the corral fence. The drivers set parking brakes and held the doors for one another. They flipped up their collars against the deluge and made their way across the uneven gravel of the driveway. An elderly couple I didn't recognize emerged from the Mercedes I had seen in the church parking lot.

Uncle Scott emerged from the passenger side of Matt's white sedan. But while his sponsor headed straight for the shelter of the house, Uncle Scott held up a hand to shield his eyes and looked around. It had been about a year and a half since he had visited, but the ranch, like the desert around it, existed on a geologic time scale, and changes, when they happened at all, were nearly imperceptible. His gaze swept over me and Joe. Our eyes met.

"I've been waiting twenty years for this," Joe said, his voice so painfully loud. He held up a manila envelope, the paper quickly collecting caramel splotches in the rain.

"Stop," I said in an admonishing whisper, waving at the envelope and willing it away. "Let's go to the barn." Behind me, I heard Aunt Christine welcoming everyone up onto the dry porch and hoped she would be too busy to search for me. I shoved open the barn door, and was greeted by Henley, the white fur of his snout against my knee. He wagged his tail as I urged him back. Joe Jared followed me in. I rested the photo of Grandma Helen on the workbench and tried to wipe the raindrops from the glass with my hand, but they just smeared.

Joe Jared took off his Stetson and flicked the water from it. He studied the space appraisingly. At roughly twelve hundred square feet, the wooden barn had more space than we needed. It had been built when my grandparents were in the meat and leather business, competing with Joe Jared for customers.

Wishbone Ranch was strictly an egg operation by the time I came to stay, but my grandmother had explained how the eggs used to be incubated until they hatched. The gangly chicks would spend their first year in the barn, living in the stalls that lined the south side of the structure until they reached their full height. At that point, they were moved out to the corral, where they waited to be transported to the slaughterhouse. That was in the eighties, before I was even born. It had been decades since an egg had hatched on our ranch, but Joe Jared would revive that business model: incubator, barn, corral, slaughterhouse.

"You got some damage to the joinery up there," Joe said, gesturing with his hat to the northeast corner of the barn. At the boom of his voice, our two goats froze midchew and gazed over from the corner where they were tethered.

The barn needed work. I knew that. Owning anything out in the desert meant fighting a constant battle against the weather. Every year, the triple-digit heat of the summer months caused the wood of the barn to swell until the winter winds froze everything, contracting and cracking the posts where they came together. A tapping caught my ear as rain sneaked through a small hole in the roof, hitting the cement floor below.

Under the ruined timber of the roof rested two hulking egg incubators, each roughly the size of a bunk bed. Wide glass doors revealed the shelves inside, stacked with vacant trays that could hold hundreds of eggs. When they were in use, the entire interior of each incubator shifted every twenty minutes to simulate the attention the eggs would have gotten from the hens if they had been left in their nests. But they hadn't been powered up in decades.

The way my grandma told it, sending the birds to their death always weighed on her. She would get attached, she said. Ostriches could live forty years, sometimes longer, and she hated to see them all butchered when they had so much life left to live.

For two decades, she ignored the nagging sense that she was responsible for so much death, but eventually, she told my grandfather it was time for a change. Eggs weren't nearly as lucrative, but Grandma Helen had taken pride in the choice, and over the years, it rubbed off on me. It wasn't that I had any great love for the birds, but it made sense to me that the meat and leather business would wear on a person after a while.

Joe Jared gave a whistle and pulled a Citori shotgun from its rack, paperwork suddenly forgotten. "I'll give you a grand to leave this when you go," he said, holding it up to admire the engravings on the side.

"It's not for sale." It had been my grandmother's, a gift from her father when she moved out to the desert, and she'd given it to me on my eighteenth birthday. She treated target practice like meditation, even when we were just shooting at empty beer cans: focus at the top of an inhale, exhale just a little and hold it, steady the aim, pull the trigger. She even showed me how to take the gun apart and clean it. She had taught me so many things, and all she had wanted in return was for me to stay and carry on the enterprise she had spent her life building.

"Two grand," Joe Jared said.

"Can we get this over with?" I snapped. I retrieved the envelope from where he'd dropped it and handed it to him.

Joe Jared reluctantly set down the shotgun and produced a slim stack of pages. Biting the cap from a pen, he laid the contract on the workbench so we could review it together.

"This outlines the basics," he said around the cap in his mouth. "Market rate for each of the birds—" Before he could elaborate, an ostrich emerged from one of the stalls in the back of the barn. Her name was Abigail, and she could be a bit of a pest. She walked with a limp due to a badly injured ankle that had never healed right. Because of it, the other birds in the corral would peck at her, so Grandma Helen had allowed her to roam the property freely. She never went far. We treated her pretty much the same as we treated the dog and, like the dog, she followed us around the ranch as we did our chores, but she did have a way of interrogating strangers. Aunt Christine had worried that the inquisitive bird would frighten the funeral guests. At her request, I had spent half an hour the day before luring the limping bird into the barn so I could shut her in until the reception ended. I'd forgotten she was there.

She crossed to Joe Jared and pecked at his giant, silver belt buckle. He chuckled and shoved her away with an oversize hand.

"Sorry." I wedged myself between Abigail and Joe Jared, trying to steer the bird into a nearby stall, but she skittered out of reach, her feet scratching against the cement floor. I scurried after her.

"Not at all," Joe Jared said with a smirk.

I hated the amusement on his face. The birds were difficult to wrangle. He knew that, but he also had a hundred pounds on me, easy, not to mention the ten extra inches and a wingspan to match. I had to compensate for my smaller size by being quick. He had probably never chased a bird in his life.

I snatched Abigail's beak and pulled her head low, forcing her to follow me into the enclosure. I latched the door and brushed my hands together as I returned to where Joe Jared waited with a condescending grin.

"As I was saying"—he chuckled again and adjusted his belt—"market rate for the flock comes in at two hundred ten, plus fair value on the land." The pounding rain overhead grew to a thundering roar that syncopated with Joe's voice until his words, loud as they were, became simply another noise.

I pictured the water flowing off the barn roof in sheets, overshooting the flooded rain gutters. It would glisten in the gray light and smooth the sand. The whole of the desert was one big basin, and though pockets of the ranch would catch runoff in pools, for the most part, the rain would rush down into the lowest part of the valley, miles to the east of us.

In my mind, I saw the path it cut to a creek bed that sat dry 363 days a year. Tomorrow, it would be a lake, and the next day, it would be dry again, the rain having soaked into the thirsty soil to replenish the underground reservoir that provided our small town with its modest supply of drinking water.

It would rain in Montana. Snow too, though I figured by the time winter came, I'd have a new assignment somewhere else. That was one of the things that appealed to me about the idea of working a handcrew. They would send me where I was needed. It didn't pay much, but I wouldn't have to pay rent and I'd have money in the bank from selling the ranch.

The thought brought me back to the barn, where Joe Jared tapped his pen on the pages before him and planted tiny check marks in the margins. When he came to the sale price, he tried to lowball me, offering a decent price for the land and the barn, but nothing for the house itself.

"It's a four-bedroom," I argued.

"I've got no use for it." He sighed, reluctant to explain himself. "Here's the thing. You can spend the next year transporting your birds to the slaughterhouse, setting up buyers, and dealing with accounts receivable while you try to sell the house, incurring all the costs that come with wrapping up a business like this. Or you can sell it all to me and be done with it."

I had three weeks to get myself to Montana. I didn't have time to sell off everything piecemeal. "Fine," I said.

He wrote the total at the bottom of the page. All in, I would walk away from the sale with almost two hundred and fifty thousand dollars, an overwhelming amount of money, though I tried not to dwell on it. My plan was to put it all in savings and buy a place of my own someday when I found somewhere I wanted to settle down.

"You hang on to this," he said, returning the pages to the envelope and handing it to me. "I'll send my inspector out to do some diligence on the barn, the rest of the infrastructure," he continued, scrutinizing the splitting wood of the joiner. "Do an official inspection. How's Tuesday?"

"Fine. The sooner, the better. I'm leaving town at the end of the month," I said, glad to have settled on a price before he knew I was in a hurry. "We'll need to wrap things up before then."

"That shouldn't be a problem." Joe Jared ducked to try to catch my eye. I avoided his gaze. I didn't want to discuss my plans with him, and I knew he didn't really care. We didn't need to pretend otherwise. We were business associates, nothing more.

I held the dog's collar as Joe Jared shoved the barn door open. The storm carried on and the crisp, cool air rushed in, the clean smell of it distinct for the absence of dust. From over near the house, I heard a squeal and saw my cousins through the deluge, dancing in the driveway, wiggling their hips and spinning in circles.

Joe Jared hesitated. "As a courtesy," he said, "would you mind firing up the incubators and collecting the eggs while we finalize the details? They're of no use to me otherwise."

"Sure," I said, trying to keep my voice light. "I can do that."

The mention of eggs reminded me again of the one lone egg that morning. It was a fluke, I told myself. It had to be. Maybe it was the pressure change before the storm, or all the well-wishers who had been coming and going with their trays of pasta. It would blow over. Everything would be fine. There was no need to worry Joe Jared and jeopardize the sale of the ranch by disclosing the details of one unusual morning.

"You heading in?" He indicated the house. Through the windows, I could see the small crowd of people gathered. The light inside looked cozy against the surrounding storm.

"I've got a few things to take care of out here."

"Yeah," he said, pulling his Stetson low. "I hate funerals too. Again, I'm sorry for your loss. Your grandmother had a good head on her shoulders." And with that, he ducked out into the driving rain and made his way to his giant truck, drops bouncing off the brim of his hat. He beeped his horn at the girls, who were jumping in the puddles beside the house, and then he was gone.

I regarded the photo of Grandma Helen. It had been part of Aunt Christine's vision for this whole reception thing, but I hesitated to bring it to the house. Grandma Helen had hated crowds. She would have been out there in the barn with the dog and me, finding any excuse to keep to herself.

Henley's tags jingled as he followed me to the workbench, where I found a nail and hammered it into the wall, leaving enough sticking out to hang the frame on. She would be safe there. The dog and I stood side by side, considering the woman who had loomed so large in our lives.

The dog whimpered and cast an accusing glance at me.

"Don't look at me like that," I said. "None of this is my fault." I pointed at Grandma Helen's image. "She made her choice."

Resentment surged in me when I thought about her leaving me alone on the ranch, followed immediately by guilt. I didn't have any proof she had taken her own life. For all I knew, it had actually been an accident. Uncertainty gnawed at me. If she had steered into oncoming traffic on purpose and it had been her last-ditch attempt to manipulate me into staying, then selling was an easy way to win the argument. If not, selling was a terrible betrayal.

Over the din of the rain, I heard a low croak from the stall where Abigail was penned in. She lifted her beak to the ceiling. She was missing the rare treat of the rainfall.

Her favorite thing in the world was when Grandma Helen turned the hose on her. She would scramble in circles, dodging the stream of water while snapping at it with her beak. In the desert, folks tried hard not to waste water, but every now and then, Grandma Helen would indulge her feathered friend for a few minutes and play. To Abigail, rain was one extended hose session. By tomorrow the storm would blow over and the rain wouldn't return for months.

"I can't let you out," I said, imagining how Aunt Christine's church friends would react to finding an inquisitive, soggy ostrich between them and their cars. "I'm sorry."

Abigail lowered her gaze to stare at me, annoyed. The small feather on the top of her head, the one that rose up like a question mark, looked almost painted in place.

The ostriches didn't have expressions, exactly. They didn't have lips to curl in anger or ears to lay back in irritation. With the ostriches, it was all about posture and sound. Friendly curiosity manifested in lilting head bobs—all the better to reach around and pilfer from the pockets of the unsuspecting. Aggression was hard to miss. A bird about to charge would lift its wings forward, suddenly appearing twice its size. Distress could be heard for miles as a low, whooping reverberation.

I grabbed Abigail's beak and pulled gently. It was a playful invitation I'd seen Grandma Helen use with her a thousand times. When Grandma Helen did it, Abigail responded by pulling away and trying to peck at her hand, initiating an oversize thumb war, but when I did it, the bird just stared at me.

"Whatever," I mumbled. I was wasting time anyway. I needed to know if there were more eggs. "Let's check on the rest of 'em," I said to the dog.

In the corner of the barn, I found the seldom-used raincoat we kept on hand and pulled it on over my dress, tucking the folded manila envelope into the pocket for safekeeping. There was something so satisfying about moving through a storm without getting wet.

The steady rain landed on the hood of the coat with hollow thumps. My boots sent sprays of water with every step. The dog trotted along beside me as far as the corral gate, then veered off to inspect a nearby sagebrush. He knew better than to come into the corral. The birds weren't usually aggressive, but they were powerful and dumb. A stray kick from a spooked ostrich could kill a grown man, let alone a dog, and he had enough sense not to put himself underfoot.

Grandma Helen hadn't let me into the corral until my fourth year on the ranch. By then, I was seventeen and strong enough to handle myself, but I never did find her level of comfort around the birds. I was forever flinching at their pecks and ducking out of their way.

Inside the corral, I fed the flock even though it was early yet for their dinner. As they gathered around the trough, I squeezed through them to survey the nests and saw a collection of empty pockmarks in the sand. I watched the birds as they fed. I just didn't understand it. They didn't appear sick. Aside from their soaked feathers, which drooped against their cheeks, they were the picture of health.

One of the hens, making her slow way to the feed trough, pecked at the shiny yellow vinyl of my raincoat. Her broad beak curled down slightly at the edges, giving her a disgruntled look that was emphasized by the sag of her wet feathers.

I pulled down her beak to inspect for any signs of respiratory trouble, but her nostrils were clear and her eyes showed no signs of swelling. She blinked.

"What the hell?" I said, releasing her. She meandered away from me with a lazy gait, shoving herself into a spot between the other birds at the trough.

One hundred forty-two ostriches and not a single egg. It didn't make any sense. Those exact birds had been laying eggs consistently for years. Biologically speaking, they should have another three decades or so of good egg-laying left in them.

Of course, when Joe took over, they would all be slaughtered. Maybe not immediately—he would need to wait until a batch of eggs hatched and a new crop of birds grew into the supply chain—but within a year or two, every bird standing there in the corral would be gone. A wave of nostalgia washed over me. Life was shifting. After nearly fifty years, our family would no longer center around Wishbone Ranch.

The oldest of my cousins might remember the family business, but the youngest was only six. At best, the ranch would be a foggy dream to her. She wouldn't remember coming out for weekly family dinners or holding out grain through the fence for the birds to pluck from her hands while she squealed at the thrill of interacting with an animal so much bigger than herself.

I shook my head to clear it. My presence was overdue in the house. I had promised Aunt Christine I would stick with her plan for the day, so I needed to get myself inside.

FOUR

In the mudroom of the main house, Uncle Scott hunched over a wooden crate containing twenty-eight custom license plates. He jumped when I burst in out of the downpour but recovered quickly. I hung my dripping raincoat on a hook near the door and joined him, suppressing the urge to reach out for a hug. That wasn't something we did anymore. Instead, I shifted my attention to the collection of license plates stacked front to back, paint chipping and rust taking hold in the cracks. It was my mother's inheritance. I had retrieved it from the barn the day before in anticipation of her arrival, a move that seemed naïve now that she was a no-show.

Uncle Scott's hair was tucked behind his ears. Up close, I could see more clearly the signs of health I had glimpsed at the church. His eyes were relaxed, if glum, and his skin was clear. I felt a familiar flicker of hope that he hadn't been lying about being sober. His father's gold watch peeked out from under his shirtsleeve, the sum total of what Grandma Helen had left him. It wasn't much, but it held a lot of sentimental value.

"No word from your mom?" he asked. He was wearing

sneakers, and the cuffs of his slacks were wet. Marlboro smoke hung on his clothes. He had probably been outside smoking while I was in the corral.

"No." The wet ends of my hair stuck to my face, and I could feel raindrops on my cheeks like cold freckles. The stuffy house made me want to go right back outside until everyone left.

"Live and let live, right?"

It was one of his NA catchphrases, I knew, but it didn't seem to fit the situation. "Right."

I was glad he had come. If he'd been on a bender, we likely wouldn't have been able to track him down. He might have gone months not knowing about his mother's death.

I ran my hand over the license plates and let my fingers walk their blunt metal edges. Flipping through the collection was like time-traveling on the highway: the way the colors shifted from authoritative blue to reflective white, the lettering of "California" at the top evolving from the utilitarian imprint of the seventies to the overly ornate art deco of the eighties to the painted-on red cursive that had been the norm since the nineties.

Uncle Scott pulled one from the middle of the stack. It was blue, with tall, yellow letters reading USDFORC. On the back, Grandma Helen had written *Honda CVCC—followed from Sombra to Baker 1982.* "I remember this one," he said.

He would have been a kid then. I could imagine him sitting next to her on the bench seat of the truck as she followed that car, patiently waiting until the driver left it unattended long enough for her to swipe the plate. She had never been a particular fan of *Star Wars.* She must have nabbed that one just for him.

"Joe Jared made an offer?" Uncle Scott asked, surprising me. The manila envelope was still folded into the pocket of the raincoat. It felt like a dirty secret. But Uncle Scott knew that

Joe Jared had wanted to buy the ranch for years. There was no reason to lie.

"Yeah."

He was studying the blue license plate with more attention than was really warranted. I worried. The ranch had been his childhood home. But Uncle Scott's life had been divided by meth. There was before and there was after. I didn't know what, if anything, the ranch meant to my uncle anymore.

"Fuck that guy," he said. "Today of all days." His voice was scratchy.

"Does Aunt Christine know you're here?" I peered past him, through the open doorway to the living room, where Aunt Christine stood making conversation. She pressed her thumbs into the small of her back and shifted her swollen body from one foot to the other. Devon had retreated to the corner of the room, where a few older men sipped beers and talked in hushed voices. Dim light gave the place a somber glow. The drumming of the rain slipped beneath the hum of subdued chatter and I could smell coffee.

"She agreed I could come if I brought Matt to babysit."

Matt, with his stupid topknot, existed apart from the other guests. He had a narrow face and square brows. The tattoos on his arms rolled down past the cuffs of his sleeves, and I knew he wore a leather band around his wrist with the word "freedom" carved into it. In his hand was a napkin stacked with grapes and cheese.

He popped a cube of cheddar into his mouth and glanced around the room. He was wildly out of place among my aunt's church friends, with their threadbare blouses and perfectly pinned hair. But he held himself as comfortably as a crow on a crowded tree branch, surprisingly at ease for someone with such a sordid history. The stories of Matt's teenage fuckups were fairly legendary in Sombra, but he had been sober for fifteen years and living in Victorville for almost twenty. He didn't come around Sombra all that often. I had only ever known him as my uncle's best friend, the guy who had pulled him up out of the muck of addiction time and time again. Even so, I didn't like him. He thought he was better than everyone around him because he was sober, like getting through the day without getting fucked up was some major accomplishment. He turned toward me and I looked away.

"Uncle Scott," I said, my voice barely above a whisper, "I'm selling the ranch." I was glad to be removed from the other guests. I wasn't ready to share the news with the whole town. "It's not official yet, but that's why Joe Jared was here. I asked him to come."

He stared at me, his expression shifting from confusion to anger. He opened his mouth to say something, but nothing came out.

"What's wrong?" Matt asked, joining us in the mudroom. I wedged myself between the washing machine and the wall. The space wasn't big enough for the three of us. I wished Matt would mind his own business.

I tried to stick my hands into my pockets, but my dress didn't have any. I shifted to brace my fists on my hips, but that felt weirdly aggressive, so I dropped my arms and stood there feeling awkward. "I was just telling Uncle Scott that I'm selling the ranch."

Matt's eyebrows lifted and he turned to Uncle Scott, assessing the response that was forming in his face and posture.

"Tallulah," my uncle finally said. "You can't."

"I can, actually." I wasn't proud of it, but I had made my decision. If I wasn't staying for Grandma Helen, I certainly wasn't staying for him. I peered again through the open door into the living room to be sure no one had caught wind of our conversation. The guests continued to talk in low voices, oblivious to the three of us tucked away in the mudroom.

"But she never would have left it to you if she'd known you'd sell it."

"She knew. I have to be in Montana by the end of August." I hadn't told Uncle Scott about the Forest Service. "I got a job. Grandma Helen knew. I have to go. I want to go."

Uncle Scott tipped his head to one side, like he couldn't quite comprehend the idea that I would sell.

Matt jumped in on his behalf. "Tallulah, what if—"

"How does this concern you?"

"Those birds were her life," Uncle Scott said.

"Yeah, well, she gave that up too, didn't she?" I covered my mouth with my hand, shocked at the bitterness I heard in my own voice. "I don't want to talk about it."

I pushed past the two men, out into the living room through the small crowd of Grandma Helen's friends and Aunt Christine's church buddies. I didn't want to talk to any of them. Despite my earlier promise to be present and polite, I just couldn't summon the energy. The best thing for everyone would be if I went up to my room and waited out the whole thing. I kept my eyes down so as not to invite conversation and was halfway to the stairs when I was pulled off-balance into the fleshy pink arms of Annie Schmidt.

The polyester of her dress reeked of eager floral perfume. She patted my hair. "I am so sorry for your loss. I have always cared about you," she said. "If you need anything, anything at all, well, I want you to call me." She held me out at arm's length. Her gray hair was done up in a soft bun. "When Mary's mother died, well, I was over there just about every night."

The short-haired women next to her nodded. "That's right. She was."

Uncle Scott grabbed my elbow and pulled me away from Annie's embrace. "Sorry," he mumbled with hardly a glance in her direction. Annie and her friends looked like they'd been slapped. Leaning close, he whispered, "It's not fair you get everything."

He was right. It wasn't fair, but I hadn't been expecting to defend Grandma Helen's decisions. I gritted my teeth and tried to pull away. Uncle Scott tightened his grip on my arm and yanked me so close that I could feel his muggy breath on my face. It smelled of cigarettes.

"What is going on over here?" Aunt Christine said in an annoyed whisper. She eyed the guests in close proximity and flashed an unconvincing smile.

"How come she gets everything?" Uncle Scott said, dropping my arm. "It's not fair." Matt appeared by his side. Our little family drama was becoming less and less private by the second.

"You sound like a dang child," my aunt said, her voice still low. "Stop complaining and take some responsibility for yourself."

"I've been sober five months."

"Yeah, well, gold star for you, huh?"

"Aunt Christine," I jumped in. "Don't."

She closed the space between her and her brother. "You want to talk about unfair?" she hissed. "Let's talk about you, with no responsibilities at all, looking for us to get all excited about you doing what we all do every dang day. Life is hard, Scott, but we deal. We don't go running off to get high."

"Stop," I said, unsure of how I had fallen into the position of defending the uncle I'd been arguing with just moments before.

"Dude, we should go," Matt said.

By then, the room was so hushed, I could hear the patter of rain on the windows and the singsong voices of my cousins stomping in the puddles outside.

"What'd you get?" Uncle Scott asked his sister, holding up his wrist to display his father's timepiece. "I got a watch."

"Scott, come on," Matt said, pressing his shoulder into Uncle Scott's.

"Go home," Aunt Christine said, meeting her brother's stare without flinching. Matt gave up any pretense of a polite exit and dragged Uncle Scott through the room. The guests cleared a path, their faces full of disdain and pity.

"She got all this." He waved his arms while Matt shoved him, more forcefully now, toward the door. "What do you figure it's worth?"

"You have no sense of decency," Aunt Christine spat at him. "We are saying goodbye to our mother."

Uncle Scott straightened and lifted his chin, his obstinate glare passing over everyone present.

"Go on," Aunt Christine said. "Get out."

Uncle Scott spun and left the house with Matt right behind him. Aunt Christine and I followed them to the door and watched them cross through the rain. Matt bent his neck against the storm, but Uncle Scott stomped across the driveway, defiant even of the weather.

The girls, who had been catching raindrops on their tongues, watched as Uncle Scott trudged to the passenger side of Matt's car. Their drenched dresses hung from their knobby shoulders. Their blond hair hung in wet ropes.

Uncle Scott scowled at me. I forced myself not to flinch. He dropped into the car and his face blurred behind the wet glass. I saw the flash of a lighter and the red ember of a freshly lit cigarette.

"Girls," Aunt Christine said, her voice firm, "get inside." The girls knew better than to argue. They filed into the house between Aunt Christine and me.

Outwardly, Aunt Christine maintained her calm, but as she held the screen door open for her daughters, I noticed her hands trembling. She faced me and gave a weak smile. "Hang in there," she said. Then she grabbed my shoulders to give them a squeeze, and any hint of a tremor had vanished. Her grip was strong and unwavering.

"You okay?" Devon asked, coming up beside me and slipping an arm around my waist. I nodded and leaned in to him.

Aunt Christine herded her girls up the stairs to change into dry clothes. The wooden floor strained under their weight as they rounded the landing at the top and they marched in a line past Grandma Helen's room at the back of the house, the adjacent room that had once been Uncle Scott's. The room in the middle was mine. At the front of the house, overlooking the walnut tree, was the room that had belonged to Aunt Christine before she married and left home. Like the good mom she was, she had brought a change of clothes for the girls, knowing they would tire quickly of their formal attire. Perhaps she had even anticipated their playing in the rain. It would be just like her to see that coming.

I found myself a little jealous that she had something to do, a task to focus on that took her away from all the well-meaning people in the living room. A few of the women from her church offered tea to the rest of the guests. I accepted a mug and sat with Devon on the couch, thankful that he didn't feel compelled to make conversation.

Later that night, after we said goodbye to the last of the guests, Aunt Christine bustled around the kitchen collecting used paper cups, stacking one into the next to form a tall tower. Mrs. Michaels, the chicken lady, had offered to help Uncle Todd take the girls home and navigate bedtime routines. He had eagerly accepted her offer and I was grateful to have Aunt Christine stay out at the ranch until everyone was gone. It was a rare glimpse of her without her girls. She seemed somehow adrift.

Outside, the rain had stopped, but the sky still hung low and sullen. By morning, I knew, it would be as if the storm had never happened. The temperature would climb back up into the triple digits, and the desert animals would hide in their underground homes to stay cool.

Devon and I sat at the table, sharing a splash of whiskey from a mug with an ostrich on the side of it. The handle was painted to resemble the bird's neck, reaching down to stick its head in the sand. The whiskey left a honey-sweet taste in my mouth. I plucked a butter cookie from a tin on the table and washed it down with another sip. From behind the couch, Griffith poked his nose out to survey the room. He was a gray, three-legged cat with hair so short he looked almost naked, and he hated having people in the house. I could see him sizing up Aunt Christine, searching expectantly for the girls. Griffith despised the girls.

"Well," Aunt Christine said, pausing in her cleaning to serve herself a plate of lasagna. "That all went about as well as could be expected." She sat down and took a few dainty bites. "Could have guessed that Scott would make a scene."

I studied her profile, trying to decide if she was upset. It had been my idea to invite him to the reception.

"He probably needs money," she continued, not angry so much as tired. "I know your grandma lent him a fair amount over the years, but that's hardly your responsibility."

"Do you worry about him?" I asked, grabbing another cookie from the tin.

She sighed. "He is in my prayers every night."

I never would have guessed. I wondered if, like me, she had the urge to hug him when she saw him, or if she had hardened beyond such impulses. We had all built up defenses where Uncle Scott was concerned. We had to, because we just never knew when he was lying. But I was painfully aware that the walls we built to protect ourselves had isolated Uncle Scott. His mother had died, and instead of being at the house with us, he had stormed off. I was grateful he at least had Matt.

Aunt Christine reached over to pat my hand. "Don't let him

get to you. This is your home. I'd have been shocked if your grandma hadn't left everything to you."

I didn't know what she made of Joe Jared's visit, or if she'd even noticed it, but apparently, it wasn't as clear a sign to her as it had been to Uncle Scott. Unlike her brother, Aunt Christine didn't stress about money. Her husband worked in commercial real estate, ran a thriving business he had taken over from his father a decade before. They hadn't always been rich, but it had been several years since Aunt Christine had clipped a coupon. They lived in a six-bedroom mansion on the outskirts of Victorville and she spent her days focused on family. She packed lunches, crafted scrapbooks, and brought the girls out to the ranch once a week for a family dinner she cooked in our kitchen. Of all of us, I expected Aunt Christine would be the most saddened to see the ranch sold. I hadn't thought Uncle Scott would care at all, and he had straight-up freaked out. I would have to think of a way to break it to her gently, give her plenty of time to pack up family photos and things. Still, nothing had been finalized, and I didn't want to upset her if there was a chance the deal could fall through. I thought of the eggs.

If Joe Jared decided not to buy the ranch, it would take months, if not years, to arrange for the sale and slaughter of all 142 birds. I didn't have the relationships set up for that line of business. And only after all Wishbone Ranch business was wrapped up could I go about trying to sell the house with its forty acres. By then, the job in Montana would certainly be filled by someone else.

No. The sale would go through. I would make sure of it. And I would tell Aunt Christine about it once Joe Jared's lawyers delivered the final contract and everything was official. I didn't want to upset her unnecessarily. She had so much on her mind.

I gazed at the urn that rested on the kitchen counter beside the vase of white lilies from the church. The dark wood had been polished and oiled until the whorls of the grain resembled a slick, topographical map. It looked far too small to contain the remains of a woman who had been such a huge part of my life.

I took another sip of whiskey and slid the mug to Devon.

Aunt Christine finished her lasagna and hoisted herself from her chair with a sigh. Over on the couch, the cat flinched and came up on his one front paw like he might bolt. "I should go," she said, tossing her paper plate into the trash. Griffith, deciding there was no cause for alarm, settled back down. Before leaving, Aunt Christine rested her hands on the sides of the urn. She closed her eyes, and I saw her lips move—whether in prayer or goodbye, I couldn't tell.

I followed her out to the minivan. Neither of us said a word. Our footsteps on the gravel driveway were muffled by the low clouds. It took her a minute to crawl up into the driver's seat and stretch the belt around her giant middle. She rolled down her window. "Trust in the Lord with all your heart," she said in a practiced way, "and lean not on your own understanding."

I hated when she spouted Scripture at me. The borrowed words put distance between us, like I wasn't really talking to my aunt anymore at all. And what did that quote even mean? Did she really believe I should disregard my own understanding of things? Was God supposed to swoop in and tell me what to do like I was fucking Noah?

She seemed to sense my irritation and dropped the sermon. "Everything's going to be okay," she said and reached through the window to take my hand in hers. "You take care of yourself, Tallulah, and I'll see you for dinner on Wednesday, same as always."

It surprised me how relieved I was to hear her say that. "Good night, Aunt Christine."

"Good night, Tallulah," she said and put the minivan in gear.

Her headlights burrowed a tunnel through the night. I watched her drive away, the darkness caving in behind her as she went.

I stared in the direction of the road long after Aunt Christine's van disappeared. Quiet returned to the ranch, and I was glad for it, but a nagging sense that something was missing persisted. It was my mom. I had actually expected her to show. Some small, foolish part of me still held out hope that she would appear, the smell of cigarette smoke wafting in her hair and a dozen excuses at the ready for why she had missed her own mother's funeral.

I had to remind myself that she was not sentimental. Mom didn't send cards. She didn't keep old photographs. And she certainly didn't come for visits. It had been stupid to think that Grandma Helen's death would bring her home, no matter what she had said over the phone. My mom hadn't set foot on the ranch since the night she'd hopped onto her boyfriend's motorcycle and run off to Los Angeles, five months pregnant with me.

She had never been interested in the family business. As a kid, I knew she grew up on an ostrich ranch in the desert, but she left out a lot of details—like the fact that I had an aunt and uncle. It wasn't until second grade, when my schoolmates and I drew family trees to put up on the classroom wall, that the question of extended family even occurred to me.

In class, I wrote my name in orange crayon over the photocopied trunk of a large tree, and then, as instructed, I drew two lines in a *Y* to form the branches of the tree. Where one line ended, I wrote "Laura Jones" for my mom, but while the rest of the kids continued working, adding fathers, grandparents, and cousins, I had nothing. The teacher suggested I finish it at home.

When I showed my mom, she tore a page from a notebook and told me to redraw the tree, but I hesitated. We were supposed to use the sheet our teacher had given us.

Irritated, she snatched the lined paper from my hand and held it over the original to trace the shape of the tree. "See," she said. "Perfect."

It wasn't perfect. The lined paper was all wrong and the frayed edge where she'd torn the page from the notebook looked sloppy.

When I hesitated, she rolled her eyes and wrote my name across the trunk of the tree. She replaced the *Y* above my name with a single line up to her name and added a line up from her to a barbell of Grandma Helen and Grandpa Hank.

I wrinkled my nose, skeptical, and asked, "That's it?" At which point she conceded and added two more names: Scott and Christine, her brother and sister. It was the first time she'd ever mentioned them. When I asked, she said Uncle Scott was older than she was and Aunt Christine was younger, but when I wanted to know more, she waved her hand dismissively and said, "I don't even know anymore." Then she poured herself another glass of wine and left the room, which was a pretty good sign that she wanted the conversation to be over. But I followed her into her bedroom.

"Who was my father?"

She set the glass on her dresser and stripped off her shirt. "It's not important," she said, standing there in her bra and flipping through the clothes in her closet. She yanked a low-cut, magenta top from its hanger and pulled it on. "The only people that matter are you"—she reached out to touch my chin—"and me."

I flopped onto her bed. "But I want to know."

"There's nothing to know." An edge came into her voice then, a subtle warning. She grabbed her wine and swallowed half the liquid in one gulp. In a pile on the floor, she found a studded belt. She swapped her slippers for three-inch heels.

I got the message, that I should drop it. Persisting would be bullying, and Mom hated being pressured to do or talk about anything she didn't want to. Not that she would hit me. When I was little, I used to wish she *would* hit me. With a fat lip or a bruised cheekbone, I expected I could go to the school nurse and gorge myself on sympathy, but my mom's response to anything unpleasant was to distance herself from it. When we fought, when I couldn't appease her, she would disappear. For days afterward, I wouldn't see her. She would leave the apartment before I got home from school and return after I was asleep. In the mornings, I would hear the click of the bathroom door, notice her footsteps in the hallway, but she was like a ghost, and I was left aching for her to take solid form again.

I considered her nearly empty wineglass, tried to guess how many more questions she would tolerate. Because even as a second grader, I knew that babies came from having sex, and that sex, as mysterious as it was, happened between people who liked each other. She had cared about my father at some point. It seemed wildly unfair that she wouldn't tell me anything about him. "All I want is a name."

"Let it go, Tallulah. He left. That's all there is to say about it." Her rings clanked against the wineglass as she grabbed it and vanished into the bathroom. I stayed frozen there on the bed, waiting. Waiting to see if she would speak to me when she came out. Waiting to see if she would look past me as if I wasn't there. Waiting to find out just how much my curiosity had set her off.

Half an hour later, she emerged. Her dreadlocks were pinned into a large bun on the top of her head, and gold earrings dangled past her chin. Her cheekbones were dusted pink, but the deep red of her lips made the rest of her face comparatively pale. She collected her things and kissed me. I felt the print of lipstick on my forehead and a sense of security washed over me. "What are you going to watch?" she asked.

"*Family Guy.*" That was a lie. I would watch *Unsolved*

Mysteries, same as every night. It gave me nightmares, but I couldn't resist.

"Don't stay up too late," she said, her voice light. "And don't unlock the door for anyone."

As soon as she left, I went to her bedroom to snoop through her drawers, hoping for a clue as to who my father was, but there was nothing. Not a snapshot or love letter or anything. If evidence of my father had ever existed, she'd long since thrown it out. For my mom, once someone was in the past, they simply didn't exist anymore. She didn't think twice about losing people because they were all, friends and lovers alike, entirely replaceable.

Every time we moved into a new apartment, which was pretty often, she would linger outside smoking until someone bummed a smoke or asked if she was new in the building. Within a day, she'd have a brand-new group of best friends. Other single moms were usually the first to come, but men flocked to her too. Parties raged into the night. Then one day, usually without warning, my mom would simply announce that it was time to go.

One time a friend of hers, a woman I could only recall as having a cascade of silky, dark hair and a necklace with a gold cross on it, asked what we did for childcare while my mom was bartending at night. The question caught my attention, though I was watching TV and pretended not to hear it. My mom told her I was fine staying home by myself. "But she's only seven," her friend said. That was the last I remembered of her. A week later, my mom found a new boyfriend, and we moved into his apartment on 14th Avenue in Oakland. It had rust-colored carpet and I slept on a futon in a small room off the kitchen.

Moving always signified a fresh break for my mom, and her genuine enthusiasm for the good things ahead made the changes feel like an adventure. Anyone from before was a hindrance to that, something to be put behind us and forgotten.

Standing there in the driveway of the ranch, I forced myself to turn from the emptiness of the night. My mom wasn't coming. The motion light over the barn clicked on, and a blaze of white light illuminated a perfect half circle outside the door. Abigail was kind enough not to peck at me while I unlatched the stall to let her wander out into the night. I fed the goats and filled the dog's water bowl. Back inside the house, Devon was finishing up the last of the dishes, drying a serving platter with an old dish towel.

"Stop it," I said, closing the door behind me. "Seriously, no more cleaning."

He dropped the towel onto the countertop and I pressed myself into his body, resting my face against the cool fabric of his formal shirt. My head fit neatly under his chin. I wanted to lose myself in the clean smell of his skin. I kissed his neck, then his jaw where the slightest bit of stubble was forming. I found his lips with mine. His mouth tasted of whiskey and lemon.

I undid the top button on his shirt, smiling because I'd never done that before. Devon always wore T-shirts. There was something endearing about the button-down, but it slowed my progress. I pulled away from him to undo the remaining buttons, and he kissed my neck.

He lifted off my dress in one swift motion and pinned me against the kitchen counter. He scooped me up onto the tile and I felt the cold through my underwear, a sharp contrast to the heat created where our skin pressed together. I closed my eyes, enjoyed his strong hands on my hips. It had been such a terribly depressing week. Not even a week. Four days. I didn't want to think about any of it. I wrapped my legs around him to pull him closer, found the buckle of his belt, and undid it.

"You're selling the ranch," he said between kisses. The words came out hot against my neck. It wasn't a question. "That's why that big guy was here, why Scott was upset."

I pushed his unbuttoned shirt over his arms and leaned

against him, the fabric of my bra pressing into his skin. I traced my fingers up his back, tickling his spine in a way I knew he liked. "Just talking." It was true. Nothing had been signed. I kissed him, hoping to distract him from that conversation.

"Why didn't you tell me?" He leaned away, pulling his hands free of his sleeves. "You never tell me anything."

"I told you," I said and tried to draw him in for another kiss, but he stiffened. I slumped and rested my head against the cabinet. "I'm supposed to be in Montana at the end of the month."

"You said a contract job." His limp hands slid down my body until they were resting on the counter on either side of me. "A few months at most, you said. Selling the ranch sounds like you're heading out for good."

I untangled my legs from around him and slid down from the counter. "Things have changed." I grabbed my dress from the floor and went up the stairs.

Devon followed. I could hear his belt buckle jangling behind me. "When were you planning on telling me?"

"I'm telling you now," I said over my shoulder.

"Because I asked." We'd had different versions of this argument before. He always insisted I was holding out on him, when usually it was just that I didn't see the point in sharing every damn thought that popped into my mind. When something was important, I would tell him, but most things, frankly, weren't that important.

I hesitated at the top of the stairs. "What do you want me to say, Devon?" But even as I spoke, I knew what he wanted to hear.

He held up his hands the way I would approach an agitated ostrich in the corral. "Don't freak out."

I groaned and spun toward my bedroom.

Devon was right behind me. "My mom was twenty-four when she married my dad. It's not all so young."

"It's not all so old either." I threw my dress into the corner of my room and undid my bra. I pulled on the oversize T-shirt I used as a nightgown.

"All I'm saying is that it wouldn't be so unusual, us getting married." His voice softened. "People do it all the time."

I didn't put much stock in marriage. At best, you got what my Aunt Christine had: a business arrangement that left you home alone with a houseful of kids. At worst, you lived a life bent by compromise until you woke up one day worn-out and bitter because you let someone talk you into a life you never wanted in the first place.

He sat on the end of the bed, then reached up and took my hand. He kissed it. "I only want to know what's going on in your head," he said. "Because from out here, it kinda seems like you're fixing to bail."

"I'm not bailing on you," I said, sitting down next to him. But we both knew that wasn't exactly true. Part of the lure of the forestry job was that it was decidedly a step away from marriage and kids, the two things Devon wanted. For him, those things were the natural next phase of life.

"We don't have to decide anything tonight," he said and kissed my hand again. "But can you try to keep me in the loop? I want to know what's going on." He kissed the skin on the inside of my arm, being careful to avoid the welts the ostriches had given me. He pushed up the baggy sleeve of my nightshirt and brought his lips to my shoulder. It was a fair request. I really didn't mean to keep things from him so often.

"I'm sorry," I said. "For not telling you."

We kissed again. I helped him out of his pants and left them in a pile on the floor. I rolled onto him and my hair fell in his face. He traced my forehead with his thumb and gathered the hair behind my neck. "I love you," he said.

"I love you too," I said and felt an overwhelming guilt for all the things I wasn't saying. How could I explain that I needed to leave? I needed to go out into the world and stand in a place of my own choosing. Devon wouldn't understand that. He had chosen the cement plant. He had his own apartment. He was building a life that worked for him. I wanted that for myself: to make choices and know that I was responsible for all the good or bad that came of them. I'd spent my life doing what other people wanted me to do. I finally had a chance to do something on my own and I wasn't going to give that up.

He kissed me and I closed my eyes. Everything was a mess, but there was nothing I could do about any of it right then. I ran my fingers through his hair and forgot myself in the feel of him for just a little while.

FIVE

"Have you changed their routine lately?" the vet asked. I had called him that morning when I woke to find the corral still empty of eggs.

Bob was a short man with a comb-over that did little to shield his shiny scalp from the sun. "Different food? Anything?" He stood in the corral with total confidence despite the fact that his head came only as high as an ostrich wing. Most people were intimidated by three-hundred-pound birds that towered eight feet tall, and only the foolhardy didn't respect such powerful legs. Tipped with prehistoric-looking claws, the two-toed foot of an ostrich could easily disembowel an enemy.

"Our schedule's been off"—I hesitated—"with all the funeral arrangements. And it's just me now." I couldn't seem to adjust to that. I picked at a hangnail, felt the pinch of it in the tender skin of the nail bed. I wasn't used to my grandma's absence.

It would be good to sell and move away, if only to be somewhere that didn't hold so many memories of her. Every doorway held an echo of her footsteps. Every bit of wire fencing had been strung by her hands. Every bird in the corral had grown up under her care. I kept being ambushed by feelings of loss and guilt and regret. Simply walking around the ranch felt unsafe. Several times a day, it struck me, again, that she was gone.

"I'm sorry for your loss," Bob said. He had wild, bushy eyebrows that looked out of place under his balding scalp. "Your grandmother was a good woman."

I nodded and relaxed a little when he refocused his attention on the birds.

He ran his hand along the spine of the nearest female and pulled down her beak to inspect closely before gently guiding her into the crook of his fleshy armpit. The hen fluffed her feathers, shifting forward on her feet, but with her head low, she couldn't kick. Bob tested each wing between his fingers, then pressed gently along her rib cage. After he inspected her from tip to toe, he had me hold her steady while he took a small blood sample.

Sweat spots formed on Bob's shirt. I followed him over to the feed trough, where he crouched to pluck up a wayward grain of corn. He pulled an empty vial from his pants pocket and took a sample of water. It looked clean and clear.

"Thoughts?" I asked.

He lifted his gaze from the center of the corral to take in the bigger picture of our surroundings. The storm from the day before was a fading memory and our little plot of land was a clean thumbprint in the sprawling sage scrub of the Mojave Desert, about a hundred miles east of the San Gabriel Mountains, with Highway 66 marking the eastern edge of the property. The gravel driveway climbed the subtle slope from the highway to where the house and the barn sat on opposite sides of the walnut tree. Every fall the branches of the giant tree sagged under the weight of its green pods. The thump of each one falling to the ground come September coincided with the dwindling of the eggs in the corral and marked the beginning of our off-season. Grandma Helen collected the fallen walnuts in paper grocery bags. In the kitchen, the medicinal scent of the green husks would infuse everything as she spent hours listening to public radio, peeling the skins and setting the exposed craggy shells on a rack to dry.

I would retreat upstairs to waste away the hours on social media, happy to have a little downtime, but Grandma Helen didn't do well with downtime. When we weren't outside fixing things that had been put off during the busy summer months, she was inside smashing walnut shells with a hammer and teasing out the wrinkled, meaty flesh. Then, after every weak spot in the fence had been mended, the barn hosed clean, the feed silos stocked, the oil changed on both of the trucks, the tumbleweeds cleared from the corral, and every last walnut shelled and packed into the freezer, Grandma Helen would pace, waiting impatiently for the birds to lay eggs again, as if the routine had varied at all in the forty-six years she had been raising ostriches. But apparently, she had been right to worry. Because there I stood, surrounded by birds in the middle of July, without a single egg in sight.

"I'll run a few tests on these samples, rule out anything serious," Bob said, "but dollars to donuts, it's stress."

"Really?" It was hard to fathom what a flock of ostriches could possibly have to be wound up about.

He rubbed the back of his neck. "A change of ownership. That storm. See it all the time with chickens. Doesn't take much to set them off."

Ostriches didn't have much in the way of brain power. They operated on instinct and flourished with routine. I thought about the many unfamiliar cars that had been coming and going. "How do I get them to start laying again?"

He pulled a notepad from his pocket and set to scribbling. "Try one of these supplements. You'll want something with folic acid and choline. Just add it to their meals." He handed me the list. "That should help them bounce back."

I studied Bob's messy scrawl. There was a farm supply store north of Victorville where Grandma Helen and I shopped. They had a section devoted to poultry care that would likely have the items on Bob's list.

"You take care of yourself," he said as he climbed into his car.

"Thanks," I mumbled, and from the shade of the walnut tree I watched him drive off.

Take care of yourself. If you need anything . . .

Stupid things to say. I'd taken care of myself all my life without anyone telling me to do it, and in my experience, asking for help was a waste of time. Depending on people was just setting yourself up to be let down.

I reviewed Bob's list again. I wasn't excited to make the ninety-minute haul to the supply store, but the sooner the birds were laying eggs again, the better. If Joe Jared discovered that the birds had fallen mysteriously barren, I'd have a hell of a time convincing him to go through with the sale. I'd be left with no source of income and 142 birds to feed.

I wished I could ask Grandma Helen for advice. Not that she would be happy to help me sell the ranch to Joe Jared, but at least she would know what was going on with the birds. She always knew what to do.

I remembered when I first saw her, when I was thirteen, through the peephole in the door of my mother's Oakland apartment. She was a thin woman with gray hair pulled into a low ponytail. Her narrow face, distorted by the fish-eye glass, had looked unnaturally stretched, her lips cut a pale line above her square chin. A series of deep wrinkles lined her forehead and traced down to encase her deep-set blue eyes. She wore jeans and a white, button-up shirt tucked in behind a large silver belt buckle. Even before I knew who she was, I knew she didn't belong in Oakland.

She peered nervously down the hall to her left, then back at the door. She seemed downright ancient to me that day, but then, when I was thirteen, anyone over twenty counted as old. She looked surprised to see me when I opened the door, but she recovered quickly. "You must be Tallulah," she said, holding out her hand. "I'm your grandma Helen."

Her hand was strong, the skin surprisingly smooth. Her thin lips spread upward in an easy smile. "It's nice to meet you."

She asked for a glass of water, so I showed her in and filled one from the tap. On the kitchen table, my cornflakes crackled in their milk. I wondered if I should offer her food, but then the door to my mom's room swung open and she emerged, dreadlocks sticking out in every direction. An oversize Raiders T-shirt hung almost to her knees. Her eyes, bleary with sleep, were circled with charcoal shadow that had smeared unevenly in the night.

"Hello, Laura," Grandma Helen said.

My mom put her hand on the wall. She'd had a late night, and she'd brought someone home with her. I'd heard them stumble through the door around four. "What the hell are you doing here?" she demanded.

"Why don't we sit down?" Grandma Helen said, motioning to the round table where my breakfast sat turning soggy.

My mom wiped at her nose with the back of her wrist and sniffed. "I gotta take a piss," she said and slipped into the bathroom.

I gave up on breakfast and waited in silence with Grandma Helen. She sat with her shoulders squared, her back perfectly straight, taking in the disarray that was our apartment.

We couldn't afford two bedrooms, so the living room doubled as my bedroom and we didn't have enough storage space. Things tended to pile up. My pillow and blanket were strewn on the couch, my clothes piled high in the corner, and my schoolbooks sat stacked on a low table by the TV. The chairs had been salvaged from a dumpster and were meant to have cushions, not folded bath towels.

I saw it all through Grandma Helen's eyes and was embarrassed. I spun the ring on my middle finger, a cheap, shiny piece of metal my mom had given me on my thirteenth birthday. The skin underneath had taken on a pale green hue. When my mom finally appeared again, she had washed her face and pulled her dreadlocks together with a rubber band.

Grandma Helen rose to her feet. "I'd have come later—I know you're not exactly a morning person—but I'm hoping to get home before dark."

My mom slumped into the chair beside me, pulling up one knee under her giant nightshirt. "Whatever," she said, cupping her forehead in her hand and peering sideways at her mother. "Why are you here?"

Grandma Helen sat and resumed her perfect posture. "Well, there's just no easy way to say it, so here it is." She cleared her throat. "I'm taking the girl to live with me on the ranch. You can come too if you want."

"Don't be stupid," my mom said, reaching over to tousle my hair. "You're not taking anyone anywhere."

Grandma Helen ignored her and spoke to me. "We've got a good middle school nearby in Victorville, lots of fresh air, and I could teach you to work with the ostriches if you want to make a little money. Since your grandfather passed, I could use the help." She waited for me to say something, but no words came. I was trying to envision the ostriches. I had never seen an ostrich in real life, let alone many ostriches. And now here was this woman I didn't even know proposing that I leave Oakland with her that very morning to go live on an ostrich ranch.

"Seriously," my mom said, her voice growing louder, "what are you talking about?" She snatched her pack of cigarettes from the table and lit one.

Grandma Helen's voice remained calm. "I'm talking about

the fact that I don't much approve of the way you're raising this girl." A rush of smoke came across the table at her. "And frankly, I'm not convinced that the money I've been sending you these last few months has gone toward the private school you said you were enrolling her in."

Private school? I didn't even know there was a private school in Oakland.

There was a shuffling behind us, and a pale man with red, curly hair came out of my mom's room. He was wearing her tattered purple robe, with one side of the collar folded under the wrong way. "What's up?" he asked.

Grandma Helen stood and extended her hand. "Helen Jones," she said. "You must be . . ."

He blinked hard a couple of times, then hunched forward with a little gag and ran for the bathroom. From the table, we heard him retching. "You might like it out on the ranch, Tallulah," my grandmother said.

"What the fuck is she talking about?" I asked my mom.

"Watch your mouth," my mom snapped, tapping her cigarette against the edge of the yellow glass of the ashtray.

Watch my mouth? She never said that to me. When I was younger, she and her friends used to throw me quarters as I made up little songs using words most parents didn't allow. I cast a sideways sneer at Grandma Helen. This was all her doing. She looked like the kind of woman who would tell a kid not to swear.

"She's not going anywhere," my mom said again, sounding tired. "She doesn't even know you."

Damn straight, I thought.

My grandmother hesitated, but when she locked eyes with my mom again, there wasn't a trace of indecision. "I'm not sending you any more money, Laura." In the silence that followed, we could all hear the man vomiting behind the bathroom door. "But the girl's my granddaughter, and I care about her well-being. I'll take good care of her." She kept her distance but addressed me directly again. "If you hate it, I'll drive you back here myself," she said. "I'd only ask that you give it three months, till the end of the school year."

I waited for my mom to protest again, but she didn't. Instead, she trudged into the kitchen and yanked the empty coffeepot from its base.

"Mom?"

Water rushed from the tap.

"Mom?" I repeated.

She spoke to Grandma Helen. "It might be worth trying for a few months."

I stared at her, disbelieving. "Are you crazy?" I wasn't moving to the desert to live on an ostrich ranch. My life was in Oakland. My school, my friends, my boyfriend. No fucking way.

"Oh, don't look at me like that," she said, a bit of her usual ferocity returning. She slipped her cigarette between her lips and it bounced as she spoke. "If you stay here, you'll be pregnant by the end of the year. Don't think I don't know that boy comes over when I'm at work. You're thirteen, for fuck's sake."

I bowed my head to hide my surprise. My boyfriend came over all the time when my mom was at work. I didn't know she knew. "Mom," I said, my voice pleading. "Don't do this."

"It's not like it's boarding school. You'll be living with family."

"I don't know her," I said, pointing at Grandma Helen, who was patiently waiting out our discussion.

My mom sighed. "Well, I do," she said. "She's stubborn and old-fashioned, but she'd take care of you."

"Right," I said. "Because she did such a fucking stellar job with you?"

The smoke from her cigarette trailed up in a perfect, unbroken line. "I'm sick of this shit," she said. "Go pack your things."

"No," I yelled, pounding the table.

I swear, she grew three inches. "Go. Pack. Your. Shit," she said. "I'm done with you." And she went back to making her coffee.

Tears threatened, but I refused to cry. Instead, I glared at her with all the anger I could muster. "I hate you."

Two hours later, I had packed everything I owned into three giant garbage bags. Grandma Helen helped me load them into the bed of her pickup. I thought about the new boots my mom had bought the month before and the expensive bottle of liquor she'd brought to her friend's birthday party—bought with money meant for me. The more I mulled over the details, the angrier I became.

She said goodbye as I slammed the heavy metal door of the pickup and I pretended not to hear, but a second before we rounded the corner onto 14th Avenue, I stole a peek and saw her wipe at her face with her sleeve. Serves her right, I thought. I hoped she felt terrible.

We drove east toward the freeway, and I wondered what my friends at school would think happened to me. And my boyfriend. He would come knocking while my mom was at work. I didn't have a cell phone, no way of telling him what had happened. I considered hopping out at a red light and running away but quickly dismissed the idea. There was no one in Oakland I trusted to take me in, no one who could afford another mouth to feed. I knew I would end up sleeping under a freeway overpass, defenseless, cold, and hungry.

Grandma Helen drove east on 580, leaving the cool air of the bay behind. Over the dry hills, we went down into the flat, bright, open expanse of California's Central Valley. The news channel on the radio grew fuzzy, and Grandma Helen tuned it to a station that came in more clearly. The reporters were all abuzz about a plane crash in New York that had killed fifty-two people. After a few minutes, it didn't seem like there was any new information to add, but the newscasters kept talking about it, interviewing different experts and calling for professional opinions. Every hour or so, the station would crackle with static and Grandma Helen would scan to find a local channel broadcasting the same news over and over.

After a couple hundred miles driving south on Highway 5, we banked east again through Bakersfield. We drove farther into the desert, through the small city of Mojave, and then deeper still into the dry expanse.

I stole a glance at Grandma Helen. It was hard to wrap my mind around the fact that I would live with her—in a house I had never seen, in a town I knew nothing about. Her gaze was locked on the road ahead. The only sounds were the drone of the engine and the news on the radio.

I kept waiting to see cacti or palm trees or something like the picture-book version of a desert, but there was nothing as tall as that, just unending clusters of bushes with stiff branches and tiny silver-green leaves. The plants lifted and dropped in great gusts of wind. The sand at the side of the road created a textured border to the expansive plain of shrubs that climbed ever so slowly to the mountains in the distance. It was beautiful, in a lonely way. We must have passed through Sombra on our way, but to me, it was just another small desert town in the middle of nowhere.

We arrived at the ranch about an hour before sunset, and the bird I would come to know as Theo raced along his side of the corral fence, escorting us up the drive. Grandma Helen set the parking brake. "Let me introduce you," she said, her voice lighter than before. There was a slightly conspiratorial tone to it, like she was about to let me in on a big secret.

It was February, and the evening wind carried a crisp chill. The hair rose on my arms. I took in the walnut tree, the simple, two-story farmhouse painted a pale blue, the red barn, but Grandma Helen steered me to the corral. I was glad when she didn't open the gate, but remained with me on our side of the fence as a tower of feathers greeted us. "This is Lady Lil," she said and reached over the wire to gently grab the bird's beak.

"How can you tell?" I asked. Looking over the corral, I could see that some of the birds were black and others were brown, but beyond that, I didn't understand how she could distinguish any one from another.

"She's got a bald patch up on her left thigh there," she said, smiling as the ostrich pulled away, then rolled her graceful neck and poked the air, inviting Grandma Helen to take hold again. The hen's luxurious tan feathers rustled as she moved, but a round spot at the top of her left leg was bare, the skin stippled with ashy spots. "Your mom named her. Did she ever read *Wind on the Moon* to you?"

I couldn't remember my mom ever reading a book, let alone reading one to me.

"It was one of her favorites when she was little." Grandma Helen didn't care that I couldn't find my tongue. Gone was the stern woman with the thin line of a mouth who had talked with my mom that morning. She looked relaxed and at ease. "Would you like to say hello?" she asked as half a dozen birds followed Lady Lil over to where we lingered.

I reached out tentatively, and one of the ostriches dropped its head over the fence to peck at my ring. It didn't hurt, but I jumped at the swiftness of it, pulling my hand away.

"Oh, dear," Grandma Helen said. "They love anything shiny. I should have warned you."

I slipped the ring into my pocket and tried again. I ran my hand over the ostrich's strong neck, felt the downy fluff under her wings. Another ostrich reached through a lower portion of the fence and gave my shoulder a friendly nudge. My mom had always preceded the word "*ostrich*" with the words "*stupid*" or "*damn,*" but I saw something sweet in their giant eyes. I found them entrancing. Looking at the way their beaks curved ever so slightly at the corners, I couldn't help but smile.

After we greeted the birds, Grandma Helen helped me drag my bags into the house. The awkwardness of our road trip evaporated. It wasn't that she was all so talkative—that was never her way—but we found a comfortable quiet. She enrolled me at Victorville Middle School like she said she would and when she picked me up at the end of every day, she asked if I'd made any new friends, if I liked my teachers. At first, her questions felt like interrogations, but I quickly came to understand that she simply cared about how I spent my day. It was an unfamiliar situation for me.

As time passed, I began to worry that I had slipped into my mom's past, that increasingly large part of her life where she put things she was done caring about. I wished that, despite my anger, I had hugged her before I left or asked her to come visit me, anything to tie a thread between us that would unspool and keep us connected as I rode away in Grandma Helen's truck. I didn't really believe she would forget me. Mothers didn't just forget their children, and yet weeks went by without any contact.

When I'd been on the ranch for about a month, I decided she hadn't called because she thought I was still mad at her. And I was. I would never find peace with the way she had sent me away, not really. But I missed her terribly. I decided to write to her.

In an email, I could choose my words carefully. Dwelling on how we'd parted would only give her reason to avoid me. I didn't need an apology. I just couldn't bear to think she could forget me. So I hunkered down at Grandma Helen's ancient computer and started typing.

I told her about my new life on the ranch. I described how I was sleeping in her old room, the walls papered with pale cherry blossoms, the bedspread a foam-green flannel. I told her about the two girls at school I ate lunch with, and how my geometry teacher had eyebrows so sharply curved that they looked like broken triangles on his forehead. I shared that I had met her brother and sister, my uncle Scott and aunt Christine, and how cute my baby cousin Gabby was. And I told her about learning to work the ranch. Grandma Helen had me shoveling bird feed and hosing down the floor of the barn. I tended the goats and took care of the dog. Once I'd written down everything I could think of to share with her, I read the email out loud to myself three times to make sure there was no trace of animosity in any of it, then hit Send.

I didn't sleep well that night and the first thing I did in the morning was to check to see if she had responded. She hadn't. I told myself she had probably already left for her shift at the bar when I sent it, and she didn't check emails after work, but she usually sat with her phone while she drank her morning coffee. She would see it then.

That day at school I was itching to get home, to see what she had written in response, but there was no reply. I told myself that she was busy. Maybe she was working extra shifts or maybe she was sick. I waited for days, refusing to believe that she wouldn't respond to my peace offering.

Six days after I sent my email, her name popped up in my inbox. Excitement flooded through me and all my justifications for her late reply felt validated. I sat forward on the edge of my chair, heart racing, and clicked to read her message.

That all sounds nice.
—Mom

I scrolled down through what amounted to pages and pages of my heartfelt sharing, then back up to her five-word response and that dash. Not "Love, Mom," or even "Best." I wanted to spit on the computer screen.

"What's the matter?" Grandma Helen asked. She was watching TV but could see into the room that had been the kitchen pantry before it was converted into the Wishbone Ranch office, baking supplies replaced with filing cabinets.

"Nothing." I closed my email, but Grandma Helen was still waiting for me to elaborate. "My mom. I sent her an email and she blew it off."

"Ah," she said, studying the glass of whiskey in her hand. "I'm afraid she gets that from me. We're not always good at saying how we feel." After a month of living with my grandmother, this was the first time we'd spoken of my mom.

"The only thing I can tell you," she continued, "is that you haven't lost her. You will always be her daughter. In the same way, she will always be mine. Nothing can change that. You don't have to be close to people to love them."

I tucked that idea away like a treasured lump of gold. The ranch became my home. My mom would call sometimes on my birthday or to let us know when she had a new address, which was pretty often, but I never saw her. One time, a week before my sixteenth birthday, she called to say she wanted to come down to visit, that I would only ever turn sixteen once and it was a special occasion. She wanted to help me prep for my driving test. I didn't tell her that Grandma Helen had taught me to drive the year before, that she let me take the truck to retrieve the mail at the end of the road. I would happily feign ignorance of the clutch and the stick shift if it meant being close to my mom, if only for the duration of a driving lesson.

But on the day she was due to arrive, she called to say she had to work. Grandma Helen took me and my friends to the movies, trying to distract me, but the disappointment of my mom's cancellation defined the day.

When I graduated from Victorville High, Grandma Helen insisted on sending announcements to dozens of people, most of whom I had never met. She took me to dinner at the Steer'n

Stein in Victorville and kept toasting my accomplishment with shots of Jameson until we both agreed that it was best if I drove us home.

We sent an announcement to my mom, but she never responded. Then, a few months later, she called. When I heard Grandma Helen say her name, I hurried down the stairs and waited to take the phone. I didn't care that it was well into the summer, that the occasion of my graduation had passed without so much as a note from her while my friends' parents threw them parties and gave them expensive gifts. She had finally called to say congratulations and that was enough.

Grandma Helen stretched the phone cord to grab her little black book, erased my mom's address, and wrote in a new one, repeating it back. "Tallulah's right here," she said, "let me—oh, okay," she said, her voice dropping. "I'll tell her." But she said the last bit in a whisper, the phone falling away. My mom had already hung up. "She's late for work. She said to tell you she loves you."

She hadn't called to talk to me at all. "Whatever," I said, trying really hard to mean it, and retreated upstairs to my room. After that, I didn't run for the phone anymore.

Sometimes, I would daydream about her arriving at the ranch, broken by circumstance and tearful at the opportunity to reunite, begging for my forgiveness. Depending on my mood, the fantasy played out either with me falling into her arms and letting her be my mom again as if a day hadn't gone by, or with me snubbing her without a word, wanting her to feel what I'd felt when she shut me out. But the time for any kind of reunion was running out. In a matter of weeks, I would be gone and the ranch would belong to Joe Jared.

"Tallulah?" Devon's voice found me standing under the walnut tree, lost in thought.

"Over here," I said, stuffing the vet's list of supplements into my back pocket.

Devon's faded shirt held the ghost of a Pabst Blue Ribbon logo and his jeans were wrinkled. He was off to work. The cement plant ran around the clock and the workers arrived in three shifts. Devon didn't often work the first shift, but he'd had to trade around with a few of his buddies to get the day off for Grandma Helen's funeral. "You okay out here by yourself?" he asked, coming to meet me under the walnut tree.

Alone meant something different out there, where you could walk in any direction and not come across another person for miles. I didn't want him to leave. Without him there, without someone else there, the house would echo. But life moved forward, and I couldn't ask him to risk his job just to keep me company. "I'm fine," I said.

"I'll come back after my shift."

"You don't have to. Really, I'm fine."

"I'll come back," he said again, leaning down to give me a quick kiss. I met his lips with mine, but I was distracted. He got into his dented SUV and drove off.

I just had to make it through the month. As soon as the paperwork was signed and the ranch was in Joe Jared's name, I could pack up and head north.

I had never been outside of California, but my route to Bozeman would take me through Nevada, Utah, and Idaho before I got to Montana. I had mapped it online. I could drive it in sixteen hours if I had to, straight through, but if I could wrap things up on the ranch with time to spare, I wanted to take a few days, see some sights, maybe stay for a night in a real hotel, one with room service. I would order pancakes direct to my bed.

But for the time being, I would have to settle for a trip to the supply store.

SIX

Before I could head out to the supply store for the supplements on Bob's list, there were chores that had to be done, and I labored under the unforgiving sun with the distinct satisfaction of someone about to be relieved of her responsibilities forever. I filled the water trough, noting that the metal had worn thin in spots and would need to be repaired; Joe Jared could deal with that. I tethered the goats in a patch of land where the sagebrush needed trimming; soon their insatiable appetites would no longer be my problem. I put out a dish of cat food to reward the strays for keeping the place free of mice; I would never deal with rodents in the ostrich feed ever again. Any task that didn't directly relate to sustaining life, I ignored.

I was about to leave when I saw a familiar brown delivery truck trundle off the highway and onto our drive. It was Friday, and a shipment of eggs was due to go out. Cursing a little, I hurried to the shed-size cold storage unit adjacent to the barn where we kept the eggs before they shipped out.

Usually, Grandma Helen boxed up the orders, carefully keeping track of which customers were due how many eggs.

She was gone, but the world kept spinning, time marched on, and clients would expect their eggs to be delivered. I could have told the driver I didn't have anything for him. Could have gone inside right then and called every customer on Grandma Helen's roster to tell them I was closing up shop, but every order I sent out was followed by an invoice. Money in the bank for me.

The driver was a beefy, tense man. He had a schedule to keep, and he got huffy when the orders weren't ready to go. I kicked the door open and propped it with a broom so he would see I was working as fast as I could, slipping eight eggs into each cushioned box, taping lids shut, consulting the list of standing orders and slapping shipping labels into place. My sweat-soaked shirt turned cold against my skin in the frigid air. The driver scowled.

"Sorry," I hollered. "Just be a minute." I considered telling him what had happened, that Grandma Helen had died, leaving me there on my own to figure things out. I almost apologized for not having the shipment ready, for not being better, more prepared, but then I couldn't think why any of that would matter to him in the least. He had a job to do and I was the cause of a delay. I bit my tongue and kept working.

He lit a cigarette and paced under the shade of the walnut tree, from time to time glancing over at me. Behind him, Abigail hobbled across the drive. She gave her billowing feathers a tousle before making her final approach, nipping at his cigarette, and breaking it to pieces. He whirled around and ran for his truck, eyes bulging. I stifled a chuckle. Abigail followed him, in no great hurry, and pecked at the keys clipped to his belt. He reeled away, dodging another lazy peck as he scampered up into the safety of his truck.

I debated if I should intervene, but she wasn't hurting anything. She was just curious, so I pretended not to see. She reached her sinuous neck into the cab to peck at the shiny gauges and levers inside. The driver desperately tried to close the door without crushing her neck. He swatted at her, but she ducked and reached around him. Finally, he managed to close and latch the door. Then he cracked the window and lit another cigarette. His truck idled, and I could hear the engine groan under the burden of the air conditioning.

It took me another thirty minutes to finish boxing up the shipment. By then, Abigail had wandered off behind the far corner of the house. I knocked on the truck window to let the driver know he could load up the boxes, which he did without a word, his head swiveling the entire time to check his surroundings for giant birds.

After he left, I went back into the cold storage room and packed up the next week's orders, stacking the taped and labeled boxes against the empty shelves so I would be ready when he came again on Monday. I wondered how many more times I would do that chore.

I ran my hands over the remaining eggs, cool and clean on the shelves. When we first brought them in from outside they were warm and covered in the fine silt of the corral floor. We dunked each one in a bucket of water, wiped it clean, polished it to a shine, and set it on the shelf with the others, where they ceased to be a part of nature and became product. All lined up against the metal interior of the cooler like that, their repetitive curves were mesmerizing.

In a way, it was regrettable that they would never grow into their potential as enormous ostriches, but if even a fraction of them were allowed to hatch, we would soon be overrun by the flock. It was better to maintain balance. With 142 birds, we made enough to cover our expenses and put a little into savings, and that was enough. I rested my palm on the curve of an egg. Joe Jared wouldn't settle for enough. He would cram the corral with birds until he had a steady stream of hatchlings bound for the slaughterhouse. It would be a very different ranch.

I climbed into my Tacoma and let the door hang open for a minute so the worst of the trapped heat could dissipate as the first rush of air conditioning came out musty and hot. Soon the cab was cool and I was on my way.

After a few minutes on the highway, I passed the first hint of civilization, a double-wide trailer with warped paneling. I had never seen anyone coming or going, but a beat-up Ford pickup was sometimes parked in front, so I figured someone lived there. Deep out in the desert as we were, it was best to leave folks alone. Homes were separated by miles of vacant land, and the people who lived in them tended to value their privacy. There were houses like ours that had been built during better times, before the economic slump of the eighties, before San Bernardino County earned the dubious distinction of being the methamphetamine capital of the world, but more recent development centered around mobile homes. They seemed to pop up overnight, with tarps slung over partially finished additions and two-by-fours sticking up from the earth like some sort of invasive species.

About ten miles down the road, I passed PFX Cement. Devon was in there somewhere, driving a gravel loader. As one of the few legitimate businesses in town, the company employed most of Sombra's nine hundred residents. Anyone who wasn't paid by PFX and still had money to spend was generally assumed to be in the crystal business, but there were a few exceptions.

Five miles south of the plant, I came to the traffic signal where Route 66 crossed First Street. It was as close to a town center as Sombra could claim. On the northeast corner sat Pat's Bar, a square box of a windowless building with a neon Budweiser sign over the door. In the glaring light of midday, it was hard to tell that the sign was illuminated, but I knew the bar was open. It saw an influx of customers at the end of every shift at the plant, and because PFX ran around the clock, Pat welcomed his first customers at eight in the morning, when the graveyard shift wrapped up. I knew without going in that there was a line of hunched, tired men sitting at the bar, covered in a coating of cement dust, drinking their monotonous days away.

Grandma Helen had taken me to Pat's for my twenty-first birthday. She almost never went there herself. She preferred to drink in the quiet of the night on our front porch, but all of my friends had moved away by then, so she introduced me around. I'd been a regular ever since. Pat had a way of making everyone feel welcome. A retired Marine, he prided himself on staying in combat-ready physical condition. He often did pull-ups in the doorframe and deadlifted full kegs.

Kitty-corner from the bar was Annie Schmidt's gas station, a squat building painted a peeling gray. A shiny new sign towering over the station reminded everyone that Exxon had bought the place years go, but it was Annie's face we saw behind the counter, so as far as anyone in Sombra was concerned, it was Annie's place.

I could see Annie from where I parked at the pump, through the wide front window of the store. She had the sturdy build of a German dairy farmer, and her pale face sported a collection of sunspots. Her gray hair hung limp around her face. She sniffed at a half-full coffeepot and put it back. My stomach growled, but I hesitated to go in, thinking about how Scott had yanked me from her arms the day before at the funeral reception, how close she had been to our distasteful family drama. I hoped she would do me the favor of not mentioning it.

A loud beep sounded as I stepped through the door and Annie came toward me with open arms. "Well, hello, Tallulah," she said, pulling me into a hug. "How you holding up?"

"I'm okay," I said over her shoulder, realizing that I actually felt like shit, hungry and tense. I waited for her to release me so I could find some food.

"Oh, you poor dear," Annie said, finally letting go when she spotted an unfamiliar red sedan waiting at the signal. In Sombra, there were churchgoers, barflies, drug addicts, and health nuts. The one common denominator was that everyone needed gas, so Annie—more than any other person in town—knew what everyone was up to. When she saw a car she didn't know, it caught her attention.

"Did you hear we got a new young couple in town?" she asked. Standing there by the glass door, peering out, she reminded me of the ostriches, their attention so easily drawn by anything shiny. "Bought the Nicholson place. I ain't met 'em yet, but I hear she's some kind of artist."

I grabbed two bags of chips and an iced tea, but Annie didn't notice when I brought them to the counter. It was only when the light changed and the unfamiliar car drove on that she came around to take her place behind the counter and resume our conversation. "You doing okay out on that ranch there by yourself?" But she continued without giving me a chance to respond. "I know when I lost my Gary, well, I couldn't afford the mortgage all by myself. Not like Edith, with that life insurance payout of hers. Did you hear about that? Boy, but she lucked out. Anyway, what I'm trying to say is, I know how hard it is, selling your place, moving on after such a loss. It's a tough time."

"How did you—" I hadn't told anyone I was planning to sell. But then, that wasn't true. Uncle Scott knew. And Joe Jared. Maybe Devon had come in for coffee before work and got to gabbing when he should have kept his mouth shut. Or maybe someone else at the funeral reception had recognized Joe Jared and put two and two together. That was how things worked in our small town.

"What's that, honey?"

"Nothing." I made a mental note to tell Aunt Christine about selling the ranch the next time I saw her. She didn't always keep up with the gossip in Sombra, living as she did out in the collection of big-box stores that was Victorville, but I wanted her to hear it from me, so I needed to tell her soon.

"I, for one, think you're smart to sell," Annie said. She finished straightening things behind the counter and scanned my items.

I dug a ten from my wallet and handed it to her.

"Truth be told," she said, leaning over the counter conspiratorially, even though there was no one else in the store to hear us, "this town's gone to shit. It's the drugs." She resumed a normal tone of voice and set about making change for me. "Now, I'm too old to go moving, but you, well, I hate to see you leave, but I understand. You need to be thinking long-term. You are thinking long-term, aren't you?"

I wasn't sure what she meant. I opened the bag of chips and plucked out one of the bright-orange triangles. The tangy, not-quite-cheese flavor had me wanting more before I had even finished chewing.

Annie went on. "Well, I'm sorry to be so blunt about it, but if I could give you a bit of friendly advice, it's time for you to consider your options."

"Okay," I said, wondering where she was going with that. I wiped orange-cheese crumbs on my jeans and reached for another chip.

"You need to be thinking about your security."

"Security?"

"Your man," she said, as if it was the most obvious thing in the world. "That Devon. He's a good one. Decent job, doesn't do the drugs. He's never . . ." She gave me an appraising stare and her gaze lingered on the fading bruises on my arms. "I mean, he's not a hitter, is he?"

"No," I said, holding my hand over my mouth to prevent pieces of chip from flying.

"Keeper. I say lock that down. Get him to marry you. You

put a wedding date on the calendar and then no matter what happens, you'll be taken care of."

"Annie, I'm twenty-four, I—"

"I know you think things are different for your generation, but some things never change. So you listen close for one second." She leaned over the counter again. "Once he thinks you're pregnant, you won't need the condom anymore, and pretty soon the truth catches up."

"Annie!"

"How do you think I landed my first husband?" She straightened and lifted her chin. "He was a good man. We raised three beautiful children together. Men are never ready for kids, Tallulah, but trust me, the good ones step up and do a fine job."

"I don't need a husband, Annie," I said, understanding why she and Grandma Helen had never been close. Grandma Helen hadn't put much stock in men. Of course, she hadn't much trusted women either. As far as Grandma Helen was concerned, the good people of the world were the ones who stayed out of her way and kept their opinions to themselves.

Annie gave a little tsk, apparently lamenting the fact that I wasn't giving her advice the attention it deserved. "I only want you to consider your options," she said. "We all need partners in life, Tallulah. It's a fact."

I thanked her, mostly so she would stop talking, grabbed my iced tea, and left. I didn't need a husband. I needed the birds to lay some damn eggs so I could sell the ranch and get the hell out of town.

Crossing the hot expanse of blacktop, I heard the hollow clank of metal on metal coming from the adjacent service garage. A dilapidated Chevy rested up on the rack, and a man in coveralls emerged from underneath it. It was Reuben Martinez. He lived about five miles down the road from us. He held up a finger, asking me to wait a minute, but it was too hot to be standing out in the open that time of day so I moved to the shade near the pumps and waited.

Reuben's neck bent against the sun as he came toward me, keeping me in sight by peering up from under his brows. His name was embroidered on a patch at his left shoulder. From a distance, you'd never guess he was in his seventies. His short hair was shiny and black, and he carried himself with the stride of a younger man, but up close, the deep lines on his face hinted at a hard life. I could see the specks of gray in his mustache. His eyes held a perpetual squint, and his dark skin had been ravaged at some point in his life, leaving his face covered in small, round scars. It was the kind of face that begged to be inspected. I always thought that if I could freeze time and crawl up for a closer look, I might understand the man better.

"Tallulah," he said, trying to wipe the grime from his hands with a grease-stained rag. "I was so sorry to hear about your grandmother." He had the slightest hint of an accent, pausing a little before the word "so," making it "eh-so." He was from somewhere down in Mexico originally, I didn't know where, but he had lived in Sombra for decades.

"I wanted to be at the funeral," he said, shaking his head. "I really did."

As our closest neighbor, Reuben was the one we called if we needed to borrow a tool or if we had a job that required a third set of hands. He had even, once or twice, stayed to join us for our Wednesday-night dinners with Aunt Christine and the girls. I had noticed his absence the day before at the reception, but only right then did I understand why he hadn't come.

For as long as I had known him, he'd made it a priority to avoid his son, Matt, Uncle Scott's sponsor. The way I heard it, through the gossip mill at Pat's Bar, Matt had gone on a bender, stolen his father's life savings, and gambled it away in one weekend in Las Vegas. Knowing what I did about addiction, I doubted that was the only trouble Matt had caused, but that was the story around town, and I had never seen the two men in the same place at the same time, so I figured there was at least some truth to it.

"Don't worry about it," I said, unsure if that was the right thing to say.

"I heard you're selling."

Of course he had heard the news. Damn, that Annie loved to gossip. I could picture her leaning against the garage doorway for hours on end, sharing her opinions on everyone in town while he worked away at whatever car was on the rack, silent except for the occasional "um-hm" to show he was listening, because he believed in good manners, whether he wanted to hear the gossip or not.

"I am," I said, silently berating myself for not anticipating how quickly the news would spread. I needed to call Aunt Christine. I had wanted to tell her in person after everything was official, but given the choice between doing it over the phone and having her hear from some distant acquaintance, the phone was better.

"I'm sorry to hear it," he said. "It won't be the same out here without the Jones family." An awkward silence settled between Reuben and me. The desert could be eerily still in the middle of the day, when even the birds and mice were hiding from the heat. I didn't know what to say. It was so hot there on the pavement that I feared the soles of my boots might melt.

"Please call me if you need any help," he said, shoving the rag into his pocket. "I know you've probably heard that a lot these past few days, but I'm right down the road if you need anything."

It was the first sincere offer of help I'd received. Reuben knew what it meant to be out there in the desert alone. "I'll keep that in mind," I said. "Thank you." Another uncomfortable silence grew, and I thought he might hug me, but he only gave a little head bob and walked back to his work.

In the truck, I dialed Aunt Christine. The loud whoosh of

the AC made it hard to hear the ringing on the other end of the line, so I adjusted the air down and the temperature in the cab jumped about ten degrees. I turned the air back up and pressed the phone hard to my ear. I waited for her to answer, but it went to voice mail. I hung up. It would be bad enough to tell her over the phone that I was selling her childhood home. I couldn't do it in a voice mail.

I drove west another thirty miles on the 66 to Victorville, where the highway spilled me onto Interstate 15 headed north behind a Honda Civic with the license plate IPMS247. I smiled, thinking of Grandma Helen's collection. She would never have taken a plate like that. She would have deemed it tacky. My grandma had a surprisingly prudish streak.

The air conditioning in the truck faltered when I took it over sixty miles per hour, so I kept to the right lane and let the faster traffic—most of it no doubt bound for Las Vegas—zip past me. It was the same route I would take at the end of the month when I drove to Bozeman. I wasn't planning to stop in Vegas but continue northeast out into the desert until I hit Salt Lake City, then due north. It was that last leg I was most looking forward to. I pictured the rise of the road into forest land, how things would grow gradually greener, wet with regular rain, the light filtered by mountainous white clouds.

My truck shuddered as I exited the freeway south of Barstow and my daydreams were replaced with worry when I heard a terrible screeching. The steering wheel jerked in my hands. Another thing I would have to deal with before I left town.

I parked and went into the supply store. It took me all of fifteen minutes to buy three bags of the supplements Bob had recommended and load the twenty-pound sacks into the bed of the truck. Then I headed back down the 15 the way I'd come, thinking about the work ahead of me.

I wouldn't be able to just sprinkle the flakes over the ostrich food. Interfering with their meals in any way was just begging to be pecked to pieces. Laying the vitamin mixture in the bottom of the troughs before I fed them could work, but I was skeptical that enough of the nutrients would be picked up that way. They needed a good healthy serving of the stuff. There was no way around it; I was going to have to lug the heavy bags up a ladder, dump them into the feed silo, then stir the whole thing with a shovel to mix it well. I wondered if I could ask Devon to help. I almost never enlisted him to do work around the ranch, but another set of hands would make the job much easier, and he had promised to come back out to the house after he got off work.

I searched my brain for anything else I needed as I passed through Victorville but came up blank. I didn't even need anything from the grocery store, considering how much food I had in the freezer from Aunt Christine's church friends. Still, I hated to come all that distance for one stop. I drove past a Starbucks and could almost smell the sweet, creamy coffee drinks. A jolt of caffeine would help me through the work I still had to get done back at the ranch.

In Sombra, if I had ever admitted to spending more than a buck fifty on coffee, I'd have been teased unendingly and probably given a nickname—something clever like "*Starbucks.*" There were no coffee shops in Sombra aside from Annie's gas station, with its stale brew and little plastic capsules of pale creamer. The quality of the coffee was judged strictly by its caffeine content.

Starbucks was the opposite of Annie's in every way. The shelves, stacked with useless merchandise, were always full. The signs were written in chalk with little artistic flares. There were comfortable chairs, and nobody spoke to you except to take your order. The folks at Starbucks wouldn't know that I was selling my grandmother's ranch. I wouldn't have to explain myself or worry about wildfire gossip.

I pulled off the highway and was pleased to see, through the large windows, that there were a couple of people ahead of me in line, just enough to get a taste of the anonymity that came with a small group of strangers. Pushing through the glass door advertising the frozen drinks of summer, I was enveloped in the bracing scent of coffee and sugar.

I took my place in line behind a woman in a beige pencil skirt and a lavender blouse. Her perfume overwhelmed the other smells of the place. Her hair was swept up in a tidy bun and she wore shiny, skin-toned high heels, her feet anchored close together as if she had been instructed to take up as little space as possible. Her attention was glued to her phone as she typed a message with incredible speed. Before her in line stood a middle-aged man in a navy blue polo shirt with an embroidered company logo on it. The young, round-faced woman behind the counter rang up his order just as fast as he could read it from the back of a receipt. The lanky, blond guy manning the espresso machine set about making the drinks with astounding efficiency.

I tried to imagine being any one of these people. How far did they commute to work? Did they go home at the end of the day to a family? Or maybe a cat? How did they spend their spare time? Maybe they took salsa lessons or played the guitar. Maybe they watched reality shows all night long.

I lifted up onto my toes, like I was wearing tall, shiny high heels, but quickly lost my balance. I wondered what it would be like to have six coworkers waiting for me to bring them coffee, or even how it would feel to make espresso drinks for people all day. I wanted to ask each of them if they were happy, if their lives had meaning.

I wanted to do something that really mattered in this world, something that made a difference. I suspected that working at Starbucks wasn't anyone's life dream, but what did I know? Maybe the skinny, blond kid behind the espresso machine was right where he wanted to be, serving the world one souped-up coffee drink at a time. I didn't understand how people found purpose in their lives, and I didn't know how anyone continued on with jobs that had no purpose.

Being part of a handcrew in Montana felt like important work. At the end of a full day, I would step back to see that my efforts had changed the world, made people safer. Clearing brush or digging trenches to slow a wildfire would save homes, maybe even lives, and that was something I knew I would feel good about.

"What can I get 'cha?" the woman at the register asked with caffeinated enthusiasm.

"A Venti Triple Mocha Frappuccino with whipped cream," I said. The guys at Pat's Bar would have a field day with that one.

"You got it," she said, smiling and taking my money.

The man in the polo shirt left, balancing two trays of drinks and backing through the door. The woman in the pale heels took a phone call while adding two packets of sugar to her drink, and then she left too. In short order, my drink was ready.

Condensation formed on the plastic cup before I even got to my truck. The sun was falling over the San Gabriel Mountains as I left the interstate and wound my way out of the suburban sprawl that surrounded Victorville. It would be dark when I got home. Grandma Helen and I usually avoided working in the corral after sunset. Flashlights were irresistibly interesting to the ostriches, but I needed to get my newly acquired vitamin supplements into their bellies as soon as possible.

The broken yellow line flashed down the middle of the desolate highway, the steady rhythm of it entrancing. I thought of Grandma Helen. Had she considered me in her final moments? In that last fraction of a second before the crash, did she have a change of heart and try to avoid the tomato truck, or did her foot fall a little heavier on the gas pedal?

I let my truck drift a little and heard the steady thunk of my tires on the dividing reflectors. Hurtling down the highway at sixty miles per hour, I took my hands off the wheel and balled them into fists at my sides. Almost immediately, the truck crossed into the oncoming lane, but I resisted the urge to right it. My heartbeat kicked up. My senses sharpened. Every spiny stem of ocotillo that flashed past the window appeared in perfect detail. The faint scent of a skunk somewhere far off found my nose.

The road ahead remained clear of oncoming traffic, but it would only be a matter of seconds before I hit the gravel shoulder. At the speed I was going, it would be enough to spin the small Tacoma. The momentum might even be enough to flip it. The thin barbed wire that traced the edge of the highway would crumple like a cobweb. I pictured how the windshield would shatter and felt the strap of the seat belt across my collarbone.

Pieces of gravel struck the undercarriage as the tires drifted over the white line on the far side of the road. The steering wheel jerked and I clutched at it to straighten it out. I pulled the truck back to the right side of the road. My body thrummed with adrenaline. In the distance, I saw the headlights of an oncoming car. I cracked the window, even though it was still hot outside. I needed the air. The lemon and camphor smell of the desert creosote calmed me down and my heart rate slowed.

Soon, I saw the small collection of lights that was Sombra. The one traffic signal was green as I passed by Annie's gas station, and without even realizing I was doing it, I scanned the cars outside Pat's Bar to see who was there. I was surprised to see Devon's SUV. I hit the brakes. The truck rattled and skidded as I pulled off the road.

SEVEN

Pushing through the gray metal door of Pat's, I saw the regulars from the day shift at the cement plant. A dozen men rested at the bar, hands wrapped around pint glasses. On the third stool sat Walter, as much a fixture as the stuffed jackalope mounted on the wall above the cash register.

The jukebox in the corner cast an orange glow over the room and played "When Doves Cry" at a low volume. There were no windows. A low white light hung over the pool table, and the rows of bottles on the shelves were lit from behind, setting the glass to glow in shades of emerald and amber. In the low light, I could see Pat bent over the sink washing glasses.

Near the end of the bar, on his usual stool, Devon sat with one elbow propped on the bar, facing the woman next to him and almost hiding her from view, but I caught a glimpse of blond and knew it was Stella, Sheriff Morris's daughter. She was a tiny little thing, coming in at about five foot two, but she compensated with really high heels that she wore everywhere. She was thin and had a way of moving that reminded me of a paper doll, never raising her arms to the side or stepping wide. Instead, she seemed only to bend forward and back. She was leaning on the bar, her body bent at a single point above the waist, as if a fat-fingered child had balanced her there. Her shiny hair fell in a flat, pale ream, ending in a blunt cut.

She was nineteen and a terrible flirt. When she'd graduated from Victorville High the year before, her dad had pulled strings to get her a job as a receptionist at PFX, away from the industrial machinery and ever-present cement dust. She knew the value of gossip in a small town, and her proximity to the sheriff gave her unique knowledge of who was in trouble for what on any given day. She often came down to Pat's Bar, looking all clean and fresh, trying to trade town gossip for an underage drink.

Pat didn't have the heart to kick her out. He served her Diet Cokes and made sure she stayed out of trouble. The sheriff kept his distance, and though no one ever said as much, I figured he knew where Stella was spending her time. In most towns, the local bar probably wasn't the most wholesome place to spend an evening, but the sheriff and Pat both knew that teenagers in Sombra with nothing else to do usually ended up entertaining themselves with meth. As long as Stella didn't come home drunk, a fragile peace was maintained.

As my eyes adjusted, I saw Stella tap a dangerously red fingernail at the screen of Devon's phone. She pulled away from him and playfully slapped his shoulder. He leaned toward her, insisting on whatever argument he was making.

"Tallulah," Pat said, smiling his toothy grin at me from behind the bar. "Welcome back." I hadn't been to the bar in over a week. It felt like a year. At the sound of my name, Devon straightened.

"Hi," I said, trying for upbeat.

"Hey, Lu," Devon said, glancing to Stella and then to me in a way that made him look guilty. He recovered quickly and slipped his phone into his pocket. "How you doing?"

"Tallulah," Stella said in her nasal drawl, leaning back to see around Devon. "I'm so sorry about your grandma?" Everything she said was a question.

"Thank you," I said flatly, wanting her to go away.

"Good to see you, Lu," Pat said, filling a frosty glass with Budweiser.

I climbed onto the stool beside Devon, hoping he would turn away from Stella to face me, but he split the difference, squaring himself against the bar between us.

Pat slid the beer in front of me. Foam slipped over the rim and down the side of the glass. I took a sip. It tasted like the end of a long day.

"I'll put that one on Devon's tab," Pat said with a mock whisper and a wink.

Stella grinned over her nearly empty glass. "Put one on there for me too, would you, Pat?"

Pat poured her another Diet Coke.

I sat elbow to elbow with Devon, staring at the mirror on the other side of the bar in an uncomfortable silence. I wanted to know why he had come to Pat's instead of coming out to the ranch like he'd said he would, but I couldn't think of any way to say it that didn't sound like whining. And anyway, I wasn't even at the ranch, so my complaint felt empty. I studied the side of my glass, wiping at the condensation with my thumb.

Sensing the tension between us, Stella unfolded herself from her stool. "I'm gonna . . . ?" Diet Coke in hand, she made her way across the room to the jukebox.

I took another sip of my beer. "She's got a thing for you."

"She does not," Devon said. In the mirror behind the bottles, I watched an embarrassed smile spread across his face.

"Oh, come on."

"What?" he said. The smile vanished.

"I thought you were coming out to the ranch after work.

Why didn't you text me or something, let me know you were here?"

"I have to check in?" Gone was the jolly guy Stella had been sitting with.

"Not check in," I said. "I just . . ." I didn't know why I was so upset to find him there, huddled up with Stella. I searched my beer for answers and found none.

We sat speechless together, shoulder to shoulder. The guys in the booth behind us laughed at something, and Pat poured more drinks for Devon's coworkers at the other end of the bar.

"Hey," Devon said, in a tone that told me he was eager to change the topic. "I asked around a bit at work today. There might be a position opening up soon in the accounting department."

"The accounting department?"

"Yeah, well, I mean, you'd be working with account managers, a support position. You don't have to know tax law or anything."

"What are you talking about?" I was genuinely confused.

"A job," he said. "A real job, not some contract position way the hell up in Montana. You could stay here in Sombra."

"I can't work at the plant," I said. Hearing the distaste in my voice, I stiffened, aware that I was surrounded by plant employees. The conversations around us faltered.

"What's wrong with the plant?" His tone held steady, but his chin lifted with the slightest hint of defensiveness.

"I can't work in an office is all I mean. You know me. I need to be outdoors." The guys around us, apparently satisfied with that, continued their conversations.

"Then why are you selling the ranch?"

"I . . ." But I couldn't say. I couldn't say that what I really wanted was to make my own decisions, to live a life I chose, rather than simply accepting what was laid out for me. I hadn't chosen to be an ostrich rancher, but it was expected that I would carry on with the business. Just like it was expected that I would marry Devon, because he was there and we were together.

Devon and I met a few weeks after he moved to town. For a year and a half, he had been living in his parents' basement and commuting the forty miles from Victorville to the cement plant, and for all that time we never met. But once he moved into his apartment above the laundromat in Sombra, he decided to join the other locals for beers after work. We met that same night. He had a kind face and an easy smile. After a month of flirting over cheap beers, he walked me out to my car one night and kissed me.

The guys at the bar, Devon's coworkers, liked to joke that our coming together was inevitable because we were the only two single people under the age of fifty in the entire town, but it didn't feel that way. We both liked Pabst Blue Ribbon and buffalo wings made spicy. We played pool and watched baseball. And at the end of the night, we went together to his apartment.

Somehow three years had gone by, and I got the nagging feeling that maybe his coworkers had been right. It was nice to have someone to spend time with, but if I had known I was signing up for forever, I might have reconsidered. Because nice was about the extent of it. Devon had no ambition, no passion. As a lover, he lacked spontaneity or playfulness. He fumbled with my bra strap so often that I finally waved him off and started undoing it for him.

He took the path of least resistance every time. I used to tease him that if someone put a hundred dollars on the stool next to him and a thousand dollars at the end of the bar, he'd take the hundred and be happy with it. He would respond that a hundred dollars was nothing to sneeze at and ask why wouldn't he take the easy money. That was Devon.

Part of the appeal of the Forest Service job had always been distance from Devon. When I'd told him about it, I had cushioned the blow by assuring him I would visit the ranch between assignments, insisting that we could make the long-distance thing work. But if I was being honest, I had hoped, even when I first proposed the idea, that we would grow apart, making the eventual breakup less painful. Or maybe one of us would find someone else and end things quickly, like ripping off a Band-Aid. There would be tears, probably, but then a fresh start somewhere in Montana. Was I really selling the ranch as a way to break up with Devon? He sat there on his barstool, staring at me with those big blue eyes, waiting for me to say something.

"I gotta go," I said. I finished my beer in one extended chug, slammed the glass on the bar, and hurried toward the door, but I could hear Devon following me. I burst out into the open desert with him right on my heels. The moon wasn't yet full, but it washed out the night sky so that only a few of the brightest stars shone overhead. I whirled to face him, unsteady on the gravel. "What do you want, Devon?"

"I want you," he said without hesitation. "Why is that so hard for you to wrap your head around?"

"Oh, I don't know," I said sarcastically. "Maybe it's the fact that I'm not the person you're sitting with after work. If I hadn't spotted your car, would I have even seen you tonight?"

He slumped a bit. "I'm sorry," he said. "I was going to come over. I guess I needed a break. It's been pretty intense at your place."

"Yeah, Devon," I yelled, raising my arms in exasperation. "It has. You don't think maybe I wanted a break too? You don't think maybe I would have liked to sit next to you at the bar and—" I detested the hysteria that was building in my voice. I didn't want to be the jealous girl yelling at her boyfriend in the parking lot of a bar.

"Don't be mad," he said. "And don't go to Montana."

"I have to go," I said, fumbling in my pocket for my keys.

"Why?" he asked. "You're set, Tallulah, more than anyone

else I know. You have everything you need right in front of you: a job, people who care about you. What's so great about Montana?"

"You don't understand," I said.

"So tell me."

Tell him that he was a boring lover. Tell him that his lack of ambition made him a friendly but dull drinking buddy. Tell him that I wanted more from life than he could possibly offer. No. The truth was far too harsh. I spun and rushed away. Tears of frustration gathered and blurred my vision as I got into my truck and wrestled it onto the highway, leaving him there outside the bar.

I fumed as I drove down the road and slapped an escaped tear from my cheek. If he loved me so much, why was he sitting at the bar with Stella? I was confused and hurt, but most of all, I felt alone, on my way to a gloomy house where nobody was waiting. I wished I'd switched on the porch light before I left. Grandma Helen had always left the porch light on for me. Even as we'd grown apart in recent years, talking less and less, the porch light was always on when I got home. On the nights when we argued, it glowed like a little white flag, that light. I was always welcome at the ranch, and the next morning would come with no mention of the previous night's disagreement. We simply moved forward. That was her way. She was as reliable and distant as the desert sun, my grandma.

I thought over our last few years working together. When I decided not to apply to college and stay out in the desert with her, I envisioned her making me a partner. She'd always shown such enthusiasm for my schoolwork, I somehow expected that would carry over to my role on the ranch. I'd hoped she would teach me to manage the books, maybe make me the point person with a few clients. At the very least, I thought she would be excited to have me working with her, but it didn't turn out that way.

Instead, I took on more and more work in the corral while she stayed indoors, only coming out when there was a task I couldn't complete without her help. She said she was taking care of paperwork, taxes, or billing, but more often than not, when I came inside at the end of the day, I found her staring at the pages on her desk and nursing a glass of whiskey. When I asked if she was okay, she said she was fine, and the business carried along as always, so she must have been doing the work.

In the months before her death, she slept late and went to bed early. When Aunt Christine came over for dinners, Grandma Helen would brush her hair and join us at the table, but her heart wasn't in it. The nights would carry on around her as she sipped her whiskey, the chaos that came with my cousins distracting from the fact that she was only there in body.

The only time Grandma Helen ever appeared content was when she greeted her birds in the morning. At the sight of her, Lady Lil would throw her giant wings up high and trot over to say hello. Grandma Helen would smile and visit with her old friend through the fence.

It was that hint of joy that had given me hope. I had thought that maybe my leaving would force her out into the corral to work with the birds again, that it would help her snap out of whatever was dragging her down, but I never got the chance to find out.

I was still thinking about Grandma Helen when the truck lurched. There was a loud bang, and the front right bumper dropped suddenly. The terrible screech of metal scraping the road filled the cab, and sparks flew up over the side windows. I gripped the steering wheel with both hands and yanked hard to bring the truck to the shoulder. It skidded to a stop.

I sat frozen behind the wheel, watching the dust rise up around my windows into the beams of my headlights. An accident. That word floated up into my consciousness again. These kinds of things happened all the time.

My guts clenched and I could taste bile. I scrambled to open my door, but when I leaned out over the road, expecting to be sick, nothing came. I staggered from the truck.

I put my hands against the hood to steady myself and get my bearings. I could see the pale sign for Wishbone Ranch in the distance, less than a quarter of a mile down the road, the white panel of it like a beacon. That, at least, was a blessing.

I pulled a small flashlight from the glove box. Aiming the beam, I could see the bald tread of the tire facing me, wrenched clear off the axle and jammed into the back of the wheel well. A flat I could handle, but this was far beyond my capabilities. I sighed, scanning the horizon. The pale wings of a horned owl flashed as it swooped down from the sky, plucked some small, unfortunate creature from the desert floor to the east of me, and flapped away.

I wasn't particularly keen on leaving my truck on the highway overnight. No one was going to drive off with it, that was certain, but a few of Devon's coworkers had had their tailgates stolen right out of the PFX parking lot, and I knew certain parts under the hood were worth something to a person who knew what to take.

I needed a tow. Thankfully, Reuben Martinez owned a truck that could do the job. And he had insisted I call him if I needed anything. I optimistically checked my phone for service, but I was too far from town. I would have to call him from the house.

I locked the doors of the cab, then hesitated, considering the bags of supplements in the bed of the truck. Each had a trio of eggs pictured on it, reminding me that the entire reason for my leaving the ranch that day was to get the ostriches the additional nutrients they needed to start producing again. I was so damn close.

Determined not to fail in my mission, I tried to lift the three sacks as one, but my palms slipped, unable to get a grip. I clenched the tough plastic in my fists and pulled, but my hands cramped trying to hold so much weight. I dropped the load before I even cleared the truck bed. I heaved a bag onto one hip, like I would carry one of my cousins, and tried to hoist another onto my other side, but I couldn't find my balance and the first slipped from my arm. The second tumbled down after it. I kicked the bag closest to me. The plastic crackled, but the unwieldy supplements didn't budge. I stared at them for a while, thinking there had to be a way to move them, but no solution presented itself. Frustrated, I lugged each sack back into the truck and slammed the gate. I hadn't even managed to complete the first step in my plan to get the birds laying eggs again.

It was getting late. I would have to feed the flock when I got to the ranch, even without the supplements. If I didn't, the birds would turn mean. I had three days until Joe Jared's inspector was due. I hoped that waiting until morning to enhance their food supply wouldn't be the difference between having eggs in the incubator come Tuesday or not.

I walked the shoulder of the road where the pavement met the pale sand. Midday in July, walking even a short distance without water would be risking heatstroke, but by night it was an easy stroll. I clicked off the flashlight and slipped it into my pocket, enjoying the way the moonlight smoothed the landscape.

The stars shimmered, their light distorted by the remaining heat of the day as it radiated back out into space. In the distance, I could just make out the shape of the barn. I checked the mailbox. Its metal hinges screeched as I opened it, revealing a stack of envelopes. In with the usual junk mail and bills were the slightly larger envelopes of condolence cards. I suspected that word of Grandma Helen's death had somehow reached her hometown of Elk Grove. The four cards that had arrived in the past few days were postmarked from that small community up north in California's Central Valley.

It was too dark to read anything out on the road under the moon, so I tucked the mail under my arm and continued my walk home. My path traced the narrow strip of land between the driveway and the corral fence. Theo the guard bird cantered up to peer at me from his side of the fence. He strolled beside me for a few yards, but I was moving so slowly, he got bored and went to curl up on his nest.

The males, with their dark coloring, tended the eggs by night, tucking the white edges of their wings under their bodies so that they blended into the landscape and became nearly invisible; come sunrise, the females took over, camouflaging the nests with their dusty coloration. It was a remarkably equitable situation.

I ducked through the fence and crossed the short distance to the feed silo, where I opened the grate. The grain poured down the sluice with a gravelly swoosh. The females turned their heads and their legs carried them with a slow, even grace. The males seemed to materialize out of thin air as they rose from their nests and exposed the white feathers along the edges of their wings.

I took the opportunity to duck low and check the nests for eggs. I didn't really expect to see any but was nonetheless frustrated when they weren't there. "Why are you sitting on an empty nest?" I asked one of the males as he approached. I tugged on his beak and pressed my forehead to his. "It doesn't make any sense." He pulled his beak free and moved around me to his dinner.

Everything just felt wrong since Grandma Helen's death. The eggs had dried up and the truck had broken down. I hated being out in the desert all by myself, and then I had managed to pick a fight with Devon, the one person who actually wanted to be there with me.

One of the females followed me as I made my way toward the gate, tapping my right shoulder and then my left inquisitively. Her attention drew others. Ostriches were like children in that way. Even midmeal, their attention was easily drawn, and once one was attracted by something, it became irresistible to the others.

By the time I got to the corner of the corral adjacent to the walnut tree and the house beyond, no fewer than fifteen hens were trailing behind me. I swatted them away and opened the gate enough to slip out. Restrained by the fence, they continued to swing their necks, each vying for a position that afforded a view, giving the impression that they were a single, many-headed beast.

The scratching of their toes in the sand, which had seemed so loud as they followed me across the corral, fell quiet. The rustle of wings, lifting and adjusting, whispered in the vast landscape. I reached up, and one of the females bent her neck over the fence to meet my hand. She had an unusual ring of iron-black skin halfway down her neck. Grandma Helen had called her Upanova, I remembered, after the cartoon ostrich in *Fantasia* that wore a bow tie. She nuzzled my palm, and the short, fuzzy hairs of her neck tickled my wrist.

Naming the birds had been part of the transition to focusing on eggs instead of meat. Once my grandparents stopped sending the birds to be slaughtered, they became familiar with the ostriches as individuals and gave them names. I only knew a few of them. "Good night, Upanova," I whispered, giving her beak a friendly tug before retiring to the house.

The abrasive kitchen light hurt my eyes. I tossed the mail onto the counter and it spread out over the tile, butting into the manila envelope Joe Jared had left behind on the day of the funeral. The elaborate cursive of the double *J*s in the corner hinted at a high-class operation. Joe Jared sold most of his meat and leather to glitzy casinos, marketing his products as exotic, expensive luxury goods. Effective branding, Grandma Helen always used to say. The logo for Wishbone Ranch wasn't nearly as ornate. Just a simple *W* inside a circle, it appealed to Grandma Helen's ideal of wholesome goodness, which was the basis of our sales pitch to the organic markets and co-ops we sold to.

A long time ago, when the competition for customers was hurting both ranches, my grandparents had considered partnering with Joe Jared, but a visit to his property put an immediate end to that line of thinking. Joe fed his flock well to ensure they grew quickly, but his corrals were overcrowded and dirty. The birds stood wing to wing, ankle deep in their own filth, which never fully dried. Because the birds were built for arid landscapes, the constant dampness led to skin problems and infections that had to be treated with intense courses of antibiotics that messed up their digestive systems and only made the waste issues worse. Whenever Joe had to go into the corral, he carried a broomstick to beat his path through the birds.

I sat at the table and opened the envelope, pulling out the paperwork for Joe Jared's offer. I wondered how long it would be, once he took over, before our serene ranch resembled his factory farm down in Yuma. I considered his efficient check marks in the margin, his tidy block print at the bottom noting our agreed-upon price.

A sour smell drew my attention to the lilies on the kitchen counter next to the urn of Grandma Helen's ashes. The withered flowers had browned at the edges and curled up on themselves, dropping a layer of pollen on the counter. I left the paperwork on the table and threw the lilies into the trash.

I polished the wooden urn with the hem of my shirt and placed it on the bookshelf in the living room, where it wouldn't be disturbed. I wiped the counter clean, trying not to think about how disappointed Grandma Helen would be that I was selling to Joe Jared.

Handing the ranch over to Joe Jared felt wrong, but there was no one else. It wasn't like there were all so many ostrich ranchers in our part of the world. If she had taken one minute to consider the repercussions of her actions, she would have known I'd sell and she could have guessed that Joe Jared would be the one to buy. If she had wanted a different outcome, she should have stuck around to see to it herself.

Famished, I ate leftover lasagna in front of the television and watched a show about adopted kids tracking down their birth parents. Episode after episode came on, and even though it wasn't good, I kept watching. After a few hours, I knew I should go to bed, but anxiety kept me planted in my chair. Grandma Helen had often gone to bed before I did, leaving me alone downstairs for hours, but even when we weren't in the same room, it was a comfort to know she was there.

Alone in the house, I kept expecting to hear the padding of her footsteps upstairs, or the gurgling of water in the pipes when she used the bathroom. My ears strained for the sounds that didn't come.

I couldn't bring myself to go upstairs, to walk past her room. Griffith was curled up on the couch, his gray head resting on his front paw. I lifted him into my arms. He regarded me with skepticism.

"Let's just stay here for a while," I said, feeling a little foolish talking to the cat, but also grateful that I wasn't talking to myself. The weight of him calmed me. I scratched behind his ears and he purred. He put his one gray paw on my chin, and I could feel the tiny pads of his toes against my skin.

On the television, a teenage girl called her birth mother's number for the first time. She hunched away from the camera, letting her wavy, auburn hair hide her face. When she spoke into the phone, her voice was so soft, closed captions were added: *trying to find my mother?* The words spoken in response appeared at the bottom of screen: *I'm so sorry. She died last year. Breast cancer.* The poor girl sat there all alone, the phone in her hand, and cried.

EIGHT

I woke to predawn light seeping through the curtains in the living room, the television playing a morning talk show. I had slept so soundly, it took me a minute to orient myself to the oversize chair in the living room. My neck ached, and as the fog of sleep cleared, I had the nagging sense of having forgotten something.

"Shit." I sat up straight. My truck was still out on the highway. And the supplements.

Griffith glared up at me, his eyes slits. I pushed him to the floor and checked the clock. It was five thirty in the morning. I burst onto the porch and strained my eyes in the direction of the highway. The sun hadn't yet risen, but filtered light spilled over the horizon, I could just make out my truck, a distant dot in the desert. I debated calling Reuben right then to ask him for a tow, but it seemed rude to call so early asking for a favor. Besides, with the sun about to come up, I guessed the risk of theft had probably passed.

Lady Lil swooped her wings into a graceful salute, like she used to do for Grandma Helen every morning. She trotted toward me across the corral, her head held high.

"Just me," I muttered, sitting down and resting my chin in my hands.

Lady Lil deflated and slowed. Her dappled wings settled flat against her body, giving the impression, as she had every morning since Grandma Helen's death, that she was disappointed. She flashed me her bald spot as she strode away from the house and became a silhouette against the corral fence.

The air was comfortably warm that early in the morning. The amethyst sky stretched for hundreds of miles over the expansive basin of the desert. Wispy clouds high above looked like a flock of doves flying north, their pale feathers peeling away and trailing out behind them.

Abigail limped up from behind the house and sat at my feet. Sunrise reached across the valley and washed orange over the tops of the mountains in the west. The color rolled down toward the desert in a lazy cascade. Closer to where I was sitting, the topmost leaves of the walnut tree caught the light in little orange pools. A bird somewhere close by chirped. In the distance, a similar call rang out twice. A finch bounced low over the brush. More birdcalls floated through the air.

Finally, the sun cleared the horizon and blasted everything with its full light. Shadows stretched out well defined against the sand, and all the pale greens of the desert shrubs emerged, completing the vast daytime landscape. There wouldn't be mornings like this in Montana. I couldn't believe there was anywhere in the world with sunrises so spectacular as in the Mojave. Warmth bathed my face and arms. I inhaled the smell of sage and distant pines. Soon, the heat would be unbearable, but those first precious moments of daylight were a gift.

Henley emerged from the barn and sat between Abigail and me. I ran my hand over his shaggy fur. As light spilled across the corral, the ostriches began their morning shift change and I could see from the porch that there were no eggs. I went inside to check the time. Five forty-eight. On a Saturday. The last thing I wanted to do was piss Reuben off by waking him, but I couldn't give the birds their breakfast until I got those supplements mixed into the feed. Days were slipping away and I needed an incubator full of eggs before Joe Jared's inspector came. I would wait until seven. It was all I could bear.

I walked around the corral to keep myself occupied and away from the phone. The land to the east was coated with a polished crust of sand that the rain had smoothed over on the day of the funeral, but the perfect footprints I left were quickly disturbed by Henley, who bounded along next to me, darting out to chase lizards into the sagebrush, then back again to sniff for whatever it was a dog could discern in the sand. Abigail followed a few paces behind us. A male bird shifted on his nest about ten yards inside the fence. He rocked left, then right, to pull his legs under him and the movement was so familiar that I paused to watch, to see if maybe he'd been guarding an egg, if perhaps the birds would start laying again just as mysteriously as they had stopped, but as he walked away I saw that the nest was empty. That made it a solid two days I had gone without collecting an egg.

"Damn it," I said.

The temperature cranked up as I made my way around the corral, half-heartedly checking for eggs and finding nothing. My frustration grew with every passing minute. I should have tried harder to drag those supplements to the ranch, should have figured out a way to get the work done before I ever went inside. I'd let exhaustion and self-pity get the better of me. I checked the time, but it was only half past six.

If Devon had just come over like he said he would, I wouldn't have seen his SUV parked outside Pat's, and I wouldn't have stopped, and my truck would have gotten me all the way home. I pictured the way Stella's hand had rested on his shoulder when they didn't know I was watching, the comfortable way they sat next to each other.

Just then, a plume of dust appeared at the end of the drive. Panic fluttered at the thought that it might be Joe Jared's inspector, but I quickly dismissed the notion, remembering it was the weekend. I peered down the road. Heat waves distorted the view, even that early in the day. As it got closer, I could see it wasn't a car. It was a truck, a big one. I would almost have thought it was Grandma Helen, towing the bird trailer, but that was impossible.

Abigail saw it too. We didn't normally welcome many visitors, and the entire ranch paused to see who it could be. Theo emerged from the flock, frantic to meet whoever was coming up the drive. His pace evened and he was about thirty yards out when I recognized Reuben Martinez's tow truck, with my pickup dragging along behind. I met him at the end of the driveway. Abigail followed.

The dirt kicked up by Reuben's tires billowed under the shadow of the walnut tree. His window was down. He gave a little nod when he saw me, then tucked his chin into the slightly guarded posture that was so distinctly his. His dark hair, as always, was combed straight back from his forehead. He squinted in the morning light, the scars on his face pulling into a new configuration, the shiny skin bunching up toward the bridge of his nose, deepening the creases by his eyes. I heard him set the parking brake before he opened his door. He was wearing the same faded coveralls as the day before, or else he had more than one with his name embroidered on it.

"How did you know I needed a tow?" I asked, relieved to see that the tailgate of my truck was intact.

But Reuben had a sour face. "You should have called me," he said. He unhooked a large metal latch and worked a small joystick. There was a low buzzing, and the tow arm lowered. I inspected the front right tire well. The wheel had come off completely and was resting in the bed all by itself. The three giant bags of supplements were gone. "Son of a bitch," I said, slapping the side of the pickup.

Reuben looked up. "I had a bunch of vitamins back there, for the birds." It sounded stupid when I said it like that. "The birds stopped laying eggs and the vet said . . . shit. I need those bags." I pictured some high ass waking up later in the day and wondering why on earth he had bothered to steal a load of bird vitamins. "Shit!" I kicked the gravel.

"They got your converter too." He bent low and waved for me to join him.

I leaned over and saw the gaping end of a metal pipe hanging underneath my truck. I couldn't have told you what was there before, but it was clear that something was missing. "Damn it."

"Used to be, out here, you could leave a car on the side of the road." Reuben moved around to the far side of the truck and pushed a lever. A motor whirred to life, and the tow chain slackened. "These days, people'll steal anything they can sell for a few bucks." I got an I-told-you-so feeling from him, but he was kind enough not to say anything more.

Abigail came over to inspect the control panel of Reuben's truck. He gently shooed her away, but she hovered nearby, waiting for him to leave it unguarded.

"Damn," I said again. "I meant to call you last night when I got back to the house." What the hell was I going to do about the eggs now? I couldn't even drive out to the feed store again until my truck was fixed. The metal bumper was all torn up from where it had scraped against the highway. In the light of day, it seemed a miracle it hadn't flipped. "Can you fix it?"

"Oh, I can fix it," he said, "but it's not cheap." He flicked off the hydraulic winch and pulled a chain loose with a chunky rattle. "That ball joint alone's gonna run you about four hundred, with labor. Then another five hundred or so for the converter."

I must have winced a little, because he hurried to add, "I'm surprised that ball joint held out as long as it did. Didn't you notice the truck shaking when you drove it?"

I had. It rattled like a son of a bitch every time I braked, but it had been low on my list of priorities. If I was being honest, I had been waiting for Grandma Helen to tire of her 2014 Tacoma. She tended to upgrade every five years or so, and though we hadn't discussed it, I was hoping she would pass on the older one to me. Sadly, it hadn't fared much better than she had in the crash.

Reuben ran his thumbnail under the nail of the index finger on the other hand. "It would have been a lot cheaper if you'd taken care of it when you first noticed something was off. Now we gotta replace the whole unit."

"Can you do it now?"

"I can work on it today," he said, irritated at my impatience, "but I'll need parts. Let me get her jacked up, take a look at what we're dealing with, then I'll swing by the shop."

The light filtered through the leaves of the walnut tree, dappling his coveralls as he maneuvered a steel plate under the front bumper and propped a jack in place. Not sure what to do with myself, I paced in the driveway. There were no eggs to collect, and I couldn't go anywhere without my truck. There weren't even any walnuts to husk. Of course, there were always things that needed repair around the property, but Joe Jared and I had already agreed on a price and I wasn't going to spend my time fixing things just to save him the trouble.

Reuben pumped the jack handle and the chassis lifted inch by inch. He and Grandma Helen had been friends for decades. Not that Grandma Helen was really close with anyone, but he knew her well enough that he might have some perspective on what had happened. It occurred to me that I might ask him what he thought about Grandma Helen's death. More than anything, I wanted to say out loud—to someone—that I wasn't convinced it had been an accident, if only to have that someone reassure me. Maybe, if I said it out loud, it would sound ridiculous and I would know I was wrong. Or maybe not. Reuben glanced up at me, sensing that I wanted to say something. "What is it?"

But when I tried to respond, I wavered. Suicide was such a terrible word. Maybe I didn't want to know. Maybe it was better to let my suspicions fade over time and get on board with the idea of it being an accident. Because if it wasn't an accident, the argument we'd had the evening before her death would play forever in my memory, accusing me of being the reason she checked out. "I appreciate your help."

"Yep," Reuben said, leaning over to inspect the inside of the wheel well.

Behind him in the corral, a flurry of feathers sprinted across the corral. It was Theo again, racing to meet a white sedan at the end of the driveway. I didn't recognize it, but apparently, Reuben did. He shifted on his feet and packed up his tools. His discomfort made sense when the car got closer. It was Reuben's son, Matt.

He parked against the corral fence, a good hundred feet from the house, in almost the same place he'd parked when he drove out with Uncle Scott for the funeral reception. He rolled down his window and hung his arm over the car door. I went to meet him.

His beard had grown noticeably in the couple of days since I'd seen him last, and he'd swapped his ill-fitting suit for a well-worn, blue T-shirt with a GPC logo. His hair hung loose around his face and his tattoos rolled freely down his arms in colorful patterns. As I got closer, I could see the scales of a snake, and a *calavera* with red roses for eyes. The name Carmen was wrapped around his forearm in an elaborate, looping script.

The birds, forever snooping, shifted toward the spot inside the corral closest to where Matt had parked. Soon, ostriches were jostling one another for a spot at the fence to see what all the excitement was about.

I couldn't think why Matt would come out to the ranch by himself. He scratched absentmindedly at his beard and I noticed the ink on his bicep: a detailed Aztec calendar with the letters NA in a double circle at the center—an interesting mash-up of symbolism. His glance shifted to where his father was busying himself.

For his part, Reuben did a great job of pretending that his estranged son hadn't just arrived. He inspected his toolbox with great focus.

"Tallulah, I . . . uh." Matt hesitated, as distracted by his father's presence as I was by his. "Sorry to interrupt. I wanted to drop by before work." He glanced at the house. "I'm trying to find Scott. He's not answering his phone, and I know service isn't so good out here. You seen him?"

"Not since you two left the other day," I said, knowing that wasn't what he wanted to hear. Grandma Helen never slept well when Uncle Scott stopped answering his phone. After a few days of not being able to reach him, the concern took its toll. In the middle of the night I would hear her footsteps down the stairs, the heavy scrape of the whiskey bottle as she pulled it from the cabinet. My heart dropped. "You're worried?" I asked.

"Yeah." Matt glanced over at his father again. If the rumors I'd heard were true, it had been years since their paths had crossed. Matt had moved to Victorville when Reuben finally kicked him out. When he got sober, he stayed there in the city, made himself a life as a mechanic, just like his dad, his fingernails always lined in grease. He looked a lot like Reuben. He had the same shiny, raven hair, the same intense eyes, but where his dad's face was a mosaic of scars, Matt's skin was smooth. The tension between father and son grew thick. Reuben kept clanking around in the back of his truck, but if he hadn't found his wayward tool by then, it wasn't in there.

Matt eyeballed my pickup and craned his neck for a better view. "Ball joint?"

"That's what I'm told."

"You need any help with it?" Matt asked. The question was directed at me, but he asked it a little louder than he needed to. "I could maybe hook you up with some parts."

Reuben grunted. "It's under control," he said, his back still to us.

Matt's car inched forward to make a slow U-turn around the walnut tree and he leaned out the window for a better view of the exposed axle. "Let me guess," he hollered. "He quoted you three fifty."

"Four for the ball joint," I said, reluctant to share the information, sensing I was teetering on the edge of an argument I wanted no part in.

"Fuck that," Matt said, shaking his head and waving an arm at Reuben. He gunned his engine and pulled his car around in a spray of gravel until the nose of the car pointed east, the way he'd come. "That's why nobody trusts mechanics," he said, not really to me. He raised his voice again. "And for a neighbor too."

Reuben burst from his stance and threw his tools through the open passenger window of his tow truck. "If you don't want my help—" He stomped around to the driver's side and climbed in.

"No, Reuben, I do. Please don't go," I said, pleading with him.

"The parts shouldn't cost more than ninety bucks," Matt said in an annoyingly calm and steady voice behind me.

Reuben's engine roared to life. He shoved at the gearshift. "He knows so much," he said, shoving his chin in Matt's direction, "he can fix it."

"Maybe I will," Matt said, directly responding to his father for the first time.

"Fine." And without another word, Reuben's tow truck rolled past Matt's car and took off down the driveway, gravel flying behind him. Abigail fluttered out of his way.

"Fine," Matt yelled after his father, but I doubted Reuben heard him.

I flared at Matt. "What the hell?" Without even getting out of his car, he had managed to ruin the one thing that was going right for me.

"He shouldn't be gouging you like that."

"So you're gonna fix it?" I pointed at my truck, up on the jack, missing a wheel.

Matt scanned the desert, distracted. "I need to find Scott."

"Damn it, Matt. You can't just leave me out here with my truck in pieces. I need a new catalytic converter too, apparently. It got stolen."

He picked up his phone, then remembered there was no service out at the ranch and dropped it on his passenger seat.

"Matt?"

"Sorry," he said. "I'll stop by the shop to pick up the parts. I'll come back as soon as I can." He glanced over at his phone again. "You don't have any idea where he might have gone, do you?"

"I don't have the first fucking idea." I was getting the sense that my problems were not a priority. "Matt, I'm stranded here without my truck."

"I'll be back," he said. "Sit tight."

And with that, he rolled up his window and drove toward the highway, leaving me alone under the walnut tree next to my broken pickup.

"Damn it," I said again, watching him go. I didn't have room in my brain for everyone else's problems. If Uncle Scott was using again, that sucked, but there was nothing I could do about it. And I certainly couldn't make Matt and his father patch up their relationship. The eggs were my only concern. But there was nothing I could do until the truck was fixed. I stomped my foot in frustration. I needed eggs.

And then a thought blew through my head like a tumbleweed: I had eggs, hundreds of them. I had been collecting eggs in the cold storage unit for half the season. I hurried over to the door of the walk-in refrigerator and considered the rows and rows of eggs. Of course, they were way past being viable. Any inspector who knew anything about ostriches would be able to tell pretty easily that they would never hatch, but a plan began to take shape.

If I stacked the nonviable eggs in the back of the incubator and I could get even a few viable ones, I could stack those in the first row. It was unlikely the inspector would check every egg. Unless he had some reason to be suspicious, he would probably check the viability of a few, pulled randomly from the front, and call it good. And the incubation period was long enough that by the time Joe Jared realized I'd left him with an incubator half full of bunk eggs, I'd be deep in the woods of Montana. The ultimate loss to Joe Jared would be almost nothing, relative to the value of the ranch. I just needed a way to fill the incubator while I dealt with the birds. Otherwise, the whole deal would fall through, and nobody wanted that.

I pulled a few of the cold eggs from the shelf, holding them in the hem of my shirt to transport them to the barn, where they slipped easily into the incubator trays. I flipped the machine on and watched through the glass door as the warm red light came to life.

It was dishonest, I knew, but I didn't see what choice I had. I grabbed the wheelbarrow and calculated how many eggs I would have expected to collect over the past two days, then added a few more, because it didn't seem likely that I was getting to the feed store before they closed, which meant another day at least. In total, I moved one hundred eggs to the incubator, but then the round number seemed to scream deception, so I pulled two out again. Better not to hit the mark exactly. It seemed more realistic that way, and I didn't want to prompt any questions. I was a terrible liar, always had been. If the inspector noticed anything amiss and asked about it, I didn't know if I could keep up appearances.

I thought of Uncle Scott. His addiction had been like an advanced course in falsehoods. I couldn't count the number of times he told us things that were later revealed to be untrue. *His car had been broken in to. He got fired for being five minutes late for his shift. Aunt Christine's church friends had turned her against him.* He always seemed to believe what he was telling us, no matter how unlikely the story. That was the trick of it. Liars had to believe their lies in order to be convincing.

I closed my eyes and imagined that I had collected those ninety-eight eggs in the corral. In my imagination, I shoved the wheelbarrow through the sand to the barn and loaded the warm, sandy eggs into the incubator. Then I blinked and tried to see the eggs under the red light as fresh, but it didn't work. I knew they would be cold to the touch, that they had come from the storage unit and not the corral. I simply had no experience with incubating the eggs, no memory to pull from. I didn't know what I was doing.

My only hope was to get my truck fixed, buy another round of supplements, get the birds laying eggs again, stack the good eggs in front of the bunk ones, and cross my fingers that nobody asked any questions, because one way or another, I was moving to Montana. It was time to start packing.

I tromped back over to the cold storage unit where I grabbed a stack of the two-foot-square boxes we used to ship the eggs. They were the perfect size for boxing up most everything in the house. Anything of sentimental value I would save for Aunt Christine. The rest would go to charity.

The act of packing sounded straightforward enough, but when I went into the house, boxes at the ready, I had to stop and think. It made sense to save the kitchen for last. I would need things in there up until I left.

I decided to tackle the most daunting room first, if only to get it over with. I trudged up the stairs, then hesitated outside Grandma Helen's door. It had never been off-limits exactly, but Grandma Helen and I had always respected each other's privacy. Standing there at the threshold, I had to remind myself that it wasn't hers anymore. She had no more use for it. Still, as I stepped into the space, I had the instinct to explain myself. I dropped the stack of boxes onto the worn daffodil quilt that covered Grandma Helen's perfectly made bed and got to work.

The room was clean and uncluttered. The white walls had almost nothing on them except for one small painting of orange hills stacked up against a red sky. On the far side of the bed was a closet with sliding doors. To my left were two tall windows facing east, framed by delicate, honey-colored curtains. A stout dresser sat between them, and on it rested a collection of framed photos.

In the center, framed in mahogany, was a wedding photograph of my grandparents emerging from what looked like a courthouse with tall cement pillars on either side. They were so young. Tiny specks of white—I assumed rice thrown by guests—blurred the image.

My grandmother was waving. She wore a crown of small white flowers and an informal, lacy gown with a high waistline. My grandfather, a handsome man with a strong chin, had on a chocolate-brown suit with a matching vest and a red tie. He braced himself with a wooden cane. They had been married shortly after he returned from Vietnam with a bullet in his leg. Grandma Helen had told me how he only needed the cane for a few years, but he had walked with a limp the rest of his life. They were a handsome couple, both smiling into the future. An imprint in the bottom corner noted the year: 1969.

There were other photographs: a senior class photo of my

aunt with filtered light pouring over her smooth blond hair; a similarly posed shot of my uncle, considerably less comfortable in a formal portrait; a school photo of my mom, presumably in her sophomore year, before she dropped out. Tucked into the metal frame was a small baby picture of me. I pulled it free and flipped it over. On the back were my name and birth date in Grandma Helen's handwriting.

Grandma Helen had not approved of her daughter running off to Los Angeles as a pregnant teenager, but she did nothing to prevent it. She figured my mom would come home to the ranch when the guy predictably left her a single parent, but my mom was too proud for that.

Next to my baby photo was a framed portrait of Aunt Christine's oldest, my cousin Gabby, as an infant, but none of the other grandkids were represented. My grandfather had died of cancer shortly after Gabby was born, and if I were to judge by how the progression of photos stopped there, it was clear that Grandma Helen had lost more than her husband that year.

Without Grandpa Hank, she didn't have the will to do all the things that life on the ranch required. She was getting on in years, living and working alone. It was less than a year after my grandfather's death that she came and collected me from Oakland. I knew she needed help running the ranch, but surveying her collection of photos, I wondered if maybe it was more than that. It was possible, despite her stoicism, that she was lonely.

I wrapped each photo in a pillowcase and carefully stacked them in a box, marking the side with Aunt Christine's name so it wouldn't get mixed up with the boxes going to Goodwill.

The contents of the dresser were much easier. I boxed them up without looking too closely, then shifted to the closet. My grandmother didn't have any need for formal wear, so there were only a few simple blouses hanging over a small collection of cowboy boots. I pulled them from the rack, revealing an old-fashioned suit and a white lace dress. The very same clothes from the photo of my grandparents on their wedding day. I ran my hand over the lapel of the suit, traced the pattern of the dress's lace with my fingers, then lifted them from the closet and folded them carefully into a box, marking that one too for Aunt Christine. I was glad to have someone who would take care of them.

My grandparents had been married for thirty-four years when my grandfather passed away. They moved to the desert and stuck by each other through the blistering summers and freezing winters, through building a business from scratch and raising three kids. I wished I had witnessed their partnership in action. I had no concept of what it would mean to share so much with one person. Long-enduring couples were not really something I had any frame of reference for. All my friends growing up had lived with single moms. Aunt Christine and Todd were the only married people I knew well, and theirs was not a relationship I wanted to duplicate.

Devon's parents were married. They lived in Victorville. I had been over for dinner once. His mom collected silly mugs with encouraging phrases on them and grew basil in a small pot beside the kitchen sink. She had tried to grow a little garden in a rectangle of dirt outside their single-story home, but the desert sun had proven to be too hot for pretty much anything. Even tomatoes withered without shade.

Devon's dad installed home-security systems for a living. He worked regular hours and watched football on the weekends. They were friendly and kind people who had taken a sincere and active interest in their son. They went to all his high school baseball games and hung framed photos of him around the house. They still insisted he come home for dinner once a month. Devon knew much more than I did what it meant to have a family.

I worried that there was something wrong with me, that I was incapable of truly loving someone. I had been raised by women who never seemed to feel anything, first my mom, then Grandma Helen. Still, as detached as she was, my grandma had managed to stay married. And then there was Aunt Christine. She had found someone to build a life with. Perhaps it was premature to assume there was something inherently broken in me, but I knew for certain I wasn't ready to settle down and start a family.

By the time I finished packing up Grandma Helen's room, it was late afternoon. I took the painting off the wall and put it with the boxes bound for charity. As soon as my truck was fixed, I would make a few runs into town to donate what wasn't going to Aunt Christine. With everything packed up in boxes, the space left by Grandma Helen—that amorphous, black hole that I had been tiptoeing around—filled in a little bit. It became less Grandma Helen's room and more just a bedroom, same as any other.

I took a break to eat more leftovers from the funeral reception, washing down some cold cuts with a beer. Then, energized by the progress I'd made upstairs, I decided to pack up the office.

Grandma Helen had been a thorough record keeper. A series of boxes on the top shelf were labeled with dates going all the way back to 1974, the year she and Grandpa Hank bought the ranch. The most recent were dated 2016. That was the year I had talked her into going digital.

It had taken me three months to convince her that a new computer would be a smart investment. Then, with cash in hand, I drove myself to the nearest electronics store in Victorville and bought a thirteen-inch laptop with a color printer. It was beautiful. Grandma Helen groused some at the expense but sat with me patiently as I downloaded a livestock management program, input our list of clients, and connected our bank accounts. Once she understood how useful it could be to have all that information in one place, her natural instincts for running the business took over. Within a few weeks, she was using the program to review trends in our expenses and do financial forecasts. Thoughts of the ranch finances brought a sudden rush of dread. No one had attended to the business side of our operation since Grandma Helen's death. I had completely dropped the ball on that one.

In the pantry-turned-office, I switched on the computer and logged on to see what accounts were due, what bills needed to be paid. Sure enough, a pop-up window alerted me that our account had insufficient funds to cover upcoming scheduled payments. Fighting off my mounting panic, I scrolled to review recent expenses and stopped short when I saw a check Grandma Helen had written for five thousand dollars. We never used paper checks for business expenses anymore. I clicked to view an image of the cleared check and saw that it was made out to Scott Jones. He'd cashed it the day after the funeral.

The date on the check suggested she wrote it a week before her supposed accident, but I couldn't think why she would have cut him a check in any amount—let alone one for five thousand dollars. It also seemed unlikely that he would have waited to cash such a large check. I examined the signature, then clicked away to find a check from before we paid vendors digitally. The loop of the *J* in Jones dropped a little deeper, while the trailing tail of the *s* lifted a bit farther. It wasn't dramatic. Uncle Scott clearly knew how to imitate his mother's handwriting. Matt had been right to worry.

Then, like anyone who's ever cared for an addict, I tried to find a way to explain his behavior, to convince myself that it was all some sober misunderstanding. Uncle Scott was terrible with money. He was up to his neck in credit card debt and had lost the deposit on every apartment he ever rented. Grandma Helen had helped him out when she could. Maybe her death was more premeditated than even I had considered. Perhaps she felt guilty for carving him out of the will and mailed the check to him before her so-called accident. It would have been quicker and easier than changing her will to leave him the money. But I knew in my heart I was fooling myself. It didn't line up with what I knew of Uncle Scott and the cycles of his drug abuse. Sobriety was such a delicate thing in his hands.

I imagined him parting ways with Matt in Victorville after the funeral. Maybe Matt had tried to convince him to stay and have some coffee. Maybe Uncle Scott had insisted he was fine, he just needed to sleep. Maybe he even meant it, but he never made it home. Instead he found a hookup and was high as the bloom on a Joshua tree before the storm cleared. The next morning, wondering why he'd ever quit, he forged a check for five grand and disappeared.

It was scary what kind of damage he could do to himself with that much money in his pocket. I hoped Matt would track him down soon. Matt had a way of talking sense into Uncle Scott that none of us could duplicate. If Matt could convince him to leave whatever skeezy crowd he was hanging out with and go to a meeting, that would be the end of the binge. That was how it had always worked in the past.

In the meantime, I put a freeze on the Wishbone Ranch checking account. I would have to use the money from my personal savings to cover the pending expenses. I had been squirreling money away for my move to Montana, but there wasn't much. After covering the shortfall for the ranch I would have just under two thousand dollars. It would have to last me until the sale of the ranch went through and the funds landed in my account. Thoughts of the bunk eggs in the incubator nagged at my conscience, but I dismissed them. I just had to stay the course. Everything would be fine.

I grabbed a trash bag from the kitchen and began pulling papers from the filing cabinets. The first few drawers were easy enough, full of invoices and receipts from decades of ranch business. I trashed it all. But the last drawer held a collection of personal papers: my grandparents' marriage certificate, birth announcements for their three children, condolence cards sent after my grandfather's passing. Anything worth keeping I set aside for Aunt Christine.

It was dark outside when I stopped to eat and my energy began to wane. There was just so much to sort through. I rested my head on the desk, just for a second, and must have dozed off. From the darkness of a dreamless sleep I heard my name.

"Tallulah."

The voice sounded far away, and it lifted the middle syllable of my name the way Grandma Helen used to do. Ta-LOOH-la. A piece of paper stuck to my cheek. I brushed it away and sat up. I was in the office. The desk lamp cast a small circle of light.

"Tallulah," the voice said again, with that same lift.

The light from the kitchen drew me out.

Standing in the threshold of the entryway, holding the door open behind her, was a thin woman in high-heeled boots, silver leggings, and a Metallica T-shirt. Her blond dreadlocks dangled down past her collarbone in a wild mane.

"Mom?"

NINE

"Tallulah, sweetheart!" She threw her hands in the air and tumbled toward me. Her dreadlocks were longer, the lines around her eyes had deepened, and her face had thinned. As she wrapped me in her arms, I could smell the cigarette smoke on her. Camel Lights. She stepped back and held me at arm's length. The collar of her shirt had been cut away, and one side of it hung down over her shoulder, exposing a lacy red bra strap. "Look at you!" Then she pulled me to her again. "You're a grown woman."

The last time I'd seen my mom, I was thirteen. I had been a pale, pudgy kid in Oakland, but that had changed pretty quickly when I started working on the ranch. I was taller, stronger, and tanner from working out in the sun.

Over her shoulder, I saw Devon come into the house and shut the door. I thought maybe I was dreaming. I didn't understand why Devon and my mom were coming through my front door together in the middle of the night. "What are you doing here?" I asked, not quite sure which of them I was asking.

"Oh, sweetie," she said, letting go. "I'm so sorry it took me so long to get here."

"The funeral was two days ago."

"I know. This must have been a terrible week for you." The heels of her boots knocked against the linoleum as she walked into the kitchen and navigated a slow survey of the home she had left behind twenty-four years before. "This place hasn't changed a bit," she said.

"What are you doing here?" I asked again, much more awake now that I was on my feet.

"I told you I was coming." She opened the refrigerator and leaned back, apparently impressed with the amount of food. She cocked her head left, then right. "There we go," she said, pulling a beer from deep inside.

"It's been a week."

"Well, of course I was coming," she said. "Want one, hon?" She held out a beer to Devon.

He waved her off.

Glancing at the clock, I saw it was two thirty in the morning, and the pieces clicked into place. "You guys have been hanging out? Drinking?"

My mom twisted the cap from her beer. "It's a funny story, actually."

I doubted it.

"See, my car broke down before I even got out of Oakland. Shitty luck, right?" She took a sip, checked out the label. "So I had to deal with that, but then I didn't have the money for the repairs, so I tried to borrow it from Tammy. She's a friend of mine. But she didn't have it. Anyway, long story short, I managed to catch a ride down the five, then hitched my way over to Sombra, but I wasn't about to walk all the way out here to the ranch. So I ducked into Pat's to see if I could convince someone to give me a lift, and I ended up having just the best time."

She leaned over to give Devon's shoulder a friendly shove. "Best place to make new friends is in an old bar," she said, taking the seat across from him. "I ran into this guy, Walter. We went to high school together. He hasn't changed a bit. Well, actually, he's a lot rounder than he used to be."

"I know Walter," I said, bridling. Where did she think she was? That was my bar. Everyone knew Walter.

"Right," my mom said. "Of course you do. Anyway, Walter and I were catching up and I was meeting some of the new faces when Pat introduced me to my daughter's boyfriend." She stretched the word "*boyfriend*" and raised an arm in Devon's direction.

Devon's eyes were bleary. The notion of them sitting together at the bar, drinking, appeared clearly in my mind, infuriating for the ease with which I'd been excluded. "Why didn't you call me?"

"Oh, don't be mad," my mom said. I didn't remember her voice being so grating. "I made him promise not to! I wanted to surprise you."

"Yeah, well, mission accomplished." I took the seat at the far end of the table, still stunned.

"But then we had to have a drink first, and next thing we knew, Pat was closing down the bar." She was hammered, and unless something had changed dramatically, it took more than a few drinks to get her that drunk.

My mom kept talking. "Devon told me all about how you're planning to sell the ranch and take that forestry job." Her expression shifted then, like she had a secret she was excited to share with me. "He also told me about how he's trying to convince you to stay."

"Jesus, Devon, you're going around telling everyone about our private lives?"

But my mom didn't give him a chance to answer. "Don't be so hard on him. I'm practically his mother-in-law. He had to tell me. But Tallulah, I can't believe you'd sell this place. It's been in the family for, like, fifty years."

"Forty-six." It was too much. I didn't know if it was my

mom appearing like a fucking ghost out of nowhere, or if it was the idea of Devon telling the whole town about our argument, or that this was all happening in the middle of the night, but I was suddenly overwhelmed. I needed to talk to Devon alone.

"Can I talk to you outside for a minute?" Without waiting for an answer, I stormed out and paced on the porch until he followed.

"Don't be mad," he said first thing. "I thought maybe, if I talked to your mom . . ." He trailed off. There was a chip in the paint of the railing, and he pressed his thumb into it.

"That she might have some idea of how to make me stay?" A warm breeze rolled over the porch. The ostriches strolled around the corral.

"Yeah," he said. "I want you to stay, Lu. Why is that such a bad thing?" It was the same argument from the night before, right where we'd left off.

"You're trying to make me do something I don't want to do, make me into something I'm not."

"Tallulah," he said, leaning against the post in the light that spilled from the kitchen window. "I'm not trying to make you into anything. I swear. I just don't want you to go to Montana."

I didn't believe him. He wanted me to be a wife and a mother and fit into the nice little space he'd created for me in his future. I crossed my arms over my chest.

"I want you here, where I can touch you." He gave me a coy, little half smile and reached out a hand to beckon me closer.

I kept my distance. "Maybe if you'd left my mom at the bar."

He perked up and hooked his thumb toward the driveway. "I could take her back."

His outstretched fingers grabbed my belt to pull me close. I could smell the beer on his breath as he kissed the side of my neck. "I'm sorry," he said, "I should have given you the heads-up, even if she did ask me not to."

"You should have," I agreed and swatted his shoulder. He nuzzled the base of my neck. I closed my eyes, wishing I could stay there and ignore the fact of my mother's arrival.

A clatter came from inside the house. "I should go in."

"No," he whispered. His arms tightened around my waist. "Stay here." I pushed against him, but he held me firmly. "Stay," he said again.

"I'm not a damn dog."

He relented and let go.

"Come inside?"

"Nah. I gotta go to work in like"— he looked at his bare wrist, where a watch would be if he wore one— "six hours. I should get some sleep. Besides, your mom is really intense." He pointed at the front door, as if afraid it might swing open, and retreated slowly.

"You sure you're okay to drive?" It was always hard to tell with Devon.

"I'm fine," he said. "Tallulah, I'm sorry. For everything."

"Call me tomorrow."

He bounded back for another kiss, then strode out to his car. He was halfway across the drive when he spun around. "I forgot," he said. "I've got your mom's bags. I'll bring them in."

Inside, my mom swayed as she leaned over the couch to inspect a portrait of Aunt Christine and her family. She waved a drunken finger at it. "I hear they got number six on the way."

Devon came in behind me with two giant duffel bags and propped them against the wall at the bottom of the stairs.

"Devon, you're a prince," my mom said with a lazy smile. Her dreadlocks cascaded down around her in a jumbled mess.

"Jesus, Mom. You sure you brought enough stuff?"

Devon ducked out the door and I snickered to think he might actually be afraid of her.

"You know me," she said, waving an arm. Her bracelets rattled. "I don't travel light."

I didn't know her at all. But there she was, standing in the living room that was hers before it was mine.

She ambled to the kitchen to retrieve another beer from the fridge and left the door hanging open. "We are so alike, you and me," she said. She twisted the cap off the beer and took a deep pull.

I closed the fridge. "How do you figure?"

"That man out there," she said, aiming the neck of her bottle at the door. "That's how I figure. You've got a good one there. He's nice, employed, and frankly, hella fun." She yanked a chair from the kitchen table and spun it around to sit with her arms draped over the back of it. "He's a keeper, and you're not sure you want him. I can relate to that. Good guys are never as interesting as the bad ones, are they?"

I sat across from her, thinking about the blur of boyfriends she'd had when I was young. I couldn't remember any of them lasting more than a month, and the images I conjured weren't flattering. Mullets and scraggly beards, dirty jeans and bloodied knuckles, a bumper sticker that read: *If it has tits or tires you're going to have trouble with it.* "When did you ever date a good guy?"

"There was one or two." She sighed. "One even proposed."

I hadn't known that.

"You were only three," she said. "You probably don't remember him, but he was a good guy. I wore the ring for months, but we never did pick a day. I fucked it up." She put her hand flat on the table, arm outstretched, like she wanted to take my hand but couldn't quite.

I remained skeptical and a little unsettled. "So I'm fucking up a good thing?"

"Eh," she said. "I just call 'em like I see 'em."

I wondered how much of this conversation had been orchestrated by Devon. I pictured him asking my mom for help, insisting that she, as my mom, could talk me into staying with him in Sombra and her agreeing, even though she had never met him before and hadn't seen me since I was a kid.

I could hear the tick of the kitchen clock. My mom gazed over her surroundings like a time traveler who's found herself in some sort of paradoxical loop. So much was the same as when she left. The yellow-flowered curtains hadn't changed in decades. The orange shag carpet was worn bald in paths around the furniture. The phone was an ancient piece of plastic hanging on the wall, its tangled cord curling from the handset to the base. The house was a monument to the seventies. At the end of the kitchen counter, my mom lifted a sheet of paper from a messy stack. I could see the JJ logo at the top.

"Mom would never have sold this place," she said, her voice nostalgic.

"She never did."

"So, what?" my mom said, leaning against the counter. "You're going to be a forest ranger?"

The dismissive tone in her voice immediately set me on the defensive. "Handcrew."

"What the fuck's a handcrew?"

I bristled. I'd forgotten how harsh my mom could be, how scornful of any opinion that differed from her own. She couldn't abide work, especially hard work. For her, jobs were a necessary inconvenience, to be held on to only until something better came along, even if that something had a beer belly and a misogynistic sense of humor.

"It's contract work, Mom. I'll go where they need me, do fire control, help out with research projects. What do you care?"

"Whoa. Down, girl. I was just asking."

"Since when?"

"That's not fair." She picked at the label on her beer bottle.

"Eleven years, Mom. It's been eleven years. You never called to see how we were doing or—"

"I called," she said, shocked.

"You called to update us on what you were doing, but did you ever ask about us? You can't show up now and pretend like you give a damn."

"I'm sorry I missed the funeral. My car broke down. What do you want me to say?"

There was nothing she could say.

She noticed the urn on the bookshelf. "Is this . . ."

I nodded.

She put down her beer and slid both hands around the urn, lifting it from the shelf and holding it out, away from her body. "It's so small."

I reminded myself that I had wanted her to come. What I couldn't conjure up was the reason why. I knew better than to expect affection, but after so many years I'd hoped she would be different. Stupid of me, really.

I sighed and got to my feet. "I'm going to bed."

She returned the urn to the shelf. "I just got here." But the buzz of her homecoming had worn off and the tired drunk in her was showing through. "Have just one with me," she said, waving her half-empty beer bottle.

"It's three in the morning," I said, "and I have to be up early."

"Ah, come on, you're selling the place, right? Blow it off for one day."

"It doesn't work like that, Mom." Running the ranch wasn't like bartending. I couldn't just not show up for work. Living things depended on me and there was no one else to do the work.

"Fine," she said, tipping her bottle to drain the last of her beer. "Help me settle in?" She drifted over to where Devon had dropped her bags.

"You can have Aunt Christine's old room." My aunt had collected all her personal belongings years ago and left her twin bed neatly made with fresh sheets. If we had a guest room, that was it, but I couldn't remember ever having a guest before.

"Sounds great." She looked down at the giant duffel bags at her feet. "Please?"

I considered telling her to do it herself, but she was so drunk, I feared she might fall down the stairs, so I grabbed one of the bags. She took the other and followed me up and along the landing. I passed the open door to my bedroom and glanced behind me to see if she would peek in, if she was at all interested in how it had changed, but she followed me without so much as a sideways glance.

I propped the bag I was carrying into the corner next to the window in my aunt's old room. My mom dropped hers and it landed with a thud in the middle of the floor. She flopped onto the bed face-first, then rolled over to give me a bleary grin. "This'll do," she said. "Thanks, honey." She closed her eyes, and I thought maybe she had passed out, but then she opened them, focusing through the booze and exhaustion. "Oh, honey, you're all grown up."

I was an adult, same as her. I didn't know where that left us. I couldn't believe she was lying there, after all this time. Strange that someone could be so out of place and yet so familiar.

She murmured something I couldn't make out and pulled the blanket around herself. I kneeled down to unbuckle her boots and was thirteen years old again. "Good night," I said, and closed the door gently behind me on the way out.

A few hours later pale light painted my window aluminum blue. I trudged down the stairs to make coffee and found my mom's empty beer bottle on the kitchen table. If memory served, she would sleep till noon at least, but I didn't know what to expect when she woke. If she thought I was going to rearrange my life to entertain her, she was sorely mistaken. I needed to get my truck fixed and get back out to the supply store to replace the supplements. I still couldn't believe some asshole had stolen them. The converter I understood—it was at least useful—but stealing a bunch of ostrich vitamins was plain stupid.

If Matt didn't come back out to fix that ball joint, I'd call Reuben and beg him to help. I didn't care if he was overcharging me. I needed to get to the feed supply store. My plan to try to pass nonviable eggs as incubating hatchlings had created a knot of nerves in my abdomen that I knew would only loosen once I had a few honest embryos in place.

Outside, the thermometer on the side of the barn sagged in surrender, its dial already a notch above ninety. As the screen door banged shut behind me, I expected to see Lady Lil's wings high in the air, her excited trot coming toward me, her eyes searching. But she didn't come. Every day since Grandma Helen's death, she had run across the corral with her feathers fluffed, and every day I had watched her deflate when she found only me. I felt a twinge of disappointment that she had given up, but I understood. The shock of Grandma Helen's absence was fading for me too. I finished my coffee, enjoying the early morning light.

I was unlatching the gate to go into the corral and feed the birds their morning meal when I noticed a trail of footprints leading away from the corral out into the desert. Looking closer, I could easily discern the two-toed footprints of an ostrich on the right, and beside them the distinct marks of cowboy boots, deeper and about a third larger than mine. The rain after Grandma Helen's funeral had smoothed the sand like a military blanket, and I could easily track my usual routes around the ranch, the earth churned up in swaths between the house and the barn and the corral. But these tracks veered off into the vast nothingness of the Mojave and the edges were crisp. They'd been made recently.

I hurried up onto to the porch for the better vantage point and did a quick head count of the flock: 141. I counted again, assuming I was mistaken but came up short again. A sinking

feeling pulled at me as I remembered Lady Lil. I ran to the corral fence and scanned each of the dusty-colored females for the distinctive bald spot on her left hip, but none of them was Lady Lil. She was gone.

But that didn't make any sense. A full-grown ostrich wasn't much good to the average person. It wasn't like snatching a chicken that could be plucked and cooked up for dinner. These were three-hundred-pound birds. A breeding pair could be sold to a petting zoo or ranch, but not one bird alone. Theft was so outside the realm of ostrich ranching that we had never taken any measures to prevent it; no locks on the corral gate, no perimeter fence. Our remote location and the fact that the birds were difficult to wrangle had always been security enough. Still, the footprints told a distinct story. Someone had stolen Lady Lil.

I had to get her back. That was my only thought as I raced into the house for a canteen. The tracks were clear enough. I would just follow them to my bird and bring her home. I was nearly to the property line before I considered that it wasn't just Lady Lil I would find at the end of the trail. Someone took her and I didn't know how that someone would feel about being followed.

I detoured to grab the Citori shotgun from the barn, just in case. Grandma Helen's voice reminded me to check the safety. I had never shot anything but a target and, in truth, I didn't know if I could fire at an actual human being. I hoped that just having the shotgun would be enough, but I also knew that not loading it was foolish, so I dropped cartridges into both barrels.

The path was easy to trace. The footprints were clear and steady, but my boots sank into the sand as I walked. It was exhausting. Dusty, hot air burned my nostrils, though the sun was still low. I fidgeted with the shotgun. Holding it in front of me, I was prepared for any possible confrontation, but it was difficult to walk in the soft sand with both hands occupied. I let

the cumbersome thing dangle in one hand, which made walking easier, but then the path dipped down into a lower section of desert, and not being able to see more than twenty feet ahead of me, I worried that I might crest the next dune to find myself face to face with whoever had stolen my bird so I held the gun close again.

Sweat dried on my face and trickled down my spine. The desert stretched out in every direction, an undulating sea of sand speckled with hardy plants that cast long shadows in the early morning light. A welcome breeze wound through the brush and the sun rose steadily, dragging up the temperature with it. All I could do was focus on putting one foot in front of the other. The farther I went, the more vulnerable I felt.

The sun climbed higher and the landscape bleached out. I kicked myself for not grabbing my hat. Every step was one I knew I would have to retrace later, when the day was even hotter and the hills were even whiter in the blinding light. My better judgment screamed at me that one bird wasn't worth the risk of heatstroke, but another part of my brain kept picturing the way Grandma Helen smiled when Lady Lil greeted her every morning and I kept going.

After what felt like hours under the unforgiving sun, I came to a shallow ravine where a confusing scene was playing out. Lady Lil stood perfectly still in front of the lowered tailgate of a black Silverado pickup. She had a white rope tied around her neck and there was a man in the bed of the truck, pulling on the rope and trying to coax her up beside him. He was bent with the effort and his back was to me. It took me a second to recognize that the man was Uncle Scott.

I had the wayward thought that maybe he planned to start a ranch of his own. Breeding pairs were expensive, but it only took two birds, and a lot of patience, to start a business. He might have come back later for a male to join Lady Lil, might have been hoping I wouldn't notice one or two missing birds.

But I quickly dismissed the idea. Uncle Scott never had any interest in being a rancher, and if he meant to transport the bird alive, he would have brought a trailer for her to ride in.

Instead, a .38 pistol rested on the roof of the cab. As absurd as it seemed, he apparently hoped to pull the hen into the bed of the truck and then shoot her, but that didn't make any sense either. A dead bird couldn't be sold to the slaughterhouse. A dead bird was of almost no use at all, unless you were hoping to feed about five hundred people. He was clearly high.

Whatever Uncle Scott had planned for Lady Lil, she was not cooperating. She was giving him enough trouble, in fact, that he hadn't yet noticed my arrival. I watched him struggle. His arms strained as he pulled on the rope again. Lady Lil's neck bowed forward, her feet skidded, and her mottled brown wings fluffed in protest. She squawked at him. Uncle Scott muttered angrily to himself, then lashed out with his fist and hit her in the eye. Her head snapped back with the force of it.

"What the hell are you doing?" I sidestepped halfway down the loose sand of the hillside toward them.

TEN

Uncle Scott jerked to attention. "Jesus, Tallulah," he said. "You can't sneak up on people like that." He eyed the shotgun.

"I'm not the one sneaking." He had on khaki cargo pants and a filthy white undershirt, the pits stained with sweat and dirt. He was no longer wearing his father's gold watch.

Lady Lil batted her eyelashes. I was relieved he hadn't crushed in her skull with that punch.

Uncle Scott leered at me. "This ain't got nothing to do with you," he said, yanking on the rope around Lady Lil's neck. He ran his free hand through his hair.

"Like hell."

He scowled and I had the urge to back away. The bird shifted beside him and he flinched, his fist jumping up again, ready to strike. For all our experience dealing with my uncle as an addict, Grandma Helen and I only ever saw him when he ran out of money and had to come begging. By then, he was agitated and uncomfortable in his skin, presumably focused on his next fix. I had never interacted with him while he was high on meth, never seen him so aggressive and twitchy. I didn't like it.

"Just let her go." I clutched the shotgun.

He leaned forward slightly, leading with his head, the way a snake might approach a mouse. "Or what?" he said, his lips curling into an ugly smile, his voice rank with derision. "You'll shoot?"

I undid the safety, cocked the gun, and swung the barrel toward the front of his truck. My hands trembled, but my aim didn't have to be precise to hit a tire at such close range. I'd be damned if I'd dragged that heavy thing all the way out there for nothing, and it seemed a safe bet he hadn't brought water. Uncle Scott straightened, shifted his line of sight to the horizon, calculating. The day was getting hotter by the minute, and even high as a kite, he knew that a hike in the desert without water was risky. He might make it to the highway. He might not. My nerves settled a little when resignation flashed across his face. He wasn't fool enough to ignore the threat of a couple flat tires.

"Just get in your truck and go," I said with an authority I didn't feel. I hoped he couldn't hear the quiver in my voice.

He glared at me, then jumped from the back of the truck. With the bird in tow, he stomped up the last few feet of the slope in my direction. I swear, the temperature went up a few degrees. I pointed the gun square at his sternum. He charged right up to me so that the muzzle pressed against the fabric of his ratty undershirt. I could smell the anger coming off him like bird shit baking in the desert sun.

He made a grab for the gun, but his hand slipped and he only succeeded in knocking it to the side. I clutched at it and managed to keep it in hand but was thrown off-balance.

He pressed in toward me, wrenched my face against him with his forearm, and grabbed a fistful of my hair. The stench of him gagged me. I slammed my knee up into his crotch and the gun shifted between us. I felt my hand slip against the trigger guard and a shot rang out. The gun kicked back against my hip and knocked me back a step. Blood sprayed across my face and neck.

Lady Lil bolted.

A metallic smell filled the air. A sound welled up from deep inside Uncle Scott—a choked gasp that transformed into a scream, then stuttered to a high-pitched whine. Blood poured down his arm as he held it up between us, staring in disbelief. The ring and pinkie fingers were gone from his right hand. Only gory, mutilated stumps remained.

"Oh my God," I said, my hands raised in a useless gesture, my mouth hanging open in horror.

He sucked a gasp through his clenched jaw and pulled a bandanna from his pocket to wrap the wound, but it soaked through in seconds. He lurched back to his truck and threw himself into the bed. His weight jostled the frame, and a dart of sunlight bounced off the .38 pistol resting on the cab roof.

My confusion hardened into panic. I kicked and clawed at the ground to scramble up the side of the dune, dragging the shotgun with me. Sand stuck to my skin where it was wet with blood. Behind me, I heard the scrape of metal on metal as Uncle Scott tried to maneuver the gun with his left hand. I threw myself over the crest of sand and lay flat on the other side of the ridge. I heard a shot, and a patch of desert exploded to the left of me.

I tried to run, but my legs wobbled and I careened like a drunk to the bottom of the shallow dune. I heard the truck's shocks squeak as Uncle Scott jumped from the truck bed. Then his engine growled to life. It would be crazy to chase me over the sand in a pickup. The truck would sink to its axle in the soft sand.

When I didn't hear anything more I lifted my head to see what he was doing and another shot rang out. His aim was terrible. Sand flew into the air far to my right and I dropped back down, waited.

Eventually, the sound of the pickup faded as he drove away. Medical attention must have taken priority over revenge—at least for the time being. I climbed up and surveyed the landscape. A fading trail of dust indicated where his truck had sped away. My knees faltered. I dropped and rested against the sandy hillside.

I had shot Uncle Scott. I hadn't meant to. It was an accident. It all happened so fast. I wanted to reverse time, to take back what I'd done. I wanted to tell him I hadn't meant to hurt him. The vision of his screaming face was etched in my memory.

I spotted the tracks Lady Lil had left when she fled and swung my battered canteen around to wash the panic from my mouth. Thick streaks of blood soaked my clothes and smeared my skin. I wiped what I could from my hands, but a rust-colored stain stretched from the collar of my shirt down the right side of my body, the blood already stiffening the fabric into a sandy crust. I collected myself, tilting my head to listen for sounds on the wind. I doubted Uncle Scott would be back, but I had never felt so exposed.

I followed Lady Lil south for a while, parallel to my property line, then veered farther west into the desert. Ostriches ran fast, but only in bursts, and the tracks were gradually falling closer together, so I knew she was slowing. I rested at a rise and took another drink from my canteen. The heat was abusive. Deep out in the desert like that, there was no shade. A lizard scurried at the base of a creosote bush, froze, then disappeared into a small hole in the sand.

Thoughts of Uncle Scott's accusing glare urged me to walk a little faster. The shallow dunes, all painted in the same pale hues, gave the illusion of flat land from afar, but a mile on the map equaled three on foot, trekking up and down the rises and falls. The tracks of off-road vehicles scratched the landscape in all directions.

Caches of spent shotgun shells and empty beer cans bleached gray by the sun told of tweaked-out teenagers passing rowdy nights in the only place the sheriff wouldn't bother to come bust them. Probably the very same assholes that stole the converter out from under my truck and swiped the bird supplements.

The pounding in my temples grew more intense and warned of dehydration. I took a small sip from the nearly empty canteen. I didn't want to leave Lady Lil out there in the desert, but I couldn't ignore my dwindling water supply and the concern that if I didn't call the sheriff soon, I would be at Uncle Scott's mercy. A gunshot wound would mean paperwork, and the last thing I needed was my uncle spreading some unfettered bullshit about how I had attacked him.

Thankfully, I found Lady Lil just over the next ridge, motionless and staring out at the far-off mountains. The rope tied around her neck dangled in the sand. "Okay, girl," I murmured, not wanting to scare her into running again, "it's been a rough morning, I know." I reached out and ran my hand along her neck the way Grandma Helen used to do. She blinked twice. "Let's go home."

She bowed her head to nuzzle my hand. I gently inspected the place where Uncle Scott had hit her. The skin was swollen and red, but there wasn't much I could do for her. I put my arm over her back and guided her gently in the direction of home. We kept up a steady pace despite the heat. I drank the last few drops from my canteen and rubbed at my temples. Uncle Scott's scream reverberated in my thoughts. I had only heard a noise like that once before, when I was ten.

My mom and I were living with a boyfriend of hers in West Oakland, and there had been a drive-by shooting. I remembered gathering outside the neighbor's house with my mom and a few others, gawking at the perfect spiderweb pattern the bullet had left in the window and listening to the whispers: a boy, a bullet to the skull. A woman inside the house kept screaming, just like Uncle Scott had screamed. The sound was pure pain.

Eventually my mom and I had gone back home, but I

couldn't sleep. I found her outside on the landing, smoking a cigarette and staring up at the BART tracks that passed so close you could see the expressions on the passengers' faces as they zipped by. Her blond dreadlocks, only a few inches long then, were lit by the kitchen window behind her. Her face was in shadow. When I told her I couldn't sleep, she pulled me to her, and I smelled the sharp scent of boxed white wine. "Don't worry, baby," she said, her voice slurring. "Bad things like that don't happen twice."

I wanted to believe her, but even at the age of ten, I knew there was no cosmic rule limiting the number of terrible things that could happen in the world. It seemed to me that bad things brought more bad things.

As I grew, my suspicions were confirmed. Dead little boys led to more shootings, which only left more bullet holes in windows. Moms drank too much and lost their jobs, which only made them drink harder. Shit happened all the time, and the closer you found yourself to the center of the trouble, the more certain you could be that bigger problems were heading your way.

I wasn't looking forward to seeing my mom back at the house. I didn't have the energy to navigate how she was feeling or to figure out what she remembered from the night before. I was covered in blood, dead tired, and desperately thirsty. It was all I could do to keep walking.

The sun baked my skin through the thin fabric of my shirt and my pace slowed. My tongue felt swollen. I focused on breathing through my nose to conserve what moisture I could, but the air scorched the back of my throat. With the bird in tow, I trekked through the sage scrub until finally, the ranch appeared in the distance.

From that far out, I couldn't see the wire strung between the wooden posts of the corral fence. It was easy to pretend that the birds had simply congregated there by chance, perhaps drawn to the oasis created by the walnut tree. The big red barn stood tall. The faded blue house looked like a little piece of fallen sky on the desert floor. I took a mental snapshot and tucked it away in my memory, then shuffled forward again, propelled by visions of an enormous glass of water.

When we got to the corral, I guided Lady Lil back in with the other ostriches. She marched directly over and pecked the bottom of the empty trough, expectant. In all the hurry of the morning, I had neglected to feed the flock.

I powered through the dehydration headache that gnawed at my skull and hurried to flip the latch on the feed silo. The grain sliding into the trough grated at my brain. I was impatient to get inside, have a drink of water, and call the sheriff, and as I watched the flock eat their belated breakfast, I considered for the first time what I was going to say.

It was an accident, or course. I hadn't meant to shoot my uncle. I had only even brought the gun with me to be intimidating, but then he'd come at me, and everything had happened so fast. I rubbed the spot where he'd grabbed me by the hair. It was self-defense. Could I claim accident and self-defense at the same time? No matter what I said, I knew it was likely I would be arrested. And then what?

Who would take care of the ostriches? They wouldn't survive more than a day or two penned up in the corral with no one to care for them. Not in the middle of July. They needed water and food. If resources went scarce, the birds could get aggressive, and then I'd have a whole other set of problems on my hands.

The edges of my vision curled up and the horizon tilted. I put my hand on the stout wooden leg of the feed silo to balance myself. I blinked hard to clear my vision and made my way out of the corral toward the house. Even in my dazed state, it didn't escape my notice that the nests in the corral remained empty.

My mom was sitting on the couch reading a gossip magazine when I burst in and lurched toward the kitchen. She had changed out of her traveling clothes into a pair of ripped jeans and a faded red tank top that clung to the cups of her push-up bra. Her bare feet were wedged between the couch cushions.

"You were up early," she said. "We should probably talk about—" She looked up. "Is that blood?" she asked with concern.

"No," I said without thinking. Then, "Yes, not mine." I put my face under the faucet in the kitchen. The cool water washed over me. I caught some in my mouth and drank deeply.

After a few gulps, the ache in my throat subsided, and I noticed flecks of red against the porcelain of the sink spiraling down around the drain. I ran my hands over my face, splashing it to scrub any remaining blood away. Still dripping, I stripped off my shirt. I was wearing a wide-strapped, matronly bra that I normally never would have shown to anyone, let alone my mother, who equated practicality with insipidness, but it was mostly free of blood, and that was all that mattered to me right then.

"Did anyone call?" I asked my mom. I needed to know if Sheriff Morris was looking for me, if Uncle Scott had gotten to him and filled his head with lies. I checked the clock. It was almost two in the afternoon. It had taken me much longer than I'd realized to find the bird and get back to the ranch.

Uncle Scott would have made it to the hospital by now, so why wasn't the sheriff at my door, waiting to arrest me? Maybe Uncle Scott hadn't gone to the hospital. What if he had gone to get high instead? How much blood could a person lose from a wound like that? Concern mixed with anger and confusion until I thought I might throw up. I braced myself against the sink, letting the bloodstained shirt fall at my feet.

My mom put down her magazine and came into the kitchen. "What happened?"

I didn't want to talk about it. There was too much to explain, too many things she wouldn't understand. She didn't know about Uncle Scott's struggles with addiction, didn't know him as an addict. With my nerves as jangled as they were, I didn't have the patience for that conversation.

"It was a coyote," I said. I leaned over and drank again, sucking down gulp after gulp. Finally, the nausea passed. I grabbed a dish towel from the counter and wiped my face with the rough fabric. "It happens sometimes," I lied.

Coyotes would never mess with the birds. They were no match for those powerful legs. In all my years on the ranch, I had never seen a coyote in the corral or even heard Grandma Helen mention them being a problem, but I figured my mom wouldn't know that.

"Shit," she said.

"I'm going to go shower," I said and went upstairs without waiting for a response. I needed a little time. I didn't know how to explain my uncle's addiction. It had evolved slowly over time, his offenses outranking one another over time. As soon as my heart rate returned to normal, I would tell her. And Aunt Christine. I needed to tell her too. Oddly enough, considering Aunt Christine's aversion to violence, I suspected she would be the more understanding of the two sisters, given her own experiences with Uncle Scott.

What if I'd killed him? There'd been so much blood, and if he hadn't gone to the hospital, where was he? What if some drug-induced paranoia spurred him in another direction or some idiot tweaker convinced him he didn't need a doctor, that the two of them could deal with the wound themselves in some filthy flophouse?

I hoped he'd gone to the hospital, even if it meant trouble for me. I had never seen him like that. He wasn't himself at all. And the grimace on his face. Those bloody stumps. I had shot off two of his fingers. He would never be the same. What the hell had he been thinking? But I knew the answer to that. He hadn't.

At the top of the stairs, I approached what used to be Uncle Scott's room. We always kept that door shut, and over time it had become a benign decoration of the upstairs. But now, with Uncle Scott's blood all over me, it was impossible to walk past blindly. Like a beggar taking up the entire sidewalk, the door seemed to demand my attention. I couldn't ignore it. I reached out and the door swung open.

While Aunt Christine had left her room like a hotel maid, ready for the next visitor, Uncle Scott had simply stuffed a duffel bag with what he needed and taken off. When I first arrived at the house, I had peeked in. He lived at the ranch then, though at the age of thirty-one, he wasn't proud of it and spent most of his time at his girlfriend's house. His room had been a mess then, and it hadn't changed.

It smelled like spoiled mayonnaise. Light filtered in through the faded gray curtains on the far side of the room, next to a low bookshelf that didn't have a single book on it. Instead, it held a wadded-up sweatshirt, a pair of brand-new hiking boots, a bottle of ibuprofen, a couple of empty Gatorade bottles, and a trash can lying on its side. An aluminum baseball bat propped against the shelf glinted in the low light.

I picked up the bat, weighed it in my hand, and surveyed the room. Clothes were scattered all over the floor. The twin bed was unmade. A battered pair of speakers rested underneath the window. A video-game controller hung by its cord from the bedpost. With the tip of the bat, I flipped open the lid of a pizza box, bracing for what I might find, but it was empty. The walls were covered with posters of half-naked women and fast cars.

Grandma Helen had never insisted he clean up his shit. I wished she'd been harder on him, for his sake. If she'd insisted he get help early on, his sobriety might have stuck. At the very least, she could have refused to keep writing him checks, but she'd looked the other way time and again, pretending nothing was wrong, and it had made him weak. That was why I was covered in his blood. He could never get control of his life and I hated him for it.

I poked at a pair of stacked Coke cans and watched them topple to the floor with a clatter. I kicked the pile of clothes at my feet. I lined up a swing and sent one of the Gatorade bottles flying. It ricocheted around the room.

Uncle Scott would be pissed I was in his room swinging at his things with a baseball bat, but it wasn't his room anymore. It belonged to me. The house, this room, and all the shit in it was mine, and I could do whatever I wanted.

I swung hard at the bookshelf, cracking the wood. I slammed the bat down on the pizza box. I tore the posters from the wall, ripping them down the middle as I pulled. All my anger at Uncle Scott had finally found a focus. I could hear myself grunting as I brought the bat down again and again. I wanted to see his room in ruins. I was enraged at him for being a fuckup, for wrecking his own life and not caring enough about anyone around him to fix it.

There was a hollow pop as I crushed an empty box of saltine crackers, and I heard a small gasp behind me. Straightening, I saw my youngest cousin, Julie, with her hand clapped over her mouth. She hovered in the doorway with all four of her sisters. Aunt Christine, slowed on her trip up the stairs by her enormous girth, appeared behind them.

"Lula," little Julie said, barely above a whisper. "What are you doing?"

ELEVEN

I saw myself through their eyes: the bra, the shadowy, red smears on my skin, the bat in my hand, my body heaving with anger and exertion. But it was Sunday. Aunt Christine never came over on Sunday. We had our family dinners on Wednesday.

"Downstairs," Aunt Christine said to the girls. Her voice was firm as ever, but her eyes were red and pleading. Something was wrong. Something she didn't want the kids to hear.

Panic gripped me. Uncle Scott had gone to her for help, or maybe the hospital had called. I dropped the bat.

When the girls didn't move, she added: "Now."

They filed down the stairs without a glance at their mom, expressions of astonishment solidly in place on their little faces. Aunt Christine closed the door, and I swallowed around the lump that was forming in my throat.

"I'm leaving him," she said, the words stuttering out into a sob. It took me a minute to understand that she was talking about her husband. "God help me, I caught him with Megan." Tears flowed down her cheeks. She glanced over her shoulder at the door to be certain the girls were gone.

"Mrs. Michaels?" I asked, remembering the chicken woman who taught Sunday school, the one who had so generously offered to help Todd take the girls home after the funeral.

"She's not the first." Aunt Christine wiped at her nose with a crumpled tissue. "She's hardly the first," she scoffed, and then relented. "But Todd and I, we always reconciled through the church. It was the one place . . ." The tears flowed again. "What am I going to do?"

If the kids had been shocked to see me trashing their uncle's room with a bat, I was astonished to hear that Aunt Christine and Todd were splitting up. She had never even hinted anything was wrong between them. She hardly ever talked about Todd, and when she did, everything was fine. I kicked a deflated basketball out of the way and wrapped her in a hug.

She leaned over her giant belly and rested her head on my shoulder. "I am so sorry to burden you," she said. Her body jerked with a silent sob. She cried with abandon yet didn't make a single sound. I wondered how many times she had practiced that skill at home with the girls in the other room.

"You're not a burden," I said, wrapping my arms around her as best I could. I had never been in the position of comforting my aunt before. Like Grandma Helen, she always stood steadfast at the center of whatever chaos kicked up around her, sturdy as the center pole of a circus tent. It was unsettling to see her crack.

"What am I going to do?" she repeated.

I let her cry her silent tears there in Uncle Scott's trashed room, then answered. "Well, you're not taking the girls to a hotel." But I hadn't told her yet about selling the ranch. I couldn't let her think that moving in with me was a permanent solution. "Stay here for a few nights, till you figure out what you want to do. We can tell the girls it's a sleepover."

"No," she said, blinking back her tears and straightening with a sniff. She wiped her eyes with her palms. "We couldn't.

There are too many of us." She said the words but kept her gaze fixed on the carpet.

"Seriously, Aunt Christine. Stop." I held her hands in mine. "Grandma Helen would kill me if you and the girls didn't stay here tonight. You know I'm right."

She met my eyes and I could tell she'd been hoping I would insist. "If you're sure."

"I've got plenty of room."

She wiped a spot from my cheek with her thumb. I had washed away the worst of the blood, but there were pale stains on my arms. She took in the chaos of Uncle Scott's room.

"I was just . . ." How to explain? "Uncle Scott stole some money. He forged a check from Grandma Helen's account. I'm pretty sure he's using again." That seemed enough to justify my behavior.

Aunt Christine gave a heavy sigh. "That's disappointing."

I knew I should confess about having shot Uncle Scott, but I couldn't bring myself to do it. It was too awful, and she had enough to deal with. I would tell her later. A squeal floated up from downstairs.

"What are you telling the girls, about Todd?"

"Nothing, so far." She waded through the junk on the floor to sit on the edge of the bed. "They know I'm mad at him. That's all." She rested her hands on top of her swollen middle and arched her shoulders in a deep stretch. "I know I have to tell them soon, but I want to work out the details with Todd first, so I can answer their questions."

Apparently, it was a family trait. We liked to have things figured out before we voiced them. Another piercing shriek came from downstairs. We both looked at the door.

"It's my mom."

Aunt Christine's mouth dropped. "Your mom? Laura's here?"

The way the house was constructed, it was easy to go

straight up the stairs from the front door. Aunt Christine had missed her sister entirely. "She hitchhiked herself all the way here. Showed up in the middle of the night last night, drunk as a skunk."

"Holy crap," Aunt Christine said, which was as close as she ever got to swearing. Her eyes, still rimmed with tears, sparkled with curiosity. We heard another squeal from downstairs, this one with an edge to it. One of the girls yelled, "Stop!"

Aunt Christine came to her feet. "I'd better get down there." She moved for the door and then turned to look back at me. "You okay?"

"I'll be down in a few," I said.

I dragged myself to the shower. The drain ran with dust and dried blood. I leaned into the stream of water and thought of Uncle Scott out there somewhere, bleeding. The cycle of anger and worry was all too familiar. I wanted to slap sense into him, at the same time that I wanted to know he was okay.

Then there was Aunt Christine. Todd had been screwing around. I never would have guessed. I was glad she had come to the ranch, that she knew she could. I could almost hear Grandma Helen's response: "Men." On the whole, she found them untrustworthy and didn't have much use for them. She had loved her husband, I knew, because he was the best one could hope for in a man: he stayed out of her way. I had always thought of Aunt Christine's marriage as an example of something more, proof that there were men out there who could be counted on, but apparently, I'd been misled.

After staying in the shower for an unforgivable length of time, I wrapped myself in a towel and went back to my room, passing the open door to Uncle Scott's room on the way. What would it have been like for Uncle Scott, as a little boy, to grow up with a mother who saw men as necessary but burdensome?

Grandma Helen had worried about him every time he relapsed, and she had given him money whenever he asked, but

I had never seen her hug him. It was easier to understand her coolness toward him in recent years. When a person lied and stole as much as Uncle Scott, it only made sense to hold him at a distance. But even before the meth, when he used to come over for dinner, I couldn't remember my grandma ever putting her arms around him like she did with Aunt Christine or my cousins. I couldn't recall her being affectionate with him in any way.

The image that came to mind was Grandma Helen with her hands clasped together in front of her, giving a curt little nod of approval. That was about as good as it got for Uncle Scott. Had she always been so cold with him? I tried to imagine him as a little boy, like my cousins. I saw how they ran to Aunt Christine seeking comfort for every stubbed toe or hurt feeling. What if, instead of kissing everything better, she waved them off and told them to deal with it themselves? Would they spend their lives searching for that tender touch? And if they couldn't find it in their mother's arms, where would they turn?

I had been old enough, by the time I came to the ranch, to take care of myself, and Grandma Helen respected that, but I think she also wanted to be there for me, to be a mother figure, even if she wasn't good at showing affection. That first day I arrived on the ranch, after she helped me carry my bags up to my mom's room and before she left me to unpack, she'd pulled me into a stiff hug and said, "I want you to think of this as your home."

I'd hugged her in return. My head only came to her shoulder then and her waist was so thin I could grab my own elbows as I reached around her. I didn't know what to say. It wasn't my home, not yet. I was still stinging from the way my mom had sent me away, but it was nice to hear that someone wanted me.

Our lives together found a rhythm pretty quickly. She gave me a lot of space and I was fine with that. I didn't need to be tucked in at night or have someone make me breakfast. I could do my own laundry. But I did miss our drives together, after I got my license and could get myself to school. That was when the distance began to grow between us.

By the time I was working full time on the ranch, we hardly spoke. Every morning, we would collect the eggs together, a routine so solid that it hardly needed a word, and then she would go inside to manage the paperwork while I did whatever needed doing in the barn or the corral.

There was only one other time I remembered her hugging me. After I drove us home from my graduation dinner, she stumbled on the porch and wrapped me in her strong arms. "I'm so proud of you," she said.

These thoughts all churned in my head as I returned to my room and lay down. My tired body sank into the comforter like it was quicksand. I surrendered to the safety of my own bed, too sluggish to fight for consciousness. I let sleep take me.

I woke confused and cold, wrapped in my damp towel. The day's events came flooding back. I saw Uncle Scott with blood pouring down his arm, heard his scream. I checked the clock. It was almost six. I hoped he was safe, wherever he was. I thought I might call the hospital in Barstow, but I didn't know what I would say. I didn't know what to do. All I knew right then was that I was hungry, and I could smell food cooking in the kitchen.

Before I was halfway down the stairs, I heard my mom.

"Okay, okay, I got it," she said. There was a playfulness in her voice that spoke of happy hour. She pointed around the room. "Gabby, Parker, Emma, Natalie, and . . . Madeline." With her finger on little Julie, she smiled. It was clear she knew her name but was teasing.

"It's Juuuulie."

"Are you sure?" my mom asked, leaning close and poking Julie's nose. The other girls busied themselves drawing pictures or reading books, except for the second youngest, Natalie, who was trying to drag Griffith out from behind the couch. Julie reveled in having my mom's full attention.

"I'm sure." Julie giggled, saying "sure" in that charming six-year-old way: "shua."

"Oh my God, you're cute," my mom said, squishing my cousin's face between her hands.

Julie's mouth fell open and Aunt Christine leaned out of the kitchen, wooden spoon in hand.

"What?" my mom said, genuinely confused.

"You shouldn't take the Lord's name in vain," my aunt's eldest recited from the couch, where she was reading a paperback novel.

Satisfied that the misstep had been addressed, Aunt Christine resumed her cooking.

"Oh, that," my mom said, relaxing. "Well, God and I have an understanding."

"Does that understanding involve you spending an eternity in heck?" Aunt Christine called over her shoulder.

My mom scoffed. "Is heck a place now?"

"Let's set the table," I said, making my presence known.

The kids had been well trained, and though they grumbled a bit, they all set down what they were doing and migrated to the kitchen with me. I doled out utensils, plates, and cups, then grabbed a stack of napkins and helped them put out everything. We were pushing the maximum capacity for the table. It was only meant for six, but as Aunt Christine's brood multiplied over the years, we had grown accustomed to squeezing.

My mom made no move to help. "Isn't it a little early for dinner?"

"It's six o'clock," my aunt said, her tone confirming that it was exactly time for dinner.

My mom rose and opened Grandma Helen's liquor cabinet. My grandmother had always been partial to Jameson whiskey.

In addition to the half-full bottle, there was an unopened bottle behind it.

"Ugh," my mom said. "Helen and her whiskey." She nudged the bottles aside, hoping for anything else. "Where's the Gordon's?"

"Mom dumped it all when Dad quit drinking," Aunt Christine said, dishing up plates of spaghetti.

"Seriously?" My mom pulled down the Jameson and unscrewed the cap. She gave it a sniff and shrugged.

"There wasn't a drop of liquor in the whole house for about a decade," Aunt Christine said. "But after Dad was diagnosed, Mom pretty much went back to her old ways."

"Pour you a glass?" My mom held up the bottle in her sister's direction.

With both hands, Aunt Christine made a little V above her belly.

"Right," Mom said. "How about you, Tallulah? I'm thinking you could use a drink."

My hands shook as I placed the paper napkins around the table. My ten intact fingers reminded me of Uncle Scott's mangled hand, the terrible way his eyes bulged in pain. It had been almost twelve hours since I shot him. Where was he?

"Come on," my mom said.

She was waiting for an answer. "What?" I said, trying to catch up with the conversation.

Mistaking my distraction for hesitation, she pressed. "When have we ever had a drink, just the two of us?"

"I was thirteen the last time you saw me." I yanked the plastic gallon milk jug from the fridge and set it on the table.

"Exactly," she said, reaching out to swat my shoulder playfully.

"Go easy on me," I said.

My mom pulled a couple of tumblers from the cupboard and moved to the freezer for ice. She had spent half the day sleeping, another few hours catching up on celebrity gossip, and now she was serving up drinks. It was like she was on vacation.

"How long are you staying, Mom?"

She shrugged. "How long *can* I stay?" She handed me one of the drinks.

From the way she emphasized the "can," I knew she was about to bring up the fact that I planned to sell the ranch. I didn't want to have that conversation. Not after the day I'd had.

"Oh," I said, suddenly thinking of the perfect way to distract her, "I've got something for you. Come on." The smoky vanilla scent of the whiskey wafted from the glass in my hand and mixed with the smell of detergent as I led my mom into the mudroom.

The crate of license plates was sitting on the washing machine, right where I left it after the funeral reception. When I first discovered it out in the barn, my sophomore year in high school, Grandma Helen had told me how she and my grandfather started collecting them when they moved out to the desert in the seventies. Her voice grew hushed and secretive when she talked about it, as if she were telling me about her time as a notorious outlaw. From what I gathered, my mom had been an enthusiastic partner in the family's larceny, and over time, collecting the plates became a thing they did together.

I pulled one from the middle of the stack at random. The renewal sticker was turquoise green and had a small 95 in the corner. The year before I was born. My mom would have been fifteen. Aesthetically, the nineties had not been a great time for the state's license plates. It was plain white with black lettering. The word *"California"* was pressed into the top in the same utilitarian font, but in red.

"Oh my God," my mom said. It only had three letters on it: DOH. The original owner had drawn an apostrophe between the D and the O. "I can't believe she kept all these." She flipped it over. The note on the back read simply: *Ford Taurus.* "I remember that," she said under her breath. She slid the plate into the stack and pushed so that they all shifted in the crate to reveal the one at the front: WHTAJRK. I knew the story of that one well. Grandma Helen had stolen it on a whim, after the guy nearly ran her off the road and they ended up at the same gas station. I could almost hear her laughing: *He really was a jerk.*

I took a sip of whiskey and watched my mom's reaction as she continued to flip through the plates, as if how she treated a box of stolen license plates would tell me something about her relationship with her mother, like it might explain the way she fit into our family.

She rested her drink on the washing machine and leaned in closely. I saw an unfamiliar expression of wistfulness on her face, but I felt none of the understanding I had been hoping for.

"Grandma Helen wanted you to have them," I said, in case it was unclear. "I'm sorry it's not more."

"No, this is great."

I wasn't sure I believed her. I knew the question of money was looming, but her sentimentality surprised me. I wanted so badly for her to ask questions, to care about the eleven years I had spent without her. I expected her to want to know things—anything, really—about her mother's last years.

"Dinner," Aunt Christine said from the other room.

My mom flipped to the very last plate, the only one I had contributed.

For her sixty-fifth birthday, I had given Grandma Helen a plate that read 2DLIMIT. I had just gotten my driver's license, and when I spotted the plate on a beat-up VW bus, I knew I had to steal it for her. *One of These Nights* was her favorite album. When she unwrapped it, she said it was the best gift she'd ever received and beamed with pride, but only a few minutes later, her mood grew dour. When I asked her what was wrong, she didn't respond right away. It took some prodding for her to admit that she was concerned about the stolen plate. It worried her, she said. Times had changed in Sombra.

Back when my mom was a kid, when the two of them had been stealing the plates, it was a lark. The sheriff knew them. Everybody knew everybody, and they only stole from tourists passing through town on their way to Las Vegas. But by the time I came to the ranch, meth had set the desert on edge. The sheriff and his men took every call expecting to be shot.

Grandma Helen hugged me and told me again that she loved my gift but that she didn't want me in trouble on her account. She asked that it be the last addition to the collection. I promised, feeling ashamed and disappointed.

"Time to eat." My aunt's voice came again from the dining room. My cousins were all sitting at the table, looking expectantly toward the mudroom. I knew Aunt Christine wouldn't allow them to eat until we said grace, and we couldn't say grace until everyone was seated.

My mom went to join them and I pulled that last plate from the crate again. Quietly, I opened the cupboard above the washing machine and slipped the plate behind a box of detergent. My mom could have the other twenty-seven, but I was keeping that one.

Aunt Christine took Grandma Helen's seat in the middle of the table. Without discussing it, the kids rotated in toward her, leaving a place for my mom at one end. We were the same number of people as we'd been the last time we all sat down together, but instead of Grandma Helen, my mom was the eighth.

Aunt Christine and the kids joined hands and lowered their heads. Out of habit, I took Natalie's hand on my left and Parker's on my right. Grandma Helen and I never said a blessing when it was just the two of us, but we played along when Aunt Christine came over.

My mom reluctantly put down her whiskey so she could

link hands with the girls. Aunt Christine said grace, the kids all repeated amen, and silverware clanked against plates.

"How's the drink?" my mom asked from across the table.

"Tastes like Jameson."

"If Mom had kept the gin around, I could've made us some fucking cocktails."

"Laura," my aunt chastised, swinging a sauce-covered spoon through the air. "Language."

My mom shrugged, not looking guilty so much as annoyed.

"Gin was Grandpa Hank's drink?" I had never really considered what my grandfather drank. I guess I had assumed he drank whiskey like Grandma Helen.

Aunt Christine gave a curt "Ha," and my mom chuckled. "Dad would drink just about anything," she said, "but gin was his favorite."

"Dad started drinking the minute he came in from the barn," Aunt Christine said.

"No," my mom corrected, pointing at her sister around her glass, "he would shower while Mom mixed the drinks. Jameson on the rocks for her. Gin and tonic for him. She handed it to him when he came down the stairs."

"Right," Aunt Christine said, remembering. "Talk about enabling."

"I think we stressed him out."

"Yeah, poor them." My aunt's voice turned sarcastic. "Three kids."

"Well, we can't all be perfect parents."

The clanking of forks against plates filled the room. Usually, the girls could be counted on to keep up a steady level of banter, even over dinner, but they seemed to sense that the arrival of their aunt was an opportunity to hear things they normally wouldn't.

I twirled my fork in the spaghetti and took a giant bite. The sauce was tangy and sweet.

"It got worse after you left," Aunt Christine said. "Scott was working by then, so it was just me most of the time."

"Yeah," my mom said. "No great surprise that we both got knocked up as soon as we could and got the hell out of here."

Aunt Christine dropped her fork. Skipping right over the word "hell," which I knew was on her forbidden list, she looked to Gabby, her firstborn, then back to my mom. "I did not get knocked up," she said.

The phone rang and I went to the kitchen to answer it.

"What's 'knocked up'?" Julie asked behind me at the table.

"Hello?" I croaked. I angled toward the wall to try to block out the conversation in the room.

"Todd and I were in love, married in the eyes of God," Aunt Christine said, growing louder.

"Yeah," Mom said. I could hear the smirk in her tone. "How's that working out for you?"

"Tallulah," said a familiar voice through the phone line. I tried to focus over the sound of the argument developing at the table. "It's Sheriff Morris. I'm afraid I have some bad news."

His words froze my feet to the floor. He'd used the same tone of voice when he'd called to tell me about Grandma Helen. I had been standing in that very spot, the phone to my ear. "What is it?" I asked, even though I knew what was coming.

"Your uncle's been shot."

A weight gathered in my gut.

"He was found in Barstow, passed out behind the wheel of his truck in the middle of an intersection. He'll live, but he's lost two fingers on his right hand and a lot of blood. I'm sorry I couldn't call sooner. He didn't have any ID on him. The hospital had him listed as a John Doe until one of my deputies ran his plates. I called as soon as I got word."

Behind me, Aunt Christine dug in. "Honestly," she said, "you have some nerve. Coming back here, after a lifetime of sin, and pretending there's nothing to say about it."

When I didn't respond, the sheriff continued. "I know you two haven't been close in a while, but family's family. I thought you should know."

I needed to say something, to respond like the concerned niece I was supposed to be. Aunt Christine and my mom continued to bicker like children, oblivious to everyone around them.

I finally found my voice. "Is he—"

"Tallulah?" Sheriff Morris asked at the same time.

We both broke off to let the other speak.

"Go ahead," we both said.

After another awkward silence, he jumped in. "Please, continue."

"Is he conscious?" If he was knocked out, it made sense that the sheriff didn't know I was the one who had shot him, but if he was awake and hadn't said anything, I didn't know what to think.

"No, he's resting," Sheriff Morris said. I heard him sigh through the phone line. "Your uncle's fallen in with a pretty rough crowd lately, but he's safe at the hospital, I can promise you that. We'll get to the bottom of this tomorrow, once he's stabilized."

"Thank you, Sheriff. I appreciate your calling." We said our goodbyes, trying not to talk over each other, and I sat down.

My mom leaned back in her chair, rotating her drink in her hand. She and my aunt regarded each other with resentment.

"Who was that?" Aunt Christine asked me. "You look upset."

It was stupid to lie. They would find out soon enough, and pretending I didn't know would only raise questions later. "It's Scott," I said.

"Scott!" my mom exclaimed, excited at the mention of her brother. She glanced over at the phone. "How the hell is he?"

"He's been shot," I said, oddly relieved at being able to share the news.

I could hear the hum of the air conditioner.

"He's okay," I said, wanting to reassure them. "I mean, he's not okay, but he's alive. He lost two fingers."

My aunt was the first to speak. "Was that him?" She dropped her fork and pushed away her plate.

"No," I said. "Sheriff Morris."

"Holy shit," my mom said, leaning forward.

"What happened? Where is he?" Aunt Christine leaned in toward my mom, their argument forgotten.

"He's at the hospital in Barstow." I told them the other details the sheriff had shared, careful not to mention anything I knew before his call. I considered telling them everything. It was dishonest leaving myself out of the story, and I didn't have any reason to think Uncle Scott would spare me the repercussions of my actions. As soon as he woke up, he would tell his side, paint himself as the victim. I would be arrested for sure. Everything would fall apart.

I might still be able to force the deal through with Joe Jared, but to what end? I wouldn't be reporting for my new job in Montana if I was in jail, and anyway, I suspected the Forest Service would revoke their offer of employment when they heard I'd shot a man. Things might go better for me if I confessed and got out ahead of it.

I was about to ask my mom and my aunt to step outside with me so I could tell them everything without having to involve my cousins, when Aunt Christine stood. "We should go see him," she said. She grabbed her purse from the counter and dug for her keys. "Girls."

"Could we—" I tried, but the momentum of her conviction carried her toward the door and I lost my nerve.

"I'm going too." My mom downed her drink with one last swig and followed Aunt Christine.

I came to my feet but knew I couldn't go to the hospital, couldn't face Uncle Scott's anger. I was too mortified by what I'd done. I couldn't seem to catch my breath. The girls stared up at their mother with blank faces, forks in hand. Aunt Christine checked the clock. It would be bedtime soon, at least for little Julie.

"You go," I said, glad to have a good reason to stay behind. "We won't all fit in the van anyway. I'll stay here with the girls."

Aunt Christine sensed the tension in my voice and hesitated.

"We're fine. Really," I said, forcing my shoulders down a notch so I would appear calm and collected.

"Make sure they brush their teeth and say their prayers," she said, and continued with motherly instructions as she kissed the cheek of each girl one by one.

My mom waited out on the porch. I could see the low light of the evening behind her. "Christine," she said impatiently.

"I got it," I said, making my voice steady. "Go."

Flustered, Aunt Christine grabbed her things, then brushed her hand over the head of each of her girls one more time. I closed the door behind them and slumped against it. The irritation I felt with myself was unbearable. I should have told them my side of the story. Why hadn't I told them? It was entirely possible Uncle Scott would wake while they were by his side and tell them everything. What's more, the sheriff was going to find out sooner or later. I had been hoping Uncle Scott wouldn't say anything, but that was ridiculous.

"Is Uncle Scott going to be okay?" Gabby asked. She was the oldest of my cousins and, like her mother, focused on practical things.

I wondered what she remembered of Uncle Scott. She'd been eight when she chanced upon him riffling through her father's desk. High on meth, he'd pulled a knife, and that was how Aunt Christine found them: her little girl with piss running down her leg, staring at Scott, who had a six-inch blade in one hand and the family checkbook in the other. That night marked the end of Aunt Christine's godly compassion for her brother. She had carved him out of their lives so thoroughly that the younger girls could have walked right past him on the street and not even known he was their uncle.

"I'm sure he'll be fine," I said. "Uncle Scott has a knack for trouble, but he always comes through okay." I did my best to pretend I had every confidence in his recovery, and I did believe he would live, but I didn't think for a second that everything would be okay. There was no coming back from what I had done.

"Let's clean up, and I'll let you guys eat the last of the cookies." Their attention was easily diverted, and once the dishes were washed, we sat at the table polishing off the tin of butter cookies left over from the funeral reception. I liked spoiling my cousins with treats. It was the best part about not being their mother.

"All right," I said when the tin was empty. "Everyone upstairs. Brush your teeth. I'll be right there." The girls shuffled around, gathering their bags and dragging them up the stairs.

I went to the phone and lifted it to dial the sheriff. I needed to come clean. I would make the call and get it over with. But I didn't even know the number to dial. Not 911. The urgency of my call had long since passed. Little Julie's voice drifted down the stairs. "Lula?"

I hung up.

The sheriff would want me to come down to the station and I couldn't leave the girls alone. I'd wait until morning. Aunt Christine would be back by then and I could go to the sheriff's office to talk to him in person. That would be better.

"Lula?" Julie called again.

"Coming," I said and plodded up the stairs. The whiskey had loosened my limbs and made me sluggish. I herded the girls into Grandma Helen's room and pulled clean sheets from the hall closet, while the two older girls made a nest of blankets on the floor and settled in to read their books under the bedside lamp. The younger three snuggled into the big bed and regarded me with expectation. I knew Aunt Christine usually read them stories, but I didn't have any.

"Do we live here now?" Julie asked.

"For tonight," I said, tucking her hair behind her ear and smoothing the blankets up around them all. "Try to get some sleep. Good night."

The girls wished me good night, their voices a small chorus. It broke my heart a little to have them there in Grandma Helen's room. I wished they could have grown up a little before losing her, that they might have known their grandmother better before she disappeared from their lives.

Then again, her love had always been distant. She'd never been one for tender embraces or words repeated until they lost meaning. She had loved us by being the anchor of our lives, grounding us with reliability, never judging a bad deed, and always being quick to tell us everything was going to be okay. I closed the door behind me and went downstairs.

Griffith emerged from under the couch, his ears flat against his head. He glared at me. He tested the couch cushions with his one front paw, then jumped up and curled into a ball.

I wiped down the table and tidied up the kitchen. Every time I tried to sit down or considered going upstairs to put myself to bed, all I could think about was Uncle Scott in a hospital bed, his hand wrapped in gauze. I wondered if he was conscious yet, if he had told my mom and my aunt what had happened. In a way, I welcomed the truth. It was the fact that I was responsible that I couldn't seem to put into words. Once they got over the initial shock, it would be easier to talk about it, but then my thoughts came around again to what Uncle Scott's version of the story would be. I should have told them.

I picked up the phone to call my aunt on her cell, then decided it would be better if I could see her eyes. I needed to know if she was disappointed or livid or blissfully ignorant of what I had done. It was possible she would land on my side, but not unless I got the chance to tell her my version of the story. As for my mom, I had no idea what to expect from her. The only thing I knew for sure was that she was unpredictable.

I hung up the phone. I couldn't let my aunt's reaction affect my decision to tell the sheriff what had happened. First thing in the morning, I would go and confess. But then I remembered my truck, still jacked up under the walnut tree, missing a wheel, which in turn brought to mind the fact that I had not replaced the stolen supplements.

One thing at a time, I told myself, and paced the living room trying to decide which one thing should be dealt with first. I decided that, come morning, I would borrow Aunt Christine's minivan and drive myself to the sheriff's office. Once I knew what kind of legal trouble I was in, I would deal with the rest. It was a plan. Not a very good plan, but it was the best I could do.

I noticed Grandma Helen's urn was perched precariously close to the edge of the bookshelf. My mom had been careless with it the night before. As drunk as she'd been, it was a minor miracle she hadn't dropped the damn thing.

I took a moment to wipe the fingerprints from the finish. Then I moved a few tattered paperback novels so I could nestle it into the shelf between the books on either side. It looked more secure that way, less likely to be knocked over or jostled.

Hoping it would calm my nerves, I decided to have another drink and poured more than I meant to. Once I added the ice, the golden liquid nearly filled the glass. I told myself I didn't have to finish it, knowing full well that I would. Whiskey in hand, I sat myself in one of the wicker chairs on the front porch, determined to settle down.

A full moon had lifted above the horizon, spilling its gentle light across the sand. I could see Abigail strolling around beyond the far end of the corral, her pale feathers catching the moonlight with each limping stride.

Henley came up onto the porch, his tags jingling in the night, and sat beside me. I scratched behind his ear, grateful for the company, and took another sip of my whiskey. It was Sunday night. Joe Jared's inspector was scheduled to arrive in less than forty-eight hours. I'd been holding out hope that I would have fresh, viable eggs to put in the incubator, but that was looking unlikely. To keep up appearances, I needed to move more eggs from cold storage to the incubator. The ice in my glass clinked as I set my drink on the porch railing and tromped down the steps. The dog jumped up to follow.

I moved forty-two eggs to the incubator, leaving the front row of each shelf vacant in the obstinate hope that the birds would lay even a few future hatchlings before the inspector came. Under the red warming light, the eggs reminded me of bloody teeth. I stared at them, remembering the way Uncle Scott had screamed at the sky, holding his disfigured hand. When the mechanical hinges on the shelves clicked, I startled, then watched as the trays lifted and tilted, wasting effort on eggs that would never hatch.

A warm breeze blew in from the east. The branches of a nearby sagebrush creaked and I smelled the acrid scent of the cement plant that sometimes carried over to the ranch. I wondered if Devon was working. He'd said he would call.

I lifted the latch on the corral gate and slipped in to see if maybe, by some miracle, the birds had managed to lay eggs again, despite the apparent insufficiencies of their diet. The males had taken their spots on the nests for the night. I approached the nearest bird, reaching into my pocket to feign possession of some treat that might lure him from his spot but was knocked off balance by a gentle shove from behind. One of the birds, a female with a wisp of a feather sticking up off the top of her head, swung her neck toward me, offering up something in her beak. The others retreated ever so slightly, which was unexpected, given how the birds were wont to crowd around at the slightest hint of anything interesting.

She nudged me and dropped a wad of duct tape at my feet. I'd never seen a bird voluntarily give up a found prize. I had once seen an ostrich try to swallow a wrench for two whole minutes before finally letting it fall from his mouth.

Stooping to grab the offering from the sand, I found a wallet made of duct tape folded over on itself. It was well worn and covered in sand, but it was definitely a wallet. Inside, it didn't have one of those clear windows that men's wallets tend to have, just two sides to carry cards in. A driver's license was tucked into one of the pockets, and as I lifted it I saw the younger, fuller face of Uncle Scott squinting at me. I flinched, as if he had suddenly appeared in person.

I scanned the desert in every direction, then remembered that the sheriff had said his guys found Uncle Scott without his wallet. He probably dropped it when he snuck into the corral to steal Lady Lil.

I slipped the license back into place. I didn't really expect that the wallet would hold any explanations of Uncle Scott's behavior, but I snooped a little anyway. I found an expired AAA card, a credit card, and two business cards: one for a strip joint and the other for a tobacco shop in Morongo Valley. There was no cash in the fold, but I did find a cheap, red-plastic poker chip. I held it up to the light and saw that the edge was raised and there was a triangle imprinted on one side with the number 5 in the center. "To thine own self be true" was written around the edge. A sobriety chip.

I ran my thumb against it, thinking about how hard Uncle Scott had struggled for those five months of sobriety, and how they were gone. Lost to another bender. I returned the chip to the wallet and put the wallet in my back pocket, hoping that someday, five months would be no big deal, that Uncle Scott would follow Matt's example and find himself fifteen years sober, free of whatever demons seemed to torment him.

I left the birds in the corral and stared down the driveway for any sign of the minivan's return. I spotted Abigail near the property line, where the ranch faded into desert. She was staring out at the mountains in the west, like crumpled velvet in the faint light. I walked over to see what was holding her attention, but saw nothing. Distant headlights appeared at the horizon, so far away that the two lights looked like one. Abigail craned her neck to watch their approach with me, her feet slowly shifting to align the rest of her body, but the car drove past the ranch without slowing.

I plucked a rock from the desert floor and held it up to the moonlight. It was dark and shiny as gunmetal. I scanned the ground at my feet until I found another. I placed the two side by side in my palm to compare them, then flicked the lighter one off into the desert.

I strolled about the wild expanse behind the house in a looping path, never straying too far. I gathered rocks and pitted them against each other to see which most closely resembled the night sky. Abigail remained by my side, taking one step to my three. When finally my aunt's minivan cut up the driveway, I pocketed the winning rock and hurried to hear what my mom and her sister had learned.

"How is he?" I asked the second Aunt Christine's door opened.

"He'll live, thanks be to God," she said with a little glance up at the sky. I could see by her posture that she was worn-out.

The passenger door slammed and my mom came around to join us. Abigail bent to pluck at her bangle bracelets and she ducked away with a yelp of surprise. "Stupid bird," she muttered and swatted at Abigail. "Seriously, Tallulah, you need to keep that beast in the barn."

My pits were sweaty despite the cool breeze and the whiskey

in my stomach threatened to come back up. I wanted to know everything they had seen, but I couldn't think what to ask.

"The girls all right?" Aunt Christine grunted a little as she lowered herself into one of the two wicker chairs on the porch.

"Fine." I retrieved my whiskey glass and sat on the edge of the chair next to her. I took a sip. The ice had melted leaving it watery.

"I need one of those," my mom said, eyeing my drink, and went inside.

"How bad is it?" I asked Aunt Christine, bracing for whatever would come.

"Well, it's not good." She sighed and crammed the heel of her hand into her belly, presumably to reposition a foot or elbow that was lodged between her ribs. "Apparently, he lost a lot of blood. He was unconscious the whole time we were there except for a few minutes, but I don't think he even knew where he was."

I hadn't realized I was holding my breath until the air rushed back into my lungs. They didn't know. He hadn't said anything.

"Every time I think he's hit bottom, he finds a way to go deeper." Brushing a stray hair out of her face, she recounted what the nurse had told her, how he'd almost made it to the hospital, thanks to the enormous amount of methamphetamine in his system, but had ultimately passed out in a pool of his own blood, slumped in his truck at an intersection. Thankfully, the driver of another car had called the paramedics. He was safe in a hospital bed. For one night at least, I knew he would be taken care of and for that I was grateful.

"Lord, give me strength," she said. "I am too pregnant for this." Aunt Christine leaned back against the wicker chair and propped her feet on the porch railing. Her ankles were ridiculously swollen. It looked like she'd swallowed a couple of ostrich eggs and they'd slid right through her body to land at the base of each leg; she didn't have ankles anymore so much as creases in the swollen skin where her feet met her calves.

My mom came back onto the porch holding two glasses. "I made you another," she said, handing me a drink with fresh ice.

"I don't really need another," I said, taking it.

She leaned against the railing beside her sister's swollen feet and pulled a pack of cigarettes from the pocket of her jeans.

Aunt Christine stiffened.

My mom rolled her eyes but took a spot at the far corner of the porch. "Better?" she asked, irritated.

My aunt didn't answer, and my mom, taking that as acceptance, lit her smoke. She was careful to exhale away from the porch, but the smell of it wafted over, bringing memories of cramped apartments and foggy mornings, the give of our funky gray couch, the pattern of red-and-orange-checkered squares on my mom's bedspread, the way I would trace the edges with my fingertip while she got ready for work. Every place we had ever lived smelled of Camel Lights from the day we moved in.

Aunt Christine sighed. "That smell." Apparently, it had evoked something in her as well, though I knew she had never visited us up in Northern California. "Whiskey and cigarettes. You're just like Mom."

On the other side of the porch, the moonlight danced through my mom's dreadlocks. "Hardly."

"Seriously. If I close my eyes right now, she could be sitting right here." Then she did, and I wondered what she saw. I never knew Grandma Helen as a smoker. She had quit by the time I came to the ranch. Even though my grandfather had died of colon cancer, not lung cancer, she said that watching him suffer through his final days had been motivation enough to get her to kick the habit for good.

My grandmother's voice always took on a melancholy tone when she talked about her husband. I knew she missed having someone else on the ranch with her, had always suspected that was why she had collected me from Oakland all those years ago, though she never would have said as much outright. She had been spot-on in all her practical reasons for me to leave Oakland and come live with her, but over the years, I also discovered that she couldn't bear to be alone.

"How much did he steal?" Aunt Christine asked, breaking the silence that had fallen over the porch.

I was still thinking about my grandparents and the question caught me off guard.

"You said Scott stole some money from Mom's account. How much did he take?"

"Oh," I stammered. "Five grand."

My mom whistled out into the night from her perch in the corner.

"He turned out so much like Dad," Aunt Christine said. "Spending money like that. Mom should have kicked him out so many times."

My mom's cigarette burned hot against the night sky. "Dad was a good man," she said. "He just—"

But Aunt Christine cut her off. "He was a lying, boozing, gambling good-for-nothing."

"That's harsh." My mom repositioned herself so she was sitting on the banister with her legs dangling toward Aunt Christine and me.

"Well," my aunt said, "he certainly didn't make things easy on Mom. She did the best she could. Lord knows it's hard keeping a marriage together and being a mother."

My mom raised her glass to me.

"And no matter how big your babies get," Aunt Christine added, squeezing my knee, "they're always your babies."

"You sure you don't want a drink?" my mom asked her.

"You stick around long enough to meet your new niece and I'll have a drink with you."

"How much longer you have to go?"

"Three weeks."

My mom waved dismissively. "Ah, you're practically done already. You could have a few sips."

"Stop."

"You look like you want a drink."

"Of course I want a dang drink." Aunt Christine's composure finally broke and she put her head in her hands. "I haven't had a drink since high school. I didn't even drink at my own wedding."

"Because you were pregnant," my mom said, leaning forward ever so slightly.

"Because I was pregnant," Aunt Christine admitted.

"Ha!" my mom said. "I knew it."

"Yeah, well, give yourself a gold star already," Aunt Christine said, flinching at some pregnancy-related discomfort and adjusting her weight in the chair so that she could rub her lower back. "You're a genius."

"You okay?" I asked her.

"It's just stress."

In the distance, Abigail made her way toward the barn, pecking occasionally at the ground. In the corral, the males blended into the night with their black feathers. Only the females caught the moonlight, like puffs of dandelion fuzz floating around in the dark.

Aunt Christine interlaced her fingers in front of her and nodded. Grandma Helen used to do the same thing. Overlooking the pregnant belly, I could see so many similarities between my grandma and my aunt, from her strong hands to the small vertical crease between her eyebrows. My mom too had been made from the same hardy mold, with meaty arms and sturdy hips. Aunt Christine was shorter, but it would have been a stretch to call her petite.

The family resemblances that the three of us shared were undeniable. An outsider could be forgiven for thinking we sat there gossiping on the porch every Sunday night after the little ones were in bed. I felt nostalgic for the moment even before it passed.

It wasn't fair to let Aunt Christine think this was our new normal, when we might never come together like that again, sharing a warm summer night and paying homage to Grandma Helen with every gesture. I had to tell her I was selling.

"Aunt Christine," I said, hating the words before I even said them. "I have an offer on the ranch. Joe Jared wants to buy it."

"Your mom told me," she said.

"Mom!"

She shrugged. "I didn't know it was a secret."

"It wasn't a secret," I said. "I just . . . I was just trying to find the right time to tell you. I should have done it sooner. I'm sorry."

My aunt stared out at the birds in the corral and I tried to read her expression, but it was blank. If anything, she looked resigned to the fact that I was abandoning the ranch.

I kept talking. "I just . . . This forestry job. I'll be doing something that really makes a difference . . . fighting fires. I want what I do to matter."

"This ranch." Aunt Christine shifted in her seat again, trying to find a comfortable position. "You've got, what, a hundred fifty ostriches out there?"

"One hundred forty-two."

"And when Joe Jared takes over, they'll all go to slaughter?"

"Eventually."

"Well, then, I'd say it matters an awful lot to them. Not that fighting fires isn't noble work. It's important, no doubt about it, but Tallulah, don't for a second think that staying here, taking care of these birds, doesn't matter. It matters plenty."

I looked out over the corral where the male birds were sitting on empty nests. "Well," I said, "even if you're right, turns out I'm not much good at taking care of them on my own. They stopped laying eggs a few days ago."

"That's weird," my mom said. "Isn't this the season?"

I stared out over the corral, clutching my glass under my chin.

"Maybe they miss Mom," Aunt Christine said.

I laughed. "You're giving them too much credit. You know their eyeballs are bigger than their brains, right?" The female birds in the corral sauntered about so slowly that in the periphery of my vision, they looked like they were drifting on some unseen lake.

Aunt Christine shrugged. "Been some big changes around here is all."

Only one big change, I thought. I could feel my pulse in my temples. "Do you . . . Am I the only one who thinks maybe it wasn't an accident? Grandma Helen, I mean."

"Tallulah," Aunt Christine said, her voice laden with concern.

"Mom wouldn't have done that," my mom said without question.

I stared at the screen door, tracing the arc of light from the bare bulb overhead that cut across the pattern of the mesh. "We'd been arguing and she'd been so down."

"Honey," my mom said, her voice light and dismissive as she mashed her cigarette butt. "There's no way."

"But you didn't know her."

Aunt Christine was silent. I expected her to be angry with me, but her eyes were fixed on something a thousand miles away. The thought had crossed her mind too.

"I'm her damn daughter," my mom said, as if that held any practical meaning after twenty-four years. Grandma Helen's absence from the ranch didn't even register for her. To her, everything was just as she'd left it: the sand of the desert rolling off into mountains, the pale turquoise color of the house, the slam of the screen door. "People don't change," she said.

"Grandma Helen did."

"It's true," Aunt Christine said. "She changed." My mom didn't argue. How could she? My aunt shifted in her seat again, lifting her giant belly to adjust her position. "She did seem out of sorts lately. But Tallulah, I just can't imagine that she would . . ." Her posture turned stiff. She was afraid of something, and it dawned on me that in the framework of Aunt Christine's beliefs, suicide was more than abandonment. It was a sin.

"Never mind," I said. "I'm just . . . I think I'm feeling guilty because we were arguing. I shouldn't have said anything. Please forget it."

Aunt Christine opened her mouth to speak, but no words came.

"It's just me," I continued. "I can't stand that the last conversation I had with her was an argument." I hadn't realized how true that was until I said it. "I wanted Grandma Helen to understand what it meant to me to take that job in Montana. I wanted her to be happy for me."

My aunt patted my knee. "I know Grandma Helen wasn't good at showing how she felt, but I'm sure she was happy for you. And whatever her feelings about your leaving, it didn't have anything to do with the accident."

And without a hitch, we were back to calling it an accident. As much as my skin crawled at the word, I couldn't deny how the panicked energy I felt dissipated when the agreed-upon story was reestablished. I shouldn't have brought it up. I looked down at my empty glass. I was drunk.

"I think you're smart to get out of here," my mom said. "What I don't understand is joining up with the Forest Service. Sounds fucking boring." She lit another cigarette.

"Devon wants me to stay in Sombra," I said, thankful for

the change of topic. "He wants me to take a job at the plant and move in with him."

Aunt Christine perked up. "Oh, Tallulah, that's so romantic."

My mom raised her eyebrows in a silent "I told you so," then looked away to pretend she wasn't involved in the discussion.

"Is it?" I pictured it: the two of us living together in his one-room apartment over the laundromat.

"Of course it is." Aunt Christine hesitated for a second, like maybe it was none of her business, but then asked, "Are you pregnant?"

My mom's head jerked toward me.

"No," I said emphatically. "What is wrong with you?"

"Only asking," she said, holding up her hands. "Babies are God's way of moving us along on our path. I left the ranch when I was pregnant. Your mom too."

"Well, I'm not."

We all fell silent for a moment before my aunt asked my mom, "Where did you go when you left?" My mom had never been one to send postcards. How strange it must have been for Aunt Christine, growing up knowing she had a sister and niece out in the world, but having no idea how we lived our lives.

My mom leaned against the porch post and, with the posturing of someone recounting a grand adventure, told Aunt Christine how I was born in Hollywood at St. Anthony's after thirty hours of labor. From there, she followed one boyfriend after another with me in tow. I knew the story well and found myself distracted, watching my mom and my aunt interact.

My mom had enough alcohol in her by then that her defenses were down. I could almost picture them as kids, though with ten years between them, they probably had never spoken so intimately in their lives. My mom had always been quick to take offense, and my aunt was usually focused on her girls.

In truth, I had almost never seen Aunt Christine without the girls by her side. To me, she was less an individual and more like the center of a small solar system. Kids gravitated close for hugs or bandages and then spun back out into the space around her. Funny, Todd had never been a part of that.

As they talked, Aunt Christine slid Grandma Helen's wedding band along the delicate chain around her neck. Grandma Helen had left all her jewelry to Aunt Christine. There wasn't much. Aside from my grandparents' wedding rings, there was a small clamshell box with a few pairs of earrings, a string of pearls, and a couple of bracelets. Grandma Helen had never worn jewelry except on special occasions, not even her wedding ring. Jewelry caused more trouble than it was worth when she was working in the corral, the birds forever pecking at anything shiny. Aunt Christine had wanted to wear her mother's wedding band when I gave it to her, but her hands were so swollen that it didn't fit, so she had settled for slipping it onto her necklace for the time being. With each flick of her wrist, the band clinked against the gold cross that hung next to it.

My mom's extended litany of her various boyfriends made me think of Devon. Again, I wondered why he hadn't called. It felt like we were in the middle of a conversation that kept being interrupted. Maybe it was the whiskey, but I wanted to hear his voice.

While my mom and Aunt Christine clucked like two old hens, I excused myself and went inside to call him. I knew his shift at the plant was over. He was either at home or at Pat's. I dialed his cell number and smiled into the phone.

"Hello?" It was a woman's voice. I could hear Pat's Bar in the background, the hum of conversation punctuated by the clack of pool balls. "Tallulah?" I recognized that rising lilt. It was Stella. The sheriff's daughter. I hung up and poured myself a glass of water, then drank it standing at the sink. He was sitting at the bar with Stella. Again.

My mom and Aunt Christine were laughing when I went outside.

"You okay?" my aunt asked.

I shrugged. "I'm going to bed."

They waited for me to say more, but all I could think about was sleep. I made my way up the stairs, being careful to step lightly past Grandma Helen's room, where the girls were sleeping, and collapsed on top of my comforter, shoes and all.

Stella's voice mutated in my mind, became the sound of Uncle Scott screaming. When I tried to sleep, I saw blood running down his arm, his teeth grinding against the pain. The room had a slight spin to it. I scooted to the side of the bed and planted one foot on the floor, a trick I had heard my mom joke about with friends. It worked. The room slowed its rotation.

I was almost asleep when I remembered the rock I had collected from the driveway. I found it in my pocket and flipped on the lamp. On my windowsill, a line of similar rocks sat side by side, arranged by color from lightest to darkest.

At the far left was a piece of white quartz, pale as a summer cloud. Next to it, a rough-textured pink rock rested against a chunk of sandstone that wasn't quite red and wasn't quite orange but held the elusive hue of a sunset. And on it went, from orange to yellow, through slate green and granite blue. There were about six shades of brown, each deeper than the last, and finally, at the end, a piece of obsidian, black and shiny as spilled oil. I had found them all within a hundred yards of the house.

The rock I pulled from my pocket had flecks of gray, and as I compared it to each of the stones, moving it from left to right, I found its place third from the end. I shifted a piece of basalt to make space for it.

I had been collecting them for over a year and was fascinated by the fact that I had yet to find two rocks that were the same color. Before seeing the rainbow on my windowsill, I would have told you that the desert was the color of coffee with too much cream in it, but after finding over twenty rocks without a single one matching, I knew that you had to look closer. The desert was purple, and pink, and orange, and green, but only if you took the time to see it. I gazed at the rocks for another moment, then collapsed onto my bed and plunged into unconsciousness.

TWELVE

"Tallulah!"

I was jolted from a deep sleep. The silhouette in my doorway yelled my name again. It was Gabby, her pale hair a wild mop in the harsh light of the hallway. "It's Mom," she said, her voice urgent, and then she disappeared. I heard her yelling from the stairs. "Tallulah, help."

I lurched from my bed, not entirely sober, and stepped from my room. Aunt Christine stood frozen on the third stair from the top, both hands on the outside banister, bracing against a contraction. She gave a terrified moan. Her eyes were clamped shut. Her pink nightshirt draped her body like a tent. Gabby hovered with her sisters just outside Grandma Helen's room. Little Julie had her rag doll in a choke hold.

"I thought you had weeks to go," I said, scurrying to my aunt's side and holding her shoulder to steady her.

"I was wrong." Her body relaxed a bit, and her grip on the banister loosened. Gabby and I each held an elbow so that she wouldn't fall as she took a few unsteady steps. "I need you to drive me to the hospital." Her voice rose on the word "*hospital*," and her body wound tight again.

Again, she grabbed the banister with both hands and bore down against the pain of another contraction. We had only taken four steps. I didn't know much about having babies, but contractions that close together seemed like a sign that there wasn't much time, and the hospital was thirty miles away. I didn't want to be caught halfway there with my aunt giving birth on the side of the road. Gabby bounced on her heels and I could tell she was scared, unsure what to do to help her mom. For all her maturity, she was only twelve.

"Gabby," I said, making my voice as steady as I could, "go downstairs and call 9-1-1."

Gabby ran.

"No," my aunt grunted.

Gabby froze halfway down the stairs.

"I want you to take me," she gasped. "I've got time."

"You sure?"

"No," she groaned.

"It'll be faster if they come to us." I waved Gabby down the stairs and she sprinted to the kitchen.

Aunt Christine opened her mouth to argue, but it was all she could do to stay on her feet as the contraction passed. Gabby's voice carried up the stairs. I could hear her talking to the dispatcher, explaining that her mom was having a baby. "Please hurry," she said and hung up the phone. "They're on their way. They said to get towels."

"Okay, good, they're on their way," I said, trying to sound reassuring as I helped Aunt Christine down into the living room. The rest of the girls came to the bottom of the stairs.

Aunt Christine crouched down as another contraction came. She let go of my arms and planted her hands so that she was on all fours. Her body clenched and she bore down. A pained wail escaped her. I knelt beside her and put my hand on her lower back, feeling entirely useless.

"What the hell is going on?" It was my mom, bleary-eyed and confused at the top of the stairs.

Aunt Christine panted. Her hair stuck to her face. "No, no, no," she said.

"What can we do?" I asked.

Another contraction crumpled her. "I want to be in a hospital," she yelled at the floor, and I could hear the fear in her voice. "With a doctor, and an epidural." The word "epidural" squeezed up into a shaky cry as she winced against the pain. She gritted her teeth to bear down again, groaning low and steady until the contraction passed. She panted up at me.

"Do you want to get off the floor?" But before she could answer, another contraction hit.

This time, as she groaned through it, she reached down with one hand between her legs. When the contraction passed, she slumped panting onto her butt and whimpered, her nightshirt hiking up over her thighs. The shock of seeing my aunt splayed on the floor was replaced by the realization of what was before me. I could see the pale crown of the baby's head.

It was happening, right there on the living-room floor. I knelt between her knees. "Okay," I said with feigned confidence.

She gave a little head bobble, like *okay* was what she needed to hear, and the next contraction washed over her, pulling her upper body forward. She reached for her knees.

"Girls," I said. "Come help. Gabby, sit behind her." The other four sat on either side and took their mother's arms, giving her something to pull against.

Only my mother remained apart, hovering at the periphery of my vision.

I was petrified, but if it was happening, we would do it together. My eyes locked with Aunt Christine's. I said as calmly and steadily as I could, "You got this. You've done this five fucking times. You don't need a hospital." For once, she didn't balk at my cursing.

Aunt Christine bore down. Gabby braced her mother's back. My heart pounded, but I believed what I had said. I knew she could do it.

Aunt Christine pushed again, her face red, the veins in her neck bulging. The spot that was the crown of the baby's head grew, then shrank. Aunt Christine panted. With each contraction it emerged farther, but each time it retreated.

One of the girls gasped as the baby's head appeared impossibly big, then retreated again. My aunt's body clenched. Her face screwed up tight and her tortured cry filled the room. She strained hard, her entire body fighting to birth the baby, and then, mercifully, the head was out.

The baby's tiny face was down toward the carpet so that all I could see was the back of her scalp, wisps of hair plastered to it. Aunt Christine collapsed against Gabby. It seemed the worst was over, but the baby was just lying there, half born. Was she supposed to be facedown like that? Shouldn't she be crying? Panic radiated out to my fingertips. I was about to ask my aunt what came next when she lifted forward to grab her knees again and pushed once more with a deep groan.

The baby's shoulders slipped free, and her skinny body slid out in a gush of liquid. Surprised by the quickness of it, I held her head gingerly between the thumb and forefinger of my right hand, catching the rest of her with my left. She was covered in fluids, and the umbilical cord pulsed. I held her close so as not to drop her and tried not to think about the blood and muck. I had never seen anything more disgusting or fantastic in all my life.

The baby unfurled her first cry and Aunt Christine, satisfied with the sound, collapsed again onto her eldest. The girls giggled with relief around me, crowding over my shoulder to inspect their new little sister. "It's a girl," I said, confirming what we'd all known for months. I was crying.

Aunt Christine undid the buttons of her nightshirt so she could tuck the infant close against her skin, not even noticing the blood.

"Mom," I said. "Can you get some towels?"

My mom broke from her trance to run up the stairs and collect a stack of clean towels. I handed one to Aunt Christine so she could wipe her baby's face clean.

She gazed down at her infant girl, then smiled up at the rest of her daughters. They all studied the baby, whose face screwed into a frown. With her thin strands of hair and her tiny eyebrows crinkled together, she looked like a grouchy senior citizen. In fact, she kind of resembled Grandma Helen. Aunt Christine rocked her and crooned. The baby's face relaxed.

It was rough business, being born. The carpet would certainly never be the same. I would deal with the mess later. The baby was here, and everyone was breathing. That was enough for the time being. From outside, I could hear the wail of a siren. I had never been more grateful for any sound. Within minutes, two men in uniforms carrying orange plastic kits rushed into the house. There was talk of the placenta and of cutting the cord. I was glad they were there.

Through the screen door, I could see the warm glow of sunrise. In the corral, Lady Lil was trotting in a small circle, her wings fluttering, apparently confused by the arrival of the ambulance. I washed up as best I could and waited out on the porch for the EMTs to finish their work. The coarse desert air calmed me. By then, Lady Lil had simmered down. My own energy was fading and a nascent headache had settled in behind my eyes.

My mom followed me out. "Holy shit," she said, dropping into a porch chair and lighting a cigarette. I had to agree. That just about summed things up. I was exhausted, but not at all sleepy. The combination of the drinks from the night before and the adrenaline from the morning had my guts all riled up. The siren light on the ambulance spun steadily, but as the sun crested the horizon, the flashing red was lost in the blinding brightness of a new day. I thought of Uncle Scott. I needed to get to the sheriff's office and deal with what had happened, but if I sat there on the porch too long I might very well fall back asleep. I stood and saw Reuben's tow truck come up our driveway. With a nod of recognition, I met him over near my pickup, still jacked up the way we had left it.

"What happened?" he asked, eyeing the ambulance.

"Aunt Christine had her baby."

"Everything okay?"

"Oh," I said, realizing that an ambulance was usually a bad sign. "Yes. She's fine. The baby's fine. It just happened really fast; we couldn't even get out the door. She was born in the living room, right on the carpet. The ambulance didn't get here until it was over."

An amused smile I had never seen crossed his face. "You delivered the baby?"

"Oh no," I said. "No. I just caught her as she came out. Aunt Christine did all the work." It sounded like a joke, but I wasn't kidding.

"Busy morning."

"Yeah."

Shifting his attention, he said, "I see we haven't made much progress on that ball joint." There was a smugness about him, and for a second, he reminded me of his son, minus the topknot. I suspected he had come to see if Matt had followed up on his promise to do the work. It was possible he had intended to sneak up before I woke, to satisfy his own curiosity.

"Matt said he would come back."

Reuben gave a little grunt. "Typical," he muttered as he opened his toolbox. "I've got the parts."

With my truck fixed I wouldn't have to borrow Aunt Christine's minivan. "Thank you," I said. Behind Reuben, over on the west side of the corral, I could see where the sand had been disturbed when Uncle Scott dragged Lady Lil into the desert. It was time to go to the sheriff. I was ready. "Thank you for coming."

Reuben gave another grunt. He had already set to work doing the repairs, and I got the distinct feeling that he didn't want me hovering over him, so I let him be. As soon as he was done, I would drive into town and tell the sheriff everything.

Inside the corral, I flipped the lever to let the feed slide down from the silo into the trough. The males lifted from the nests and joined the hens, gliding toward their breakfast. I ducked through the birds and walked the length of the corral. On either side, from end to end, were empty nests.

It was Monday morning. I had one more day before Joe Jared's inspector showed up to peer into all the cracks of the ranch. Twenty-four hours for the ostriches to produce a few viable eggs.

The birds continued to peck at their feed, oblivious to the world around them. "Why aren't you laying eggs?" I asked them. I ran my hand along the back of the bird closest to me, letting my fingers sink into her umber feathers. I thought about Aunt Christine's suggestion that they missed Grandma Helen. I wasn't sure I believed they had the brain power required for mourning, but in many subtle ways, the ranch was different without Grandma Helen.

I didn't want her to be gone. I wanted her on the ranch with me and the birds. I wanted her to wish me well as I went off to Montana. I wanted to see her light up at the sight of her newest granddaughter. I wanted to hear her argue with my mom. She had abandoned us all.

The baby's wail floated from inside the house, through the

screen door and out over the desert. Grandma Helen would never know this little one. Life marched on.

Lady Lil left the feed trough and strolled toward me. She planted her feet and lowered her head until it was level with my own. A few more inches and our foreheads would touch.

"She's gone," I said. Tears rolled down my cheek, but I held the stare. "We have to let her go." A long moment passed in stillness. Finally, the bird blinked and walked to the far end of the corral.

I wiped at my eyes. What an idiot I was, talking to a bunch of stupid ostriches. I had work to do. I moved more eggs from the storage unit to the incubator. I didn't know what else to do. I was about half-finished with the awful chore when I heard my mom call out, "Tallulah, phone."

"Who is it?" I yelled.

"Bob something." The screen door knocked against its frame as it shut behind her.

The vet, with the test results on the birds. I hurried inside. If Bob had found something unusual in the blood work he might change his diagnosis. The supplements wouldn't matter at all if it was some sort of infection.

The paramedics were still in the house, but the pace of things had slowed. Both Aunt Christine and the baby were exhausted but in good health. "Are they taking her to the hospital?" I asked my mom as she handed me the phone. She shrugged.

One of the paramedics pulled a stack of paperwork from his bag and came toward me.

"One second, Bob, sorry," I said into the phone, then clamped it to my collarbone.

The paramedic held out a stack of papers for me to take. "I've got some basic information on postpartum care."

"This is not her first rodeo," I said, smiling at the sight of my aunt surrounded by her five older daughters, all of them cooing at the infant.

"I gathered," the paramedic said. "All the same, if she's going to stay here, I need you to take these and sign here."

I did.

"Mom," I said, "hang this up once I've got it upstairs?" There was too much going on down there to hear what Bob had to say. I handed the phone to her and hurried up to Grandma Helen's room. "Got it," I yelled.

"Bob?" I heard the click of my mom hanging up the other line in the kitchen.

"Tallulah, hello. Sounds like you've got a full house there. I won't take up your time." This was one of the reasons Grandma Helen always hired Bob. He wasn't one for small talk. "As far as the blood work goes," he said, "the birds are healthy as can be. The water tested clean as well." I could hear some papers shuffling on his end of the line. "No viral infection, and it's not age. Did you get those supplements?"

"I did, but—"

"Well, that should take care of things."

"They got stolen."

"The eggs?"

"The supplements."

The other end of the line went quiet.

"It's a long story," I said. I heard a commotion at the bottom of the stairs. Stretching the phone cord as far as it would reach, I could see one of the paramedics supporting my aunt as she climbed.

"Well," Bob said through the phone, "all signs point to stress. You get those extra nutrients into their food and they should be back to full production in a few days." He promised to send me a copy of his full report, and we said our goodbyes as my aunt made it to the top of the stairs.

"This will do," she said, crossing the threshold into Grandma Helen's room, her body bent at the waist and her feet wide apart. She approached the bed with both arms out to catch herself and crawled up onto the blankets, resting against the headboard.

My mom came up the stairs with the new baby. She handed the bundle to Aunt Christine, then followed the paramedic back downstairs. We could hear the shuffling of gear as they packed up to leave. I followed Aunt Christine's gaze out into the blazing bright day.

"Still no eggs?" she asked.

"There's nothing wrong with the birds," I said, surprised that she had had the wherewithal to track anything beyond what she had been going through herself. "I don't know what I'm doing wrong." I scooted closer to peer down into the little bundle and smiled in spite of everything that was wrong. She was so peaceful. "Do we have a name yet?"

"I'm thinking Grace."

The baby's tiny hand wiggled loose from her swaddle and she curled her delicate fingers, pale as daisy petals, around the edge of the blanket under her chin. "Grace," I repeated. "I like it." Aunt Christine smiled down at the baby too, her happy expression contrasted by the dark circles under her eyes. Her face was puffy, her hair a mess. "You should sleep," I told her.

"I should call Todd." And tears ran down her face. "Oh, I'm a wreck," she said, wiping at her cheeks with her hand. "Every time, I forget how much these hormones send me for a loop." She laughed through her tears. "You'd think I'd be used to it by now." Her voice cracked a little, and she wiped at her face again. "I wish your grandma was here to tell me I'm doing the right thing, but I guess, in some ways, losing her was the thing that finally convinced me to leave him. Life's too short, you know?" She let the tears fall. "But everything just feels wrong."

I grabbed a box of tissues from the bedside table and handed it to her. "Are you considering going back?"

"No," she said with resolve, shaking her head to clear her tears. "He's never been faithful. Not even when we were first married. And I'm used to it at this point, I am. But it was always a private thing. With Megan . . . I can't go back to that church. It's more than humiliation; it's like he took my congregation from me."

Grace shifted and Aunt Christine placed her hand on the baby's belly to soothe her. "What kind of example am I setting for my daughters," she whispered, "if I continue on like this? Gabby is going to be a teenager in December. And this little one," she said, tracing the curve of the baby's ear. "Another girl. What am I going to do?"

"Want to buy an ostrich ranch?"

Aunt Christine laughed again.

"You should rest," I said. "We'll have time to figure everything out. I'll set the girls up in Scott's old room." Then, realizing that two rooms weren't really enough for her and her brood, I added, "We can boot my mom to the couch if she outstays her welcome."

Aunt Christine sniffed. "Did she say how long she's staying?"

"As soon as we run out of booze, I'm guessing she'll be on her way." I'd meant it as a joke, but it wasn't funny.

"I'm sorry, Tallulah."

"You've got nothing to be sorry for." She looked like a wounded animal sitting there with her shoulders hunched and her eyes sunken. "Don't worry about calling Todd right now," I said. "Sleep first. Take care of yourself for a few hours. There'll be plenty of time to hash things out later."

She closed her eyes and nodded.

"I'll check on the girls," I said, "make sure my mom's not teaching them to gamble."

As I left the room, she snuggled down to curl her body around her newborn.

I changed clothes in my room and was halfway down the stairs when I heard the television. For half a second, I was impressed that my mom had found a way to be helpful, but then I saw the confused expressions on the girls' faces. My mom had chosen a soap opera. On the screen, a muscled man was kissing the cleavage of an overly made-up woman who clutched at him with a dramatic moan.

"Mom!"

"It's educational," she said.

What my mom considered life lessons, Aunt Christine would call pornography. "You can't . . ." I grabbed the remote and handed it to Gabby. "Find something appropriate for a first grader, would you?"

Gabby perked up at being put in charge and immediately began surfing the channels.

There was a knock at the door. Reuben wiped his hands on a grease-stained rag. "All fixed," he said. "The converter too. I found a good used one for you."

"Thank you," I said, but the gratitude I'd felt earlier had been replaced by a deep sense of dread. My truck was fixed. I had to go to the sheriff. I didn't have any more excuses. "What do I owe you?"

Behind me, the girls bickered about what program they wanted to watch. Parker lunged at the remote and Gabby held it high.

"One hundred's fine," he said, shifting on his feet.

I found my checkbook. "For everything? The converter too?"

Reuben shifted on his feet, clearly uncomfortable with the discussion of payment. The dramatic drop in price led me to believe that Matt had been right when he called out his father on gouging me. I wrote him the check, thanking him again, and he left quickly.

The girls had finally landed on a cartoon show I knew their mother didn't hate. They would be fine. I hesitated at the door, keys in hand. It was time. I held the screen door so it wouldn't thunk against the frame and draw attention as I left.

The hum of the truck's engine soothed me, and I sat there waiting for the AC to turn the scorching gusts cold against my face. I told myself I wasn't stalling, but that was a lie. I had the sudden impulse to drive to Mexico, or Canada. I could run away and leave everything behind, let my mom and Aunt Christine work it all out, but that wasn't what I wanted either.

I put the truck in gear and rolled down to the end of the driveway. What would I say? Where should I start? I decided to go with self-defense. Uncle Scott had been stealing my property, I caught him, he attacked me, and I was defending myself. All true. So why was I so nervous?

I pulled out onto the highway and drove south. The sun was high, and the light reflected off the sand, chasing even the smallest shadows from sight. I cracked the window and let the roar of the air fill the cab. I could smell clay baking in the sun, the scent of heat itself. Midday in the Mojave was how I pictured the bottom of the ocean: nothing moving, the craggy bushes like coral in the bleached-out landscape. The intense pressure of the sun pinned everything down, trapping every lizard and mouse in its den. Not even a whisper of a breeze stirred the sand. The only things moving were the cars on the highway, like sharks passing through in search of their next meal.

After about twenty minutes, I came to the place where cell service improved. My phone buzzed, signaling messages that had finally come through. Holding the phone over the steering wheel, I could see they were all from Matt. *Still no word from Scott. Please let me know if you hear from him. I'm worried.*

That last message had been sent the night before, while my mom and Aunt Christine were at the hospital. I should have called Matt to tell him. I came to the traffic light at the center of town. There was no one else there, so I typed out a response sitting right there at the intersection, ignoring the light when it changed. *He's at Barstow Community Hospital. Tell him Christine had her baby.* I wasn't sure what else to say. There were too many details to text, and I didn't want to call. I was afraid my voice would give me away.

I passed Pat's Bar and knew a drink would help. A drink would give me the courage I needed to say out loud that I had shot my uncle, but then I thought of my mom, sitting at the table drinking whiskey before noon, and it made me uneasy. What was more, I didn't want booze on my breath when I confessed.

Out of habit, I scanned the parked cars to see if Devon was there. He wasn't, but he had been there the night before. I remembered Stella answering his phone with that whiny little voice of hers.

The way I figured it, there were two explanations. The first was that she answered because he was off in the bathroom or playing pool or something. The other was that he was sleeping with her and he let her answer because he was drunk and being a pussy and he hoped I'd get the message and break up with him so he wouldn't have to do the dirty work. I heard them mocking me as she climbed into his car at the end of the night and went home with him to his apartment over the laundromat.

When the light flashed green again, I continued down Route 66 for about a mile and pulled into the parking lot of Devon's building. His silver SUV was there.

I didn't want to believe Devon would sleep with Stella. She was so annoying. And yet my suspicion was undeniable. The metal stair railing leading up to his apartment burned my fingers. My footsteps rang out like the tolling of an iron bell. At the landing, I hesitated underneath the tiny awning. I hated myself for doing it, but I leaned in to listen at the door. When I didn't hear anything, I knocked.

THIRTEEN

There was a muffled rustling before Devon opened the door. He blinked in the bright light and ran a hand through his hair.

"Tallulah. What's wrong?"

"Nothing," I said reflexively. "I just wanted to see you." There was no sign of Stella. He didn't seem nervous or cagey the way I imagined he would if she'd spent the night with him. I felt foolish for being so suspicious.

He pulled the door open and it was wonderfully cool inside his studio apartment. A large bookshelf took up one whole wall, with paperbacks lined up above vintage records. An afghan lay over the end of the orange couch. His bed was unmade but empty. The place smelled like something had recently been cooked with a lot of butter.

"Hey, what's up?"

I wanted to tell him about what had happened with Uncle Scott, how Aunt Christine had had her baby, how the birds weren't laying eggs, but it all got jumbled. I traced my thoughts back to when I had seen him last.

"I never said thank you for driving my mom out to the ranch

the other night. I'm sorry if I was short with you." I plunked myself at his tiny table and leaned forward on my elbows. The kitchen was little more than a corner of the room that had been tiled over with yellow and given a counter. The fridge was barely big enough for some milk and a six-pack. There was a two-burner stove and a cabinet. A small window over the sink had been covered by a pillowcase, pinned up to keep out the sun.

"Your mom's not quite what I expected," he said. He dumped the soggy grounds from the basket of the tiny coffee machine and set to making a fresh pot. "She's not at all like my mom."

His mom would never, ever, have hitchhiked three hundred miles and ended up drinking in a bar until two. Our families were different.

"Aunt Christine moved in, with the girls." I was stalling. "She left Todd. And she had her baby. On our living room floor, early this morning."

"Seriously?"

I nodded. "And one other thing." The biggest thing. The thing I couldn't bring myself to say out loud. "It's not good." I buried my face in my arms.

"What is it?"

"It's . . . really not good," I said to the Formica of the tabletop. My words made a little spot of condensation. "My uncle Scott was shot." It was easier to begin there. I lifted my head, expecting to see a look of shock on his face, but his expression held steady.

"I heard," he said. "I'm sorry."

"What? How? Sheriff Morris only found out last night."

"Stella."

"Of course." The sheriff's daughter. Not that simply being the sheriff's daughter entitled her to know everyone's business, but she was nosy and had a way of finding things out. "You guys are tight these days."

"Don't be like that," he said, going to the cabinet for some Cheerios and eating a handful right out of the box. "She's a sweet kid."

"Yeah, well, you should tell that sweet kid not to answer your phone in the middle of the night."

"What?" He swiped his phone from the counter and tapped the screen a few times, no doubt seeing the log of my incoming call. "What the hell?"

"A girlfriend could get the wrong idea."

"Lu," he said evenly as he put down the phone, "I was at Pat's. You know there's nothing going on between me and her. Wait. Is that why you're here?"

"No," I said. "I was just—" *Stalling.* "I was passing by. I gotta go talk to the sheriff, about my uncle."

"Why?" He scooped another handful of cereal into his mouth. "Stella said—"

"Ugh." If I heard him say that name one more time, I would scream. Stella didn't know everything. I grimaced and forced the next sentence from my mouth. "I did it. I'm the one who shot him."

"What?" he sputtered through his Cheerios. "What happened?"

I savored the surprise on his face, but immediately regretted what I'd said. I should have told the sheriff first. I was about to make some lame attempt to take it back when my words found momentum in spite of me and the confession spilled out. I told him everything.

He sat across from me, listening without interrupting, his fist still full of uneaten Cheerios, and my regret faded a bit. It was cathartic to lay it all out on the table. The hardest part had been getting started. It wouldn't be as difficult to say it all a second time, when I went to make my official confession.

"You need to tell the sheriff."

"That's what I said. I'm going now."

"But you're not going now. You're here. You shot him yesterday, Lu. What have you been waiting for? You can't just ignore this."

I opened my mouth to explain that I wasn't ignoring it, but the truth was I hadn't reported it to the sheriff, hadn't gone to the hospital, hadn't even told my family what happened. I had gone about my life like nothing was out of the ordinary. How had twenty-four hours passed so quickly? In a dizzying moment of clarity, I understood how my grandmother had overlooked seemingly unavoidable problems like her son's addiction or her teenage daughter's pregnancy. I was doing the exact same thing.

I suddenly longed to be at Pat's Bar. The instinct to hide from it all was overwhelming and I felt trapped by my own confession. I'd admitted what I'd done and now I had to deal with it. There was no going back.

"Lu?" Devon stared at me, waiting for a response.

"I guess I was hoping you would be supportive," I said, which sounded weak and wasn't even true, but I could hardly say I came over to see if I could catch him sleeping with Stella.

Devon's voice jumped an octave. "Of you shooting your uncle?"

"No. Of my going to tell the sheriff." Though I had, in fact, been using him as another distraction. Even an argument about Stella was preferable to confessing to shooting Uncle Scott.

"You should be there right now!" Devon went to the door and pulled on his sneakers, hopping a little as he balanced on each foot.

"Stop yelling."

He lowered his voice. "Tallulah, you have to go." He never called me by my full name. "If you don't tell the sheriff, I have to. We have to go right now." When I didn't stand, he took my hand and pulled me up from my chair. "I'll drive you."

I couldn't move. "I need a minute." I would go to the sheriff. I would. But I didn't like being pressured. "Devon, wait."

"We can't wait, Lu. You've already waited too long. Even if it was self-defense—"

"It was," I said.

"Waiting makes you look guilty." He tugged on my hand. I kept my feet planted, but the apartment was small enough that he could reach the door without letting go. He twisted the knob and flung it open, and we were both shocked to see Sheriff Morris there at the top of the metal staircase, poised to knock.

"Sheriff Morris," Devon said, dropping my hand.

"I'm sorry to interrupt," the sheriff said, "but I was on my way out to the Jones ranch to talk to Tallulah when I saw her truck parked out front." When I didn't say anything, he continued. "I went to see your uncle this morning, to get an official statement of what happened."

I stood stunned, like a bird that's flown into a plate-glass window.

"But . . . it would seem your uncle has declined further care and left the hospital." He pulled a notebook from his shirt pocket and flipped it open. "I was hoping you might have some idea where we could find him."

"'Declined further care'? What does that mean?" Devon asked.

I knew what it meant. It had happened before. "It means he's gone to get high," I said.

"That seems a fair assessment," the sheriff said. "The nurses told me he said your name a few times in the night before regaining consciousness. You haven't heard from him?"

"No," I said.

The heat from outside was pouring through the open door. "Do you want to come in?" Devon asked. The space wasn't really big enough for three people, but it was too hot to keep talking through the door, so the sheriff came inside.

"Mind if I . . ." He put his hand on one of the two chairs at the table.

"Please," Devon said, pulling out the other chair for me.

The sheriff crossed one ankle over the other and sat forward on the edge of his seat. His daughter often adopted the same posture on her barstool. I searched his face for other similarities, but while Stella had the fragile bronze eyes of an anime character and the perfect complexion to match, the sheriff's eyes were slits under his bushy eyebrows and his checks were splotched with red. The nose was the same as his daughter's, narrow and straight, as was the blond hair. I wondered if he knew that Stella and Devon were spending so much time together. "When was the last time you saw your uncle?" he asked.

"We had an argument last week at Grandma Helen's funeral." That wasn't the last time I'd seen him, but it felt important to give a little context. The sheriff stared at me expectantly. "He was upset," I said, "about me selling the ranch."

"You're selling the ranch?" Sheriff Morris uncrossed his legs and sat back.

"Yes, I've been offered a job in—"

"That is a shame," he said. "Those birds have become quite a landmark."

"Well, the birds aren't going anywhere," I said. The ostriches were not what I wanted to talk to him about.

"Did your grandmother approve of this?"

"No, she—"

"Man, she loved those birds." He smiled to himself. He was making it surprisingly hard to say what I needed to say.

Devon gave me an encouraging look. "Yeah, so as I was saying, Scott was pretty upset when he left the funeral reception, and . . ." I steadied myself. "He was clearly high when I caught him trying to steal one of my birds."

Sheriff Morris checked his little notebook. "When was this?"

"Yesterday morning." I watched his brow furrow as he tapped the paper.

Devon cleared his throat. "She shot him."

I spun in my seat. "Damn it, Devon." That wasn't how I'd wanted to say it.

The sheriff straightened, looked from Devon to me with a hard stare.

Panicked to tell my side of the story, I implored him. "It was an accident. He was trying to steal my bird and there was a struggle. It was self-defense." I glared over my shoulder at Devon.

He flinched. "You were dancing around it like you weren't going to say."

"For fuck's sake. I was getting to it. Why do you have to push all the time?"

Sheriff Morris held up his hands. "Let's take a second here."

Devon and I shut our mouths, but I was fuming. It was so typical of him to try to take care of things for me.

The sheriff pinched the bridge of his nose. "You should have come to me sooner."

"I know, and I'm sorry, but if I file charges against him, can you arrest him?"

"You want to press charges against the uncle you shot?"

"Attempted theft. And check forgery. He stole Grandma Helen's checkbook. I can prove at least one forgery."

"We could put out an APB, but let's back up a minute here. I'm afraid we have to talk about the seriousness of your confession. Self-defense or not, you shot a man."

"He attacked me." My voice was defensive, whiny.

"I understand the context, Tallulah, but I have to bring you in. As soon as we track down your uncle and get his side of the story, we can sort this whole thing out." He came to his feet, adjusting his uniform with a tug.

I stayed in my chair.

"Sheriff, I can't go to jail. With Grandma Helen gone, there's no one else to take care of the birds." The room felt hot and my neck itched. "Please. There must be something . . ."

"Let's take this one step at a time," the sheriff said. "Come on down to the station with me now. We'll do the necessary paperwork and see what we can do about getting you arraigned as soon as possible."

I hesitated, helpless, trying to process the fact that I was being detained.

The sheriff opened the door and looked to me expectantly.

I came to my feet, but my limbs felt sluggish.

"What can I do to help?" Devon asked.

You've done enough, I thought, but then changed my mind. "Will you go to the house? Tell my mom and Aunt Christine what happened?"

"They don't know?" he asked, incredulous.

"And the birds." I hated to ask for his help with the flock. Going into the corral could be dangerous if you didn't know what you were doing. "Someone has to feed them." The sheriff waited patiently as I gave Devon quick instructions. "Just do it and get out of there," I told him, worried that something would go wrong.

"I'll take care of it," he said, squeezing my hand.

I pulled away and followed the sheriff down the stairs. He held open the back door of his cruiser for me and I climbed in, grateful that he hadn't seen fit to handcuff me. The hot vinyl seat burned me through my clothes.

I squinted through the hard light that reflected off the building, watching Devon lock his front door as we drove away. I had been about to confess. The fact that he had jumped in like that pissed me off.

At the station, the sheriff took my official statement and relinquished me to a stout woman in a crisp brown uniform. She had white hair pulled into a tight twist. Her face was clean of makeup and a burst blood vessel had left a crimson web over one cheek. She asked me to empty my pockets. I handed over my wallet, keys, and cell phone. She took my fingerprints and a mug shot. I felt numb as she guided me through the motions.

When all the paperwork was done, she walked me down a hallway to an empty cell. As the bars closed behind me, I took in the space. It smelled of industrial cleaner. There were two beds, one suspended over the other. A toilet rested in the corner with a matching sink set into the adjoining wall. Both were discolored, stained with orange streaks where the water flowed. The walls were resignation beige and I could trace the lines of the cinder blocks underneath the paint. There were no windows. A single fluorescent bulb cast an unforgiving light.

"We'll bring you some dinner in a few hours," the woman said, patting the bars between us before she left. I sat on the bottom bunk, bent forward so as not to hit my head, and listened to her shoes squeak on the linoleum as she walked away.

I was still rattled by Devon sticking his nose into things, telling the sheriff what I had done. Agitated, I paced the cell. I had wanted to confess, in my own way, in my own time, not because he thought I should. I was tired of navigating what he thought was best for me and I wasn't taking some stupid accounting job at the cement plant because Devon wanted to get married. I knew he was patiently waiting for me to settle down. I had known it for a while, but I had no intention of ever marrying him. I never had.

It was diverting, being with Devon. We got drunk and threw corn nuts at the TV when the Dodgers lost. The sex wasn't great, but even mediocre sex was better than none, and he was always so grateful afterward. He actually thanked me the first few times, until I told him to stop.

More than anything, Devon was a way to avoid going home at the end of the night. By the time I turned twenty-one, I'd been working full time at the ranch for three years and Grandma Helen was like a ghost. We rarely spoke. She was drinking a lot. After finishing my work for the day, my options were to microwave a burrito and eat it alone in my room or to go to Pat's and have a burger with Devon and the guys he worked with over at the plant. From there, the natural course of things just seemed to lead to Devon's apartment.

And I liked sleeping at his place. I felt independent driving to the ranch for work in the morning, like it was just a job and I had other things going on in my life, even if those other things were drinking beer and sleeping with Devon, neither of which I found terribly exciting on their own, but both of which were entertaining enough to pass the time.

Once I investigated getting my own place in town, but all I could find was a room for rent in the home of a large Latino family, and that didn't seem like much of an upgrade from the ranch, which was free. For a while, I harbored fantasies that Devon would find a job in some other town and I would rent his apartment after he left, but Devon had built his life around PFX Cement, Pat's Bar, and his apartment. He was never going anywhere.

I leaned against the cool cement wall of the cell and pictured myself driving away from Sombra, never coming back. I felt all my anxieties float away, it was almost like I'd already done it, left it all behind and gone off to the Northwoods. I craved hard, meaningful work that required little thought. I wanted to labor shoulder to shoulder with like-minded people and sleep easy every night because I was too tired to stay awake worrying. I even craved the cold weather, the novelty of gloves and scarves, my nose red from cold instead of sunburn.

I sat on the cot and held my head in my hands. I had to accept the fact that I couldn't just drive away from what had happened with Uncle Scott.

I rolled onto my back and tried not to think for just a little while, but my mind continued to race. I thought again of how Grandma Helen had spent her life ignoring her problems and how I had tried to do the same. I had shot my uncle and then gone on about my business, as absurd as it seemed in retrospect, pretending that nothing was wrong and harboring some delusion that the problem would go away. Confessing felt like stepping in front of a firing squad, but I had survived.

Granted, I was in jail. I didn't have money for bail and I didn't know if the court would believe me when I claimed I'd acted in self-defense, but the angst over being found out had lifted. The muscles between my ribs relaxed and I took a deep breath for the first time since my fight with Scott.

Dinner arrived with the news that my arraignment would take place the following morning. I accepted the plastic container of soup, a bread roll, and a glass of water thankfully, eating in silence and lying down again. I wanted to sleep. I willed it to come, but my eyes wouldn't close. I stared up at the cot above me imagining Devon trying to feed the ostriches. It was a terrible idea to send him into the corral, but I hadn't had any choice.

Joe Jared's inspector was due at the ranch the following morning. As I was being arraigned, he would be poking around the property compiling his report. I cringed as I pictured him in the barn candling the eggs, not that anyone used candles anymore. He would balance an egg on the head of a powerful flashlight, setting the whole thing to glow and illuminating a web of healthy blood vessels running up the inside of the shell. Only the eggs in the incubators would have none. They would glow a smooth orange like giant Christmas lights, without a sign of life in them. Joe Jared would back out of the deal. I would have to sell the ranch off piece by piece to cover my legal expenses. I'd be left with nothing.

The next morning, after a granola bar and a tiny carton of milk, I changed into a clean pair of jeans and a white, button-up, short-sleeved shirt, clothes packed up by Aunt Christine and delivered by Devon via the guard.

I was led down the hall to a high-ceilinged room with tall windows. I'd never been in a courtroom, but it resembled the ones I'd seen on TV, with two tables for the lawyers facing a raised platform for the judge. Behind a low railing, three rows of seats were empty except for my mom and Devon, who perked up when I entered. When I saw Devon's face, his encouraging smile, part of me wished he wasn't there. The thought that came to me clear as day was *I don't love you.*

How many times had we swapped those words? *I love you, I love you too.* Rote confirmations that we cared for each other. I hadn't lied intentionally, but the disparity between the meaning we each put into that phrase was suddenly clear. He loved me and I considered him an entertaining way to pass the time. It was even possible I loved his apartment more than I loved him.

The judge was a dour, gray-haired man with bushy white eyebrows and a black robe. Behind him on the wood paneling hung a mounted bighorn sheep's head. He made me nervous, but my appointed lawyer, a tired, brunette woman in a navy pantsuit, leaned close and told me not to worry. The proceedings began with little ceremony, and when it was time to speak, my lawyer simply said, "*Not guilty.*" The topic of bail was raised and she argued for something called a PR bond. "Ms. Jones is an upstanding member of the community with a pristine record. She is the sole proprietor of a ranch that's been in her family for three generations. There's no flight risk here." The judge consulted some papers on his desk, told me to report for trial in nine days, then banged his gavel to signify he was done with me.

My mom came to her feet clapping. The sound reverberated in the empty room. My lawyer handed me a stack of papers and said we'd talk soon. "What's a PR bond?" I asked her. I hadn't heard a sum mentioned for bail. Everything happened so fast.

"Personal recognizance," she said. "It means they trust you to come back. No bail." She grabbed her briefcase and left me there. *They trust you.*

Those three little words suggested to me a version of myself that I hadn't considered before. Objectively, I was just as she'd described: a hard-working, law-abiding young business owner. Nobody cared that I'd spent the first half of my life being dragged all over the state by my mother and nobody suspected that I would run away and leave important matters unattended to. They trusted me. I held my head a little higher as I signed the remaining paperwork and collected my things.

Feeling a little stupefied by the whole experience, I stepped out into the mild July morning with my mom and Devon by my side. After spending a night in the intensely air-conditioned jail cell, the warmth enveloped me like a welcome embrace. I let my eyes scan the distant horizon and felt insanely grateful just to be outdoors. We crossed the parking lot to Devon's car and a diesel truck slogged past, its exhaust dense, and I wrinkled my nose at the stink of it. My mom crawled into the back and I took the passenger seat.

"We should celebrate," my mom said, bouncing a little in her seat. A sour smell floated around her, the odor of the previous night's cocktails seeping from her pores. In the rearview mirror, I could see her dreadlocks framing her face. "Let's go to Pat's." It was ten thirty in the morning. Pat's Bar would be open, but I couldn't think of anything I wanted to do less than go drinking with my mom and Devon before noon.

"I shot your brother," I said, staring out the window as we passed the post office with its faded flag. I wasn't happy about what I had done, but I wasn't going to go drinking and pretend it hadn't happened.

"Well, shit," she said. "When you put it like that." I heard her slump against the seat, deflated.

"My truck's at your place," I said to Devon. He kept glancing over at me, then back at the road. I found a loose thread in the hem of my shirt and wrapped it around my pinkie, pressing the tip as it turned purple, thinking about what had happened at the courthouse.

Facing my problems honestly had given me a feeling of control. The hardest part was spitting out those first few words. Once the truth was spoken I could own it. I lifted my head. "Devon . . ." I had to do it. I told myself that it would be just like confessing to the sheriff. Getting started was the biggest hurdle. "Devon, we have to break up." I kept my gaze forward, watching the sandy lots and chain-link fences that lined the main street of town.

"Lu, I'm so sorry about yesterday, I thought—"

"It's not . . . It's not about yesterday."

"Then what is it?" he asked, growing impatient.

I couldn't bring myself to tell him that I didn't love him; it sounded too cruel. But when I looked at him, all I felt was trapped. "I don't want to be your girlfriend anymore."

"Since when?" He slowed the car to avoid a mangy mutt as it trotted across the road.

"Since now."

My mom thankfully kept her nose out of it, but I could feel her watching us.

"Why?" Impatience became insistence. "Tell me why."

"I don't want to get married. And you do. And if I keep dating you, I'm just leading you on. It's not fair."

His smile was patronizing. "Why don't you let me decide what's fair?"

"No," I said. Because he would choose what was easiest

and least painful, and that was to stay together. Even though I didn't love him and on some level he must have sensed my pulling away, he would stay with me to avoid the discomfort of a breakup.

"What is it you're worried about, exactly?"

"I'm not worried . . ." I faced him and saw pleading in his eyes. *Please*, they seemed to say, *please let's just move forward and forget anything bad ever happened and pretend we love each other because it's so much easier than breaking each other's hearts.*

But I couldn't pretend anymore. "I don't love you." He flinched and I knew immediately the pain I had inflicted with those words. It wasn't just that I didn't love him—that would have been bearable—but to say it out loud was to break the fantasy that we could last, that we could make our relationship work. "I'm sorry." And I was. I hated to hurt him.

"Tallulah." He was upset. If the problem had been him spending time with Stella, or him telling the sheriff I'd shot Uncle Scott, we might have found a way through together, but it wasn't about any of those things. I just didn't love him.

We rode in silence the few blocks to Third Street. He pulled in behind the laundromat. My mom fled the back seat without a word and went to wait for me next to my pickup. She looked around for shade, but there was none.

Devon reached over and took my hand in his. "Lu, please. We can work this out."

"No," I said, gently slipping my hand out from under his. "I don't want to." I kept my eyes down and tried to focus. I didn't want the grief I was causing him to overwhelm me and make me change course. "I'm sorry," I said again.

I got out of the car and hurried to my truck. My mom climbed in too and we shifted uncomfortably against the hot seats. I blasted the AC and adjusted the vents.

"Damn, Tallulah," my mom said. "That was cold."

I had nothing to say about it. My thoughts were clear for the first time in as long as I could remember and I pulled out onto the highway with a rare sense of having made the right choice. I wasn't hiding anymore. Not from difficult conversations, not from the repercussions of my mistakes. It was my life and I was taking charge. I sat tall in the driver's seat, as if good posture alone could shield me from my mother's opinions.

When we got to the ranch, a sparkling-white SUV was parked in the drive, the words "*Southwest Regional Inspections*" painted across the side and the spacious optimism I had enjoyed on the way home collapsed into a tight knot behind my belly button.

The barn doors were open, and in the shadows, I could see a lanky figure with a headlamp and kneepads. He held a clipboard and looked up at the corner where Joe Jared had noted the failing joiners.

My mom, who had remained surprisingly mute after we left Devon's place, went inside without breaking her silence. I hesitated in the truck, bracing myself against the feeling that I was about to be caught in a lie.

But before I could decide how to approach the inspector, Aunt Christine emerged from the house, dish towel in hand, concern on her face. The front hem of her purple maternity dress hung almost to her ankles without the nine-month bulge of pregnancy to give it shape, but otherwise, she looked surprisingly well for someone who had given birth the day before.

I jumped from the truck to meet her but had no idea what to say to her now that she knew I'd shot her brother. Thoughts raced through my head: *I'm so sorry, it was an accident, I was so scared.* What came out was, "Please forgive me."

"Oh, honey, I was so worried about you." She came down the steps with obvious discomfort, holding the railing for support. "I'm sorry I couldn't come this morning. I wanted to be there . . ."

I rushed to her side. "You should be in bed. How are you even on your feet?"

She rested against the railing. "I'm hanging in there," she said. "Gabby's been helping out. I only just got dressed. I really did want to be there for you, but I didn't have the energy to get everyone out the door."

"No," I said. "I'm glad you didn't bring the girls." They didn't need to be involved. This would never be a story we told at family gatherings. Gunshot wounds weren't the kind of thing that grew funny with the passage of time, no matter how much whiskey had been passed around the table.

"Are you okay?" she asked, and I felt guilty that she was the one asking me.

"Scott left the hospital."

"Devon said."

"And I broke up with Devon." It felt good to be forthright with the facts. I'd never realized how much energy I wasted carefully doling out information in an attempt to spare other people any discomfort.

"What? When?"

Behind Aunt Christine, through the open doors of the barn, I saw Joe Jared's inspector move around the incubators. The beam of his headlamp bounced in the dim space.

"Just now," I said, distracted. "Let's get you back inside." Holding her elbow, I guided her up onto the porch.

"Why did you break up with Devon?"

The inspector emerged from the barn and waved. He wore thin-rimmed glasses and had a tidy line of a mustache. He reached to turn off his headlamp and consulted his clipboard as he approached.

"Why?" Aunt Christine asked.

"What?"

"Why did you break up with Devon?"

The inspector joined us on the porch. "Miss Jones?" He

looked back and forth from me to my aunt, unsure which of us to address.

"Tallulah," I said, shaking his hand.

"I'll wait inside," Aunt Christine said, abandoning her inquiry about Devon and folding the dish towel as she retreated into the house.

"I apologize for starting without you, but Mr. Jared did say you were in a bit of a hurry."

I nodded. I could hardly focus on what he was saying. When I didn't respond, he continued.

"I'm afraid there's a problem with the incubator." He pushed up his glasses with his pinkie finger and beckoned me to follow him into the barn. I knew what he was going to say. I hadn't collected a single viable egg. Every muscle in my body wanted to walk in the other direction, to avoid the conversation that was about to unfold. I recognized the feeling. It was the same way I'd felt before saying out loud that I'd shot Uncle Scott and I realized this was another opportunity to do things differently, to tell the truth. I would admit to moving the eggs from cold storage and spill my guts about the barren birds. Just get it over with. But as I opened my mouth to speak I noticed that the red light inside the incubator was dark. I hurried over to the unit and flipped the power switch off and on again with no change.

The inspector waited patiently as I put my hand on the glass, then opened the door to confirm that the shelves were not warm, as they should have been. I ducked behind the unit to check that it was plugged in. The cord was in place.

"It would appear to be a thrown circuit breaker."

I came back around, and he pointed with his pen at the metal panel in the corner of the barn.

"I took the liberty of candling a few of the eggs. I don't know how long the incubator's been down, but I'm afraid the eggs have been affected."

Bewildered, I opened the door of the breaker panel and saw that the two small switches with the word "*incubator*" beside them were off. The electrical system in the barn was ancient. The power draw had been too much for it.

"Then there's this joiner." He switched on his flashlight and directed it at the cracks in the ceiling beams. "You're looking at some major repairs in the next year or so. And I assume you know about the broken water pipe?"

"What water pipe?" I was still trying to wrap my head around the thrown breaker. I had been prepared to speak the truth and face the consequences. My head was spinning.

"This way," he said.

I followed him back outside to the corral, where he twisted the handle on the water spigot. Normally, the water gushed into the trough, but instead, I heard a wet hiss and a spray of water hit my ankles. Bending, I saw that the metal pipe that came out of the ground had separated from the spigot and the bulky nut that had held the two pieces together was gone. The sand around the trough darkened as water sprayed in every direction.

He shut off the spigot. "See how the pipe's a little askew there?" he said. Where it came out of the ground, the pipe was tilted at a slight angle. "My guess is that the nut came loose and one of the birds inadvertently kicked the lower piece, dislodging it." He spun around slowly, scanning the floor of the corral. "I didn't find the nut. I'm guessing it's in the belly of one of your birds by now."

As peculiar as the explanation was, it actually seemed plausible.

"I can fix it," I said, but I didn't have a replacement nut that size. I would have to jury-rig a fix with some duct tape. The birds were well suited to the dry climate, but even they couldn't go long without water in triple-digit heat. "Maybe you could leave that off your report?"

"I'm afraid I have to include what I find as I find it, but I will note that you plan to make the repair." He scribbled on his clipboard. "That breaker panel should be a fairly easy fix too, but those ceiling beams, that's a big project."

My heartbeat slowed. I didn't have to confess my attempted deception. I could still make things right. A trip to the supply store for more supplements, a few days' time. I could get the birds producing again and sell to Joe Jared with a clear conscience. I couldn't believe my good luck.

The inspector continued listing the items he would include in his report: a stubborn latch on the barn door, a crack in the cement slab of the foundation. "Mr. Jared instructed me not to inspect the residence," he said.

"Really?"

"It's a teardown," he said with a shrug.

Joe had said he had no use for it, but I hadn't realized he planned to tear it down. My family had lived in that house for forty-six years. My cousin had been born on the living-room floor not thirty hours ago. It wasn't just some *residence*. It was our home.

"That leaves the flock," the inspector said, oblivious to my rising indignation. "Most everything seems to be in order out here, but I did notice that a few of the ostriches are showing signs of sickness."

"What? What do you mean?"

"I'm sure you're aware," he said. "A few have red swelling around the eyes."

"No, I just had them tested. In preparation for the sale, I mean. They're healthy as can be. I spoke to the vet yesterday. I can forward the report to Mr. Jared."

The inspector chewed the end of his pen and then jotted something in his notes. "Well, Mr. Jared will want to confirm that. Would you mind if I took some samples?"

I helped him wrangle a few birds to draw blood, and I noticed it too: red rims around the eyes. While the inspector was distracted, I saw one of the hens on the far side of the corral falter, her wings flapping wildly, but she regained her footing before the inspector looked up.

I followed him to his SUV, where he slipped the vials of blood into a tiny cooler. "That should do it," he said. He grabbed his clipboard and riffled through the pages.

Behind him in the corral, I saw another bird totter, a male this time. His knees buckled. He didn't fall, but his wings swung out wildly.

"This is for you," he said, handing me a pink carbon copy of a form he had filled out. I forced myself to ignore what was happening behind him in the corral where the bird continued to flail. "Of course, I will send you a PDF of my final report as soon as it's ready. How about you write your email there at the top for me?" He handed me the clipboard, and I wrote as quickly as I could.

"When could I expect that?" I asked, desperate to keep his attention away from the corral.

"Give me a few days," he said, taking the clipboard. In my peripheral vision, I saw the bird swaying like a drunk, and it was all I could do to keep focused on the inspector. I tried to think of a way to speed his departure but came up blank.

He slipped off his right kneepad, then the left. With great care, he stowed the small cooler with his samples on the floor of the SUV beside the clipboard. Finally, he left.

I waited until he was completely out of sight before I rushed into the corral. By then, the bird had recovered and I couldn't tell which one it had been. I watched for a bird with an uneven stride or unusual posture, but they all looked equally baffled. Granted, that was more or less their natural state, but something still felt off.

I did a quick head count to make sure Uncle Scott hadn't made off with another bird while I was in jail. I counted 142, including Abigail, who was pecking at something near a sagebrush off beyond the barn. They were all accounted for.

I fed the birds their morning meal and surveyed the floor of the corral, unsurprised by the empty nests and giddy that the inspector had dismissed the bunk eggs with the flick of his pen. I would get back out to the supply store right away for more supplements. The birds would lay eggs, the sale would go through, and the rest of the repairs around the ranch would fall to the JJ Ostrich Operation.

One fix couldn't wait, though. I grabbed a roll of duct tape from the barn and set to patching the gap in the pipe that the inspector had brought to my attention. It wasn't pretty and a fair amount of water leaked out around the tape, but enough rushed through to fill the trough. A few of the closer birds lowered their beaks for a sip.

I was turning off the faucet when, a few yards to my right, one of the male ostriches wobbled and collapsed. He didn't lower himself, folding up his legs like ostriches normally did when they sat. His legs simply gave out from under him. A small cloud of dust puffed up around his feathered body. I ran over and crouched down next to him. His neck lolled. He blinked groggily, and I could see that the whites of his eyes were tinted red. He put his head in my lap and let out a sorrowful call. I considered rushing into the house to call the vet, but even as I had the thought, the poor bird's rib cage shuddered and relaxed. The delicate black filaments of his feathers settled into stillness. "No," I said.

A female near the east end of the corral dropped. I raced over to her. "No, no, no," I said. I lifted her head in my hands, but her eyes stayed shut. I inspected her body from beak to tail but found no outward sign of injury or abuse.

Frantic, I searched the corral for anything that would explain two birds falling sick like that at the same time. I suspected that Uncle Scott was somehow responsible and I hoped against hope that I was wrong, that there was some other explanation.

But when I saw the familiar imprints of cowboy boots about a third larger than mine, my fears were confirmed.

I debated whether to grab the shotgun from the barn as I followed the tracks to the first small rise of desert. In a shallow dip between the dunes—low enough that someone could have used a flashlight without it being noticed from the house—the boot prints muddled near a pile of trash, then went off toward the highway. I scanned the surrounding desert to make sure I was alone before moving closer to inspect the mess.

The garbage consisted of five cigarette butts, two crushed beer cans, a pillowcase, and an empty box of gopher poison with the top torn off. I flipped the pillowcase inside out, and a few alfalfa pellets scattered in the wind. He had given the birds poisoned food. "No, no, no."

I rushed to the corral and elbowed through the birds around the feed trough. With one arm raised up to shield myself from their pecks, I squatted low next to the large bin and ran my free hand through the grain, reaching around the hungry pecks of the birds and searching for the small, green, pill-like alfalfa pellets, but there were none. One of the females nudged me, annoyed to find me between her and her breakfast. I struggled to keep from falling. The birds pressed in around me. I shouldered my way back through the crush to get out of their way.

Slowing down to think rationally for a minute, I decided there wasn't enough in one box of poison to make the whole flock sick. Uncle Scott must have fed the birds individually. They loved alfalfa. He could have just held the pillowcase through the fence and let them gobble up the poison treat.

I walked around the flock. Most of the birds pecked at their meal, but a male and a female stood dazed. I moved closer, watching them carefully. The other birds dispersed once the food was gone, but those two swayed on their feet, struggling for balance. Approaching the female, I ran my hand over her neck. Her eyes were bloodshot.

"How you doing there, girl?" She blinked at me.

Right then, the male collapsed with a thump. I rushed over to him and lifted his head from the sand to rest it in my lap. "I'm sorry," I said. I felt so helpless.

The female, rooted in place near the feed silo, kept her gaze fixed on the horizon. I sat there with the fallen male and watched her. "I should never have left you alone," I said. "I'm so sorry."

Eventually, the dazed hen fluttered her wings and moved to the water trough for a drink. She moved slowly but stayed steady on her feet as she joined a group of females near the fence. A little sob of relief burst from my chest, but by then, the male beside me had passed.

FOURTEEN

I wallowed on the floor of the corral, mourning my birds, hating Uncle Scott, and feeling deeply responsible. If I had gone to the sheriff sooner, he could have arrested Uncle Scott and kept him away from the ranch. It was my fault the birds were dying.

I let my hand linger on the fallen ostrich. It was hard to believe he was dead. His body was still warm, but I waited in vain for the rise and fall of his rib cage. He was gone.

My attention was drawn to a cloud of dust at the end of the driveway. I jumped up, afraid that it might be the inspector returning for some reason, but it was Matt's white sedan. I stormed toward the corral gate. If he knew where Uncle Scott was, he needed to tell me. I was calling the sheriff and adding new charges to the list for when they finally arrested him.

I flipped the latch on the corral gate and gave it an angry shove. It came loose in my hands and slipped right off the hinges, landing on the ground with a thud. I stumbled, carried forward by my momentum, and my boot went through the gate as it toppled. I caught one of the planks in the crook of my arm and struggled to keep my footing. Profanity poured from my mouth. The ostriches, drawn by the commotion, approached on all sides.

I managed to pull the gate more or less into place, but there was nothing to prop it against, no way to keep it upright. One of the birds nudged me from behind and I lost my balance again.

"Matt," I yelled when I heard his engine cut off in the driveway. "Damn it." The birds pecked at my hands and I couldn't keep my footing with the weight of them pressing against me. A large gap opened where the gate had been attached to the fence.

Matt rushed to help me. We lifted the gate into place, repositioning the hinges, but the pins were gone. "Can you hold it?" I asked.

Matt put his weight against the metal frame. "For a minute."

I ducked through the side fence and hurried to the barn. I had some baling wire that would do for a temporary fix. I hurried back to where Matt was struggling. One of the ostriches was pecking at his studded belt. Another had his topknot in its beak. He swatted at them and the gate slumped.

I threaded the wire through the hinges, twisting to secure it, then slapped the latch closed so Matt could finally let go. Loose strands of hair hung down around his face and his topknot slumped over one ear.

"Tallulah—"

I shoved him. "Uncle Scott did this." When he didn't fight me, I pushed him again, harder. "He killed my birds."

"I know," Matt said, stoic in the face of my anger.

"You knew? And you didn't do anything?"

"I only just—" He caught my arm midshove. "I came straight here."

"Let go," I said, yanking away from him. "He killed my birds." I hated that he could see the tears gathering in my eyes.

"I'm sorry I couldn't stop him. I tried. I looked for him all night." He pulled the rubber band from his disheveled hair and slipped it over his wrist as he tamed his wild mane back into place. "I found him this morning, down at Meadowbrook. He was by the creek, ranting. I've never seen him like that. He said . . ."

Matt hurried over to my pickup and I followed. I expected him to mention the repairs he never did, but there was something else on his mind.

"Pop it for me," he said, tapping the metal impatiently.

Apparently, he had forgotten all about the busted ball joint. Thank goodness for Reuben, or my truck would still be up on the jack.

I reached inside the driver's door to release the hood and he raised it. I expected him to ask about the work his father did, but he leaned over the motor. "He told me he cut your brake lines, but they're fine."

"I wasn't here last night. My truck was at Devon's."

We hurried over to my aunt's minivan. The severed brake lines were obvious under the hood, cut clean through and left to dangle. I pictured Aunt Christine and my cousins all loading into the minivan on their way to the courthouse that morning, Aunt Christine's foot tapping the brake at the end of the driveway and nothing happening. They might have plowed across the highway and launched into the desert on the other side, suffering bumps and bruises. Or they might have met a freight truck sailing down the highway at sixty miles an hour. I couldn't speak.

Matt pulled at some wires. "I'm going to disconnect the battery cables so it won't start." He wiped his hands on his jeans. "I'll fix it, I swear."

"Why would he do that?" I was shocked that Uncle Scott could be so vicious.

"I'm sure he didn't realize it was Christine's van."

"That doesn't make it better," I said.

"You fucking shot him, Tallulah." He leaned against the minivan, narrowing his eyes against the sun.

"I was defending myself. This is all his fault. I understand that he's mad about the inheritance, but I didn't write Grandma Helen's will. Why is he so angry with me?"

Matt sighed and glanced at the house. "I don't think it's about you at all. I think it's about the birds."

I blinked back tears of frustration. "What are you talking about?"

"I mean, he's pissed off about getting shot, don't get me wrong, that shit went all fucking sideways, but before that . . ." He crossed his arms and looked out at the horizon. "I don't know, Tallulah, I just . . . okay, I know this sounds crazy, but I think . . ." He hesitated again before finishing the thought. "I think Scott's jealous of the birds, always has been."

I didn't know what to say to that.

Matt seemed to sense my skepticism and pushed away from the minivan to avoid my stare. He waved his arm in the general direction of the ostriches. "I'm not saying he wanted to sleep in the corral or anything," he said. "More like they got a lot more attention than he ever did."

"He said that?" Oddly, it made sense to me on an intuitive level.

"Not in so many words, but we've been friends a while now. We've been through some shit. I just got the impression, hearing him talk about your grandma, that he had a lot of pent-up anger. Then, when you said you were gonna sell, he kinda freaked out."

"Ya think?"

"And the meth just amplifies everything. I never should have let him out of my sight after the funeral. He was a mess."

I wondered if it was a coincidence that Uncle Scott had tried to kill Lady Lil. She had always been Grandma Helen's favorite, the one she greeted every morning with a fond hello. That wasn't how she'd greeted me. As soon as I got my driver's license and could take myself to school, she was out in the corral before I even woke each morning. She had probably been the same with Uncle Scott. Grandma Helen was so much more attentive to the birds than she was to the humans in her life.

"Did he say anything else? About last night?"

"He wasn't making much sense. He said something about a water pipe, a breaker box. I don't know. He was rambling."

Of course he had flipped the fuse breaker. He was trying to sabotage the sale of the ranch. How ironic that it had worked so well in my favor. It was a small consolation. The ranch seemed so vulnerable without walls or fences. The corpses of my three dead birds lay in heaps inside the corral like a warning. "Where is he now?"

"He was talking about Fresno, some girl he knows up there."

I faced Matt and saw his concern. He and Uncle Scott had been the best of friends for years. "I should tell you, I'm pressing charges. If the cops catch up with him—"

"Do you have to?"

"I can't look the other way anymore, Matt. I won't. I'll own my part in all this, show up for my day in court, but he has to do the same." It was a shitty thing, to set the authorities on my own uncle, but I believed it would be better for him in the long run. "I don't want him to go to prison, but—"

"It doesn't matter," Matt said. "He's halfway to Fresno by now. He'll keep his head down."

We were both unhappy about how things had worked out and equally frustrated at our inability to do anything about it.

I sighed. I still needed to bury three giant birds. I considered waiting until the sun went down to avoid working in the hottest part of the day, but the other birds would peck at the fallen ones and I couldn't bear to see that.

"What is it?" Matt asked.

I explained what I needed to do.

"Let me help."

"No."

"Why not?" He fished a wide-brimmed hat from the trunk of his car and tugged it into place over his topknot. It was the kind of canvas hat you saw all the time on people who worked on farms, but it was out of place on Matt, with his colorful tattoos and studded belt. He looked like a hipster imitating a ranch hand. "What?"

"Nothing," I said.

"You think I'm afraid of a little hard work? Come on. I need something to keep my mind occupied."

I wasn't used to working with people. I didn't want to have to make small talk or worry about how he was holding up in the heat, but it was foolish to refuse help.

"Fine," I said and led the way to the barn, where we each collected a shovel. But back outside I hesitated, looking over the expansive landscape. I had never buried an ostrich. Had never needed to. Abigail came up beside us, as if she too were contemplating the task at hand. Matt looked at her. She considered him. Our shadows pooled like puddles at our feet. A tumbleweed bounced by in the distance and Abigail strode off to investigate.

I decided that the north end of the property would be best and Matt followed me without a word. The graves didn't need to be long, just deep enough to keep the scavengers away. I drew a square in the sand, about three feet on a side, and we set to digging. The soil was sandy and heavy but not hard. The scraping of our shovels set a rhythm. I found myself recreating the scene I had missed on the ranch the night before. I pictured Uncle Scott unscrewing the nut on the water pipe and tapping free the pins from the hinges on the corral gate. He must have thought ahead to bring something to muffle the noise or else someone in the house would have heard him.

It was the premeditation that upset me most. Particularly

with regard to the birds. I didn't even have alfalfa pellets on the ranch, which meant he drove all the way to the supply store to get some. He brought beer, as if it were a summer picnic. The more I thought about it, the angrier I got, until my insides were burning.

Sweat coated my skin as I worked, itching in the creases of my elbows and collecting on my face. When the hole was about a foot deep, we both stepped in, but it quickly became apparent that wouldn't work. Our elbows kept bumping as we shifted with the weight of the shovels.

"I'll get started on the next one," Matt said, moving about five feet to the east, where he plunged his shovel into the top layer of sand.

As the grave grew gradually deeper, I found the damp chill of the earth around me refreshing. When eventually the hole was about four feet deep and I could stand in it with only my head sticking out, I was reluctant to climb back into the heat to dig the third grave. Part of me wanted to sit in there and hide from the world forever. It was so cool, and the sun had fallen halfway toward the horizon, so that when I crouched, the light didn't reach me at all.

A shadow appeared over the opening of the hole. "Water break," Matt said. He offered his hand, and I took it so he could hoist me out.

We drank deeply from the hose at the side of the barn and rested for a minute in the shade. "Why are you friends with my uncle?" I asked.

Matt pulled at the dry stalk of a dead sagebrush. "That's a weird question."

"No, it's not." I could smell the sweat baked into my shirt and taste salt on my lips.

"Why is anybody friends with anyone?" he said. The stalk came loose, and he whacked it against the barn, watching the earth fall from the roots. "We get along. Dude makes me laugh."

I tried to remember the last time I'd shared a joke with Uncle Scott. For so many years, my interactions with him had centered around trying to decide if he was lying and waiting for the next relapse. "Isn't it hard, being friends with someone so . . . unpredictable?"

"I've been in his shoes. I'm not one to judge."

It was hard to imagine Matt on a binge, irrational and fuming like Uncle Scott had been. Again, I saw my uncle's face, contorted in pain. "When you see him again, you know, even if I'm gone from here and he hates my guts, will you tell him I'm sorry?"

He nodded. "Absolutely."

We sat there staring out at the rolling landscape, each of us lost in our own thoughts. I was glad he'd come. I was still mad, but talking with Matt helped me understand things a little better. Uncle Scott was hurting. It was likely he'd been hurting for a long time.

Matt groaned as he came to his feet. He turned on the hose again and took another deep drink, then doused his head before passing the hose to me. I rinsed my face and let the water run over my neck. We walked back over to where we had been digging, resigned to our task. I began work on the third grave while Matt finished digging the second. When he was done, he came over to help with the last grave, but as before, we found we didn't both fit at the same time. Climbing out of the hole to let him work some, I sat at the edge with my back to the sun.

One of the females in the corral stared at me. I met her forlorn gaze. "I'm sorry," I whispered, hoping the wind would carry the words to her. She stood perfectly still, her eyes unblinking. "Matt," I said. "My turn." He climbed out and I took his place, hiding from the bird's chilling stare as I worked.

When the plots were ready, Matt and I lugged the bodies of the murdered ostriches out of the corral. It was awkward. They were too heavy to pick up, but if we dragged them by their feet, their wings splayed out beside them, scooping sand and making them even heavier. When we pulled them by their shoulders, their necks dragged in the sand and their cheeks bumped against rocks. It was upsetting. I cursed Uncle Scott with every step.

Thankfully, filling the graves proved to be much easier than digging them in the first place and the work went quickly. The sun sunk low in the sky. The sweet smell of chili peppers wafted from the house.

When the three graves were little more than patches of freshly disturbed earth, Matt and I considered them. "Should we mark them in some way?" he asked.

"No," I said, thinking about what Joe Jared would say about fresh graves on the property. "I'd rather not."

We carried our shovels to the barn.

"You should come inside. Let me at least feed you as thanks for all that work."

"No," he said, walking toward his car. "I gotta get home." High clouds on the horizon blazed orange with the setting sun. The heat of the day persisted. "I was up all last night driving around, trying to find Scott. I'm dead on my feet. But I'll come back tomorrow to fix up Christine's van."

"Promise?" I asked, skeptical.

"I promise. Tomorrow." He touched the brim of his hat in an old-fashioned farewell, dropped into his car, and drove away.

I dragged myself inside, where my mom and my cousins sat eating plates of enchiladas. It was the mole sauce I had smelled from outside. Aunt Christine made excellent enchiladas. They all stared up at me with uncharacteristic silence and I wondered if the meal had been quiet before or if they had all shut up when I came in.

"Come eat," Aunt Christine said, handing me a plate. "You must be starving, working out there all day in this heat."

I took the empty seat without a word and dug in, thinking about how Uncle Scott's sabotage had given me an excuse I hadn't even considered. The fact that I had collected the eggs in the incubator had satisfied the inspector that the birds were laying eggs and everything was fine, which it would be, just as soon as I got those supplements.

I was curious about what the inspector's blood tests would show. Would gopher poison be detectable in the blood samples? Probably Joe Jared would think I had been careless with how I stored the grain in the barn. But so what if he did? As long as he saw it as a problem he could easily fix, the sale would go through.

"What's it like in jail?"

"Parker, hush," my aunt said, scolding her second born.

That was why they were all so subdued. Around the table, curiosity simmered. I could see it in the faces of my cousins. Even my aunt and my mom appeared to have questions they were afraid to ask.

"It's quiet," I said and took another bite of my enchilada.

"Will you have to go back?" Gabby asked.

"I don't know," I said honestly. "I hope not. Next week, I'll tell the judge my side of the story and he'll decide." I didn't know how much to say about Uncle Scott.

"Leave her alone, girls," my aunt said, her voice firm.

My cousins all resumed eating but kept stealing glances at me. I scarfed down the last few bites and excused myself. Their eyes all followed me as I moved across the room.

I thought about the bird who had stared at me as Matt and I dug the graves, like she knew that her death was coming too, like she understood that all of them would go to slaughter after Joe Jared took over. I couldn't shake the image of her, even as I washed up and combed the tangles out of my hair. I didn't want the ostriches to die.

With the towel wrapped around me, I padded down the hallway to my room and found my mom slouched in the corner armchair, gazing out the window to her right. The lamp was on near the bed and I could see her reflection in the window. She didn't hear me come in and I studied her face. Her lips were set in a hard line and her gaze held on something far away. I could see that she had been beautiful when she was younger, but age had done more than carve wrinkles in her skin. It had set her adrift in the world, untethered. I wondered what she was thinking.

Her face brightened when she saw me in the glass. "Tallulah." Breaking from her reflection, she grabbed the bottle of Jameson from where it rested unevenly between two glasses on the carpet. "Let's have a drink."

"No." I slipped on my nightshirt and let the towel drop.

She ignored me and poured two large glasses of whiskey, then balanced the bottle on the windowsill, where it dislodged the rocks I had so carefully lined up from lightest to darkest. A handful of them toppled to the floor and I hurried to scoop them up.

"Damn it, Mom," I said, moving the bottle and trying to put the rocks back in order. I plucked the obsidian from the pile and set it at the end, but I was too tired to arrange them all properly. It would have to wait. I set the rest of the displaced rocks in a pile on top of my dresser.

"You're way too sensitive, my girl." She slumped into the chair.

"I'm not your girl," I said.

"Like hell." She pushed a glass of whiskey into my hand, clinked her own glass against it, and downed hers in one gulp. Only when she moved to refill our glasses did she notice that I hadn't taken a sip. "What's wrong?"

"I don't want a drink." I shoved the whiskey back into her hand and she struggled to hold both drinks along with the bottle. "I need sleep." I picked up my wet towel and hung it on the doorknob.

"But I gotta tell you about the whiskey glass theory," she said, insistent, "and it's really not the same if you don't have a glass of whiskey." She held out my glass to me.

When I didn't take it, her voice dropped to a whisper. "You're hurting. I know. And I haven't been much of a mother, but if there's one thing I can give advice about, it's moving on." She thrust the glass an inch closer. "Please."

I rolled my eyes, but I took it and sat on the edge of the bed.

With a satisfied smile she pulled her cigarettes from her pocket and slipped one from the box.

"You can't smoke in here."

"I was smoking in here before you were born," she said.

"It's not your room. Just say what you need to say. I'm fucking tired."

"Fine." She put the cigarette away with a sigh and swirled her glass so that the whiskey climbed the sides. "Okay, see, things can seem real crazy sometimes, right?"

I stared at her, irritated and impatient.

"Right," she continued with an exaggerated lean. "But if you choose one thing to focus on, say a glass of whiskey"—she held up hers—"you'll find the one thing you need to get through anything life throws at you."

"And what's that?"

"Trust."

"In whiskey you trust? Jesus, Mom."

"Let me explain," she said, the alcohol softening the word to "*essplain*." "See, pretend you're an alien. And you have to learn everything you can about the human race, and Earth as a planet, and the only thing you have to go on is this glass of whiskey.

"Start with the glass itself. Where does glass come from? What's it made of? How is it made? How many people were involved in getting the glass to this time and place, and why do they do what they do? What does it mean to have a job? And then ask why I used a glass instead of a plastic cup. I found this particular glass in a cupboard in a house in the desert. How was the house made? What kind of animals live in the desert? Why is the desert so fucking hot? See what I'm doing here?"

She was so emphatic. I kept quiet.

"The whiskey itself. How was it made? When did humans figure out how to make it? Who was the lucky son of a bitch who first discovered what it was to get a little buzz on? How does alcohol bring us together? And don't even get me started on ice."

"How do the ostriches tie to your glass of whiskey?" I asked, trying to bring in something completely unrelated, but she didn't miss a beat.

She sat forward in the chair, perching on the edge of the worn cushion. "Where did the money come from to buy this particular bottle? Ostrich ranch. And what's money anyway?"

"What's your point?"

"My point is that no matter where you are, there's nowhere you can't go. That's the whiskey glass theory. You just gotta trust that one thing leads to another and you'll get there. You just need that one next thing to move toward."

She read the skepticism on my face.

"It doesn't have to be whiskey," she said. "You could use birthday cake, or running shoes, or pandas. It doesn't matter. It's all connected. You gotta find trust, especially when things get tough."

"Trust in what? Sounds like something Aunt Christine would say."

"Don't do that." She frowned.

"What?"

"I'm not talking about blind faith. Faith is believing something because someone told you to. I'm talking about trust, knowing something is true because you've experienced it and all logic says it'll happen again." My mom held up her glass to tap mine. "And when all else fails, drink up."

I could hear a version of Grandma Helen's own logic in what she said. The faith Aunt Christine had in God never suited my grandmother, but trust was a different matter. When she spoke of the rhythms of nature being her church, that was what she meant. She knew that sunshine would follow rain, that goats would keep the weeds under control, and that the moon would rise full every month. These were the things she trusted.

"I know things are bad right now," my mom said. "And I'm sorry I haven't been here for you. Really, I am. But you're strong; you always have been. And you have your next thing. You will sell the ranch and move on with your life. Leave this all behind. Just let it go. One thing connects to another, and somehow you get to the place where everything is okay."

I took a sip of whiskey and winced at the wash of it over my tongue. I wanted to believe her. It would be so easy to just leave all my problems behind. "Is that why we moved so much when I was a kid?"

She raised her glass again. "Exactly. If shit doesn't work out, just move on. Don't look back. Find the next thing, which will lead you to the next, and before you know it, your past is in the past and it doesn't hurt so much anymore."

"And when exactly did you find the place where everything was okay?" I thought over the thirteen years I'd spent growing up with her. It never felt like we were moving on to something better. We were always running from something bad. "Was it the time we were living in the car because that guy stole our rent money? What was his name? No, wait, it was the time that one guy's wife threw a rock through our window and I cut my foot and bled all over the carpet. Was that the place where everything was okay?"

"That's not fair." She dropped her chin like a pouting child.

"Fair? What's not fair is pretending that our life was anything but the shit show it really was, Mom. Whiskey glass theory, my ass. You're justifying bailing on anything that doesn't suit you. You quit jobs, moved cities, left men. And you dragged me along."

"And you breaking up with Devon this morning?" Her lips pulled into a satisfied sneer. "A good guy who wants to be there for you?"

"That's different," I said.

"Like hell. You think you're better'n me?" She rose from her seat and paced to the other side of the room. "You think you're facing up to your problems? Is that why you're selling the ranch to the first buyer you could find, even though you know it's pretty much the last thing your grandmother wanted? You are my girl. And you're doing just what I would in your shoes. Only I got a few years on you and I'm trying to share some fucking wisdom, so you can at least understand what you're doing. It took me a while to come to peace with the world."

"Yeah, Mom," I scoffed, "you're the fucking Buddha."

Her brow furrowed. Absentmindedly, she pulled her cigarettes from her pocket again, fidgeted with the box, and then put them away.

"Why did you even come back here?"

"My mom died," she said, tossing her dreadlocks behind her shoulders.

"But you missed it. You missed the funeral, the reception. You missed everything. You've missed my entire adult life so far. Why are you here?"

"Maybe I thought you might need some help with things."

"Because you're so eager to do ranch work? Come on. In the time you've been here, have you even been outdoors in the daylight?"

"I came to the courthouse this morning."

"Can we just say out loud that you need money?" I wanted

the remark to jolt her into being honest with me, but she didn't flinch.

"About that."

"Shit," I said, bracing myself. I'd known this conversation was coming from the minute she appeared at the front door.

She returned to the chair by the window and sat facing me like she was leading some kind of formal meeting. "You're gonna have a fat stack of cash after you sell this place, Tallulah."

"She left it to me," I said flatly and focused on her reflection in the window. I refused to debate Grandma Helen's will.

"Scott got five grand," she said defensively.

I couldn't quite believe that this was the argument she was going with. "Uncle Scott *stole* that money. The sheriff has an APB out on him."

"It's not fair that I don't get anything but a stack of dirty license plates."

I set my whiskey on the dresser. "It's not a soup kitchen, Mom. You don't just line up with your hands out and expect the same as everyone else."

She considered her next words before she spoke. "Well, I wasn't going to say anything, but I could always lawyer up, you know. You said yourself she wasn't in her right mind."

"No," I said, anger flaring inside me. "Don't you do that. Don't pretend you know anything about what Grandma Helen was like these past years. You don't get to do that. You have no right."

"I have every right." Her voice had slipped into that dismissive tone that drove me crazy. "She was my mother."

"Get out," I said.

"Tallulah . . ." She held my stare for a second before she reached down and grabbed the bottle again. "I'm not gonna just let this go." She poured herself another round.

"Get out of my room!"

When she still made no move, I lunged at her. We were about

the same height, but I was stronger from my years of work on the ranch. I scooped her out of the chair and shoved her toward the bedroom door.

I was so sick of her shit. She couldn't blunder into my home with her fucked-up philosophy of life and tell me what I owed her. I didn't owe her a damn thing. The bottle clanked against the drink in her hand and she hunched her shoulders protectively. "Tallulah, stop!"

But I couldn't. I shoved her out the door and slammed it shut. Blood pulsed at my temples. I growled at the closed door and the sound grew into a wordless yell. I bent at the waist, falling with the force of it, then crumpled to the carpet.

Her voice came from the other side of the door: "We're not done talking about this." I heard her retreat down the hall.

I crawled up onto my bed and pulled the blankets over my head. I stared at the frayed edge of the comforter and watched as my breath made a loose thread dance with every exhale.

She had no right. Nobody did. It was my life and I would do what I wanted to with it. I wasn't running away from my problems like she always did. I was making a choice—my own choice—to live the life I wanted. There was a big difference.

Slowly, my breathing slowed and exhaustion wound its way around me. I pictured my mom downstairs, pouring herself another drink. She would leave soon. I had screamed at her. She would lean into her stupid whiskey glass theory and put me in her rearview. *Just let it go.* She had survived a lifetime of adversity by simply moving on when things didn't suit her.

Maybe she was right. There was a logic to moving on. But then I remembered the despondency I'd seen in her face when she hadn't known I was looking and decided no. She was an unhappy person.

I thought about Grandma Helen and wondered for the first time if her bringing me out to the ranch was about more than assuaging her own loneliness. She must have seen, with the perspective of distance and time, how my mom was floundering. Taking me in would have been a sort of do-over at parenting, a chance to fix the mistakes she'd made in raising her own kids. But then, once she got me out to the ranch, the reality of taking care of me set in.

For someone who despised neediness, it must have been a nightmare. I had seen how needy my cousins were. Not because they were unusual in any way; kids just required a lot of attention. They needed food and clothes and trips to the doctor. And more than anything, they needed love.

Grandma Helen had never been good at giving affection. She was a good provider, but intimacy and warmth were beyond her. And so, like my mom before me, I had sought those things elsewhere.

I found friends at Pat's Bar and affection in Devon's arms, but what I wanted more than anything was a feeling that what I was doing with my life mattered. Around the ranch, Grandma Helen didn't seem to care if I came or went. Instead of bringing me into the business side of the ranch, she treated me like an employee and so I had acted like one. Grandma Helen had been left more alone than ever.

Of course, to send me back to Oakland would have been to admit defeat, so she simply withdrew. She buried herself in the paperwork of the ranch, shucked walnuts endlessly, or sat on the porch drinking whiskey while I took the laptop up to my room, spending hours online.

The distance between us had only grown after I graduated and was home all the time. We became like magnets flipped the wrong way, pushing each other out of rooms as if there wasn't space enough for us both. It must have been so painful for her to see that her faults as a parent hadn't magically corrected themselves with time. Her flaws had grown with her over the years and for all her best intentions, she had grandparented me the same way she had parented my mother: from a safe distance.

I wondered if, like me, her kids had wanted to work on the ranch. Probably not my mom, and Aunt Christine didn't seem the type, but Uncle Scott might have. As the oldest kid, he probably saw himself as the man of the house, especially if his dad, my grandfather, had been a drunk. Uncle Scott would have done everything he could for his mom, would have bent over backwards to make her happy. And the grandmother I knew wouldn't have appreciated his efforts. I thought about what Matt had said about Uncle Scott being jealous of the birds, of all the attention Grandma Helen gave to the flock when she all but ignored the people in her life.

If I hadn't seen the ad for the Forest Service job, I might have ended up just like my uncle, taking a series of minimum wage jobs in Victorville, living at Grandma Helen's but crashing at my boyfriend's place, trying to convince myself that I wasn't some overgrown child. I might have even turned to drugs to numb the frustration of a life that seemed to go nowhere. And from what I gathered, messing around with drugs led pretty quickly to needing them. Uncle Scott and I weren't all that different. Only I was lucky to have found something to run toward. In Montana, I would pour myself into my work and I would be good at it. I might even hear someone say, "Good job today, Jones."

But then Grandma Helen had flipped the whole situation upside down by dying and giving me the one thing I had wanted in the first place. She had waited until I had thoroughly talked myself out of any desire to stay on the ranch and then handed it to me on a platter. It was mine, every square foot of it. And the despair I'd felt when those birds died in the corral that day was unexpected.

I pulled the pillow over my face and waited for sleep to take me.

In my dreams, I was running from something I couldn't see. I splashed through a puddle that grew deeper and deeper until I could only slog forward in a panic, checking over my shoulder every few steps. A spatter on my lip tasted of whiskey. Soon, I was waist deep and the sharp smell made my eyes water. I didn't want to go any farther, but I was still being chased. The whiskey got deeper until I was swimming and gagging, my sodden clothes tugging at my arms. I spotted a life preserver floating in the darkness and swam to it, but the moment I touched it, it dissolved into a sandy ostrich nest and sank.

FIFTEEN

I woke with a gasp.

Rubbing the dream from my eyes I listened for signs that anyone else was awake, but the house was hushed. I tiptoed downstairs to the living room. My mom was passed out on the couch in the spotlight of the lamp, fully clothed, with a fashion magazine on her chest, her whiskey glass on the floor next to her and the bottle on the coffee table. It was empty. My anger at her reared up again. I wasn't like her, no matter what she said.

As quietly as I could, I unlatched the front door and slipped outside. The landscape was cast in silver tones and I moved away from the house to see the moon shining down impossibly large, like I could climb right up onto it and sail away over the night.

A strong wind whistled low and steady over the land. It wrapped my nightshirt against my body and I could hear the creaking of a nearby sage plant as a gust of air slammed against the branches. Sand blew against the side of the barn with a sound like scratching claws.

I almost never came outside without my boots on. The

gravel was hard against the bottoms of my feet, but it wasn't unpleasant. Another flurry of wind blew my hair into my face, reminding me of the way my mom used to tousle my bangs when I was a kid. With both hands I smoothed my hair back over my head, enjoying the tickle of warm air as it slipped through the sleeves of my nightshirt.

The female ostriches ambled around the corral and the males sat on the nests. In the crowd of birds, I sought out the ones I knew by name: Theo, Upanova, Lady Lil. I was troubled by the way the female ostrich had stared at me the day before as Matt and I dug the graves for the three dead birds.

I reached through the corral fence to catch the beak of one of the hens and pulled at it playfully. She moved away, then circled back to peck at my hand while I tried to trap her beak again. Just like Grandma Helen used to do. Our game caught the attention of a couple of the other hens and they came over. The males joined in, their black feathers mixing with the pale brown ones of the females. I reached for each of them, wanting to share a touch with every ostrich in the corral. I stretched around and over the beaks I had already greeted. I felt like a rock star at a concert, grazing the hands of my adoring fans. Eventually, my arms grew tired. The birds dispersed. The females grouped up and the males made their way back to the nests.

As one of the males lowered himself to the sand, I caught a glimpse of something round and white beneath him. I ducked through the fence, holding my nightshirt so it didn't shift up around my waist in the wind, and hurried over to the nest. The male tilted his head as I approached.

I held out my hand, offering an imaginary treat, and he craned his neck to reach for it. He lumbered to his feet and I saw it: a perfect white egg, practically glowing in the moonlight. I led the bird a little farther, then pretended to throw the make-believe snack. It was enough to distract him. I rushed to the nest and grabbed the egg, taking in the reassuring weight of it in my hands. I held it up and inspected its strong, dusty curve in the moonlight. I rubbed it clean with the hem of my nightshirt and held it up again. It was perfect.

Bright beams cut the night, sweeping across the corral before settling in my direction. I pulled the egg close, surprised at the speed of the approaching car. It was careening up the drive, closing the distance from the highway at a reckless rate.

The headlights veered wildly. I saw the silhouettes of the ostriches and retreated instinctively as a truck plowed through the fence opposite from where I was standing. The metal wire screeched against the grille of the truck before breaking and springing away. Ostriches leaped out of the truck's path. Wings flashed in the night. A riotous cloud of sand lifted from the tires and I held my arm up to shield my eyes. My birds panicked, sprinting past one another in a flurry of feathers. It was Uncle Scott's black Silverado.

I crouched and almost dropped the precious egg, but feared the frantic birds would trample it. I clutched it to my chest and moved deeper into the corral. The flustered ostriches camouflaged me, but the shelter they provided thinned with each passing second as they found the break in the fence and sped away into the desert.

An upstairs light went on in the house. Uncle Scott pitched out of the truck. "Tallulah," he yelled. His back was to me. "Come on out here, you bitch." His bandaged hand hung at his side.

I didn't want to face him alone, barefoot in my nightshirt and clutching the delicate egg, but I couldn't let him go into the house. Aunt Christine and the girls were in there. I thought of baby Grace, so defenseless. "Over here," I said.

He spun around like a weather vane in a tornado, but he didn't spot me right off. He looked up to the house again, like he wasn't sure he had really heard me.

"Here," I said again and he turned. Behind him, up in the second floor of the house, another light went on.

Uncle Scott staggered toward me and as he cleared the glare of the headlights, his body became a silhouette, anchored by the red spot of a cigarette dangling from his lip. I saw the smoldering point of it bounce from side to side as his vision adjusted and he saw me. "What the fuck you doing out here?" His voice cut through the wind.

"I'm so sorry I hurt you."

"Little late for that," he said.

"I know. I'm sorry," I said again. "But you have to stop," my voice was pleading. "You killed my birds. And you could have killed Aunt Christine and the girls, cutting their brakes like that. This is crazy."

"No," he said. With his good hand, he reached to pull something from the back pocket of his jeans. The headlights behind him reflected off metal blades. A pair of garden clippers. "I'm seeing things real clear."

"Uncle Scott," I said. It had been a bad idea to try to reason with him. I stepped away. He followed. The red ember of his cigarette shifted in the darkness. There were maybe fifty yards between us.

I gave up talking and ran. The shotgun was in the barn. If I could get there a few seconds before Uncle Scott, I'd have time to load it. I hoped a warning shot would be enough to snap some sense into him. At the very least, Aunt Christine would know to stay inside and keep the girls safe.

I reached the far end of the corral and the floodlight over the barn door flashed on. I dropped the egg as I ducked through the fence, but it didn't fall far. I didn't have time to collect it. I was scrambling to right myself when I felt Uncle Scott's hand around my ankle and tripped.

I landed in the sand and saw his face in the harsh white light. His skin was pale. Stubble shaded his jawline. His eyes were sunken into slits. I kicked hard. My foot glanced off his chin but connected with his neck. His grip loosened enough for me to clamber away and keep running. I raced into the barn, grabbed the shotgun, and rushed to pull shells from the drawer of the workbench.

He hit me with the full force of his body and we both went down against a bale of hay. The gun slid from my grasp. I heard the shells scatter against the cement floor. His body pinned me. I managed to twist around and hit him in the jaw with my elbow, but he didn't even notice. I thrashed against him, my bare feet scraping uselessly against the cement floor. His bad hand hampered him a little, but he pressed his knee onto my wrist and immobilized my right arm.

The clippers passed over my face. I screamed and bucked, but he was stronger than I was. He moved with steady focus, his cigarette miraculously clinging to his lip. Then it dropped, landing on my face and burning my cheek.

The sharp blades of the clippers sliced through my pinkie finger. Pain exploded from my hand and my vision went dark around the edges. He adjusted to keep me pinned and repositioned his grip on the clippers. He wasn't finished. He wanted another finger. "No, no, no." I heard the pleading words fall out of me, felt tears stream down my face. "Please," I begged.

I strained against him with every bit of strength I had. I stretched my neck to try to bite him. But all my struggling amounted to nothing. He wedged the clipper blades against my ring finger. I braced for more pain, but instead heard a hollow thump and his weight shifted on top of me. His body went slack and he lurched to one side.

My mom crouched above us, a shovel held high. "Tallulah."

Panicked, I pulled my arm from under my uncle and scrambled to my feet. With my good hand, I held the stump of my pinkie in front of my heart. Blood oozed down my wrist, and a shiny smear covered the cement floor between me and where

Uncle Scott lay collapsed. Bits of straw were stuck in the mess, spelling out a message in some language I didn't understand. I spotted my severed finger in the bloody mess and plucked it from the floor.

"Oh my God," my mom said. "I thought . . ." She dropped the shovel with a clatter.

I realized what it must have looked like when she came running: my bare legs flailing from under a man who had me pinned.

In a flash of feathers, an ostrich ran past the barn under the floodlight. The wind whistled against the wooden frame of the barn.

"My birds." I wobbled toward the door, surprised at how unsteady I was on my feet. Only a handful of birds remained in the corral, pacing at the corners, distressed and unable to find the break in the fence. The rest had escaped, streaking across the desert like ghosts in the moonlight.

"Shit," my mom said, joining me at the door to take in the scene.

"I have to get them." But even as I said it, I knew it didn't make any sense. I was in no condition to wrangle ostriches, but I couldn't just watch them scatter to the winds.

"Fuck the birds. I'm calling an ambulance," my mom said, racing for the door.

My hand throbbed. A sharp pain lanced my cheek where Uncle Scott's cigarette had burned the skin. Dazed, I followed my mom toward the house, but a crackling pulled my attention back to the barn. Flames surged a few feet from where Uncle Scott lay unconscious.

"Mom! Help me!" I yelled.

We rushed to grab him by the feet and pull him over the threshold of the barn. In the bright floodlight, I could see an unnatural dent in the side of his skull. The flames in the barn grew, fanned by the wind that blew through the open doors, gaining purchase with every second.

Fighting a wave of nausea, I blundered forward into the barn. I ducked against the ferocious heat of the flames and grabbed the fire extinguisher from the far wall. Blood flowed freely from the stub of my finger and slid down my arm. I managed to yank the pin, but when I pressed the lever, nothing happened. "Damn it," I yelled, throwing the useless thing to the ground as the flames grew higher.

A bleating came from the corner of the barn. The goats. I fumbled to untie them and they trotted outside to join the rest of my animals in the wild of the night. I backed out of the barn to where my mom sat stooped over her brother, her hands cradling his face.

My knees weakened and I landed in the gravel, holding my injured hand close. Through the barn door, I watched the fire grow, replacing the shadows with orange light.

Aunt Christine came out onto the porch in her pajamas, brandishing a cast-iron pan. I could see the faces of my cousins pressed against the glass of the windows. "Call 9-1-1!" I yelled and she disappeared into the house.

The horizon in the east had lightened ever so slightly with the coming day, and against the denim sky, I could see the silhouettes of my birds scattered across the desert. A few still took long strides, but most had slowed. Some stood frozen in place. I counted ten birds inside the corral. Accounting for the three killed by Uncle Scott, that meant 129 birds loose in the desert. How would I ever get them all back in the corral?

My mom hovered over Uncle Scott's crumpled body. "I have to . . ." She seemed to consider her surroundings for the first time: the chaos of my birds, the fire, her brother, me. And without another word, she ran toward the house.

I tried to follow, but tripped on my nightshirt. My head throbbed and again my vision faded. The gravel of the driveway welcomed me as I fell forward. I heard the scrape of footsteps on gravel nearby and opened my eyes.

My mom kneeled over me with concerned murmurs, then stared out to the horizon at something I couldn't see. Behind her, the barn bloomed like a poppy in the fading night, all orange and red flames. The fire had burst through the roof and was jumping into the wind. An ostrich crossed my line of sight with a slow, even strut, like something out of a dream.

My mom's dreadlocks tickled my face as she leaned forward to kiss my forehead, like she used to when I was little. "I love you," I heard her say. And then everything went dark.

I woke on a stretcher in an ambulance, the fluorescent light blinding me. My mom was gone. My hand was wrapped in gauze and a red spot had formed in the white fabric over my pinkie finger. A bag of fluid hung from a metal hook, attached to an IV in my arm. They must have given me something, because I was aware of the pain, but it registered more like a blanket of uneasiness with a focal point vaguely centered on my hand.

The ambulance doors were open and I could see a fire engine parked at the end of the drive. The firemen waltzed around it, opening panels and pulling hoses without ever running into one another.

The fire roared through the roof on the north side of the barn, but the south end held strong. I could see the wild flames whirling in columns, reaching from under planks of scorched wood, ebbing and growing again in a cadence that matched the work of the firemen. The men and the flames danced together.

The north side of the barn caved in with a loud crack. The fire lost its rhythm and sent sparks flying into the night sky. The firemen braced against their hoses and the water flowed. I wondered where it was coming from.

How long had I been sitting there? Why were we not going to the hospital? I needed to get my finger back on. I snickered. It wasn't funny.

The sheriff's cruiser pulled into the frame of my window on the world. One side of the white car was lit orange by the intense glow of the fire, while the other held the crystal blue of early morning.

I could see Uncle Scott's body under the walnut tree. There were no EMTs, no gauze bandages or IVs. There was just one lone figure sitting cross-legged in the sand beside him and it wasn't my mom. It was Matt.

I remembered my mom's kiss, her voice saying she loved me. Where was she?

Matt came to his feet when two men with a gurney appeared. A slow-moving figure approached beside him. It was a man with the same build as Matt, his chin tucked to the right and his eyes cast down. Reuben.

One of the men with the gurney pulled a white blanket over Uncle Scott.

Matt's head hung low. He was crying. Reuben hesitated, then reached out and put his hand on Matt's shoulder.

Father and son stood together like that for a few seconds before Matt took half a step toward his father. I saw both men in profile, their faces so similar. Then Reuben pulled Matt close and wrapped his arms around him. Matt's fists curled against his father's back. His shoulders shook as he cried.

An EMT climbed into the ambulance, causing the whole thing to jostle disconcertingly. He slammed the door shut behind him. I closed my eyes and let the ambulance take me.

SIXTEEN

I woke to the astringent smell of disinfectant. The tidy sheets of a hospital bed were tucked in snugly around my legs and my hand was wrapped in clean gauze. I could hear bustling from behind the industrial blue curtain that hung close to my bed, suspended from a metal track. Then the fabric parted and Reuben appeared. The smell of coffee wafted from the cup in his hand. He smiled when he saw that I was awake.

I shifted, trying to sit up. Memories of my ostriches streaking across the open desert assaulted me like a bad dream. "My birds."

Reuben hurried to put his coffee on a short table beside my bed and helped me to a sitting position. "It's okay," he said.

"No," I said. "No, it's not. They were out. They were everywhere."

"Matt's dealing with that," he said. "He got a few buddies to help him fix the fence and they've been working all day to wrangle the birds back into the corral."

"No," I said again. They would get kicked if they didn't know what they were doing. They could be killed. I couldn't allow any more carnage. I needed to be there. I shifted again, but I was attached to the bed by a tangle of tubes and cords. I tried to extract myself, but the simple act of tracing a given tube away from my body proved befuddling. Exhaustion washed over me. "Buddies," I echoed, the word foreign in my mouth. I saw Matt standing over Uncle Scott, his body shuddering with sobs. "Uncle Scott is dead."

"Yes," Reuben said solemnly. "I'm sorry."

I had known it the night before, watching the scene through the doors of the ambulance, but saying it out loud made it real. I put my good hand to my cheek where his cigarette had burned me. Uncle Scott was gone. He would never attack me or the ranch again, never rain fear down over our family or come to take another of my fingers. I shuddered. The solace of knowing he couldn't hurt me anymore came hand-in-hand with overwhelming regret. Everything had gone so terribly wrong. I was grateful to my mom for saving me, but he hadn't deserved to die and she hadn't meant to kill him. "My mom?"

"We're not entirely sure where she is." Reuben recounted how he had come over to the ranch when he heard the sirens pass by his property and saw the fire in the distance. The firemen had managed to contain the blaze. Then there had been the ambulance. Sheriff Morris had shown up right as I was driven away. Reuben told me no one had been able to find my mom. In the chaos of the night, she had simply vanished.

"Your truck went missing too," he said. "But Sheriff Morris found it this afternoon in Victorville, near an on-ramp for the 15."

I could picture her, thumb out, heading north. Mexico was the obvious choice, but she couldn't handle the hot weather and didn't speak a lick of Spanish. She could disappear more easily into the woods of Northern California, drifting through a network of disgruntled hippies, living off the grid in the forests. I remembered her kissing my forehead as I lay in the driveway, bleeding. *I love you,* she had said. And then she was gone.

An attractive, confident man in a white coat came through the curtain, followed by a short nurse in pink scrubs. His badge said his name was Allan Stavros and he sported an impossibly bushy mustache. Reuben made room for the pair.

"Tallulah Jones," Dr. Stavros said, flipping the top page on a clipboard. The brown pelt that was his mustache bounced around as he spoke, distracting me. As he explained about delicate veins and tendons, I slowly came to understand that they had not, as I had assumed, sewn my severed finger into place.

"What do you mean? You didn't—" I heard the anger and disbelief rising in my voice. "How could you not sew it back on?" I demanded. That was his damn job. I was disfigured. For life.

Dr. Stavros remained perfectly calm in the face of my disbelief. "Let's take a look at what we've got here, shall we?"

I didn't want to see my hand with four fingers. It wasn't right. But as he gently rolled away the gauze, it was impossible not to look. All that was left was a short stub with the skin drawn up around it and sewn into place.

He examined the stitching. "The swelling will go down," he said. "I am very sorry we weren't able to reattach it."

I remembered Uncle Scott's weight pinning me to the floor of the barn, the blades of the clippers cutting my flesh. "Wrap it up," I said. As kind as he was, I didn't want Dr. Stavros turning my hand in his, trying to soothe me with his condolences. "Please."

I closed my eyes as he pulled a fresh roll of gauze from a drawer. I felt a length of it wrap around my palm. My breath caught in my throat. I would live the rest of my life with a little stub where my finger should be. I wondered how my mom's whiskey glass theory would deal with that reality. There was no avoiding the incomplete digit, no moving on or pretending things were different. It was a bullshit theory. The only way to really deal with anything was to look directly at it.

"Wait. Stop."

Dr. Stavros let go and the gauze unraveled. I lifted my hand and forced myself to inspect it closely. This was what was left of my finger. I touched it. I traced the bump of the lowest knuckle, the only remaining joint, and prodded the skin above it, being careful to avoid the stitches where the red stump came to a sudden and unnatural end. It was ugly, but the loss of my pinkie finger wouldn't affect my day-to-day life, not really.

I could see how, with time, I could even forget that a little part of me was missing. The longer I studied it, the more my distress over disfigurement sloughed off and tumbled away. All things considered, it wasn't so bad. Maybe it was the painkillers, but I suddenly felt grateful just to be alive. Finally, the doc insisted it was best to wrap it up to protect it from infection.

It was late afternoon when I rode home in the passenger seat of Reuben's tow truck. The painkillers Dr. Stavros had prescribed for me to take home made me groggy and the diesel fumes that permeated the truck gnawed at my sinuses. My bandaged hand hung in a sling. I dreaded what I would see when we got to the ranch. There would be no ignoring the reality that waited for me there. No whiskey glass theory would change the fact that my uncle had died and my barn had burned to the ground. My birds had scattered to the desert like butterflies in a hurricane. There was no running away from all that.

But what I saw as the truck pulled up to the house was a corral full of ostriches. Uncle Scott's pickup had been moved to the driveway. The fence was in perfect condition.

Near the house, Matt held his arms wide and approached a lone hen while three other men created a loose circle around her to keep her from bolting. The bird's head raised high and her wings flapped. She was not happy about being surrounded. She stepped back and I recognized Abigail's distinct limp.

I burst from Reuben's truck and ran toward Matt. "Wait," I called. Abigail took advantage of the distraction to bolt behind the house.

"Damn it," Matt said, his arms dropping. He met me in the driveway, followed by the other three men. "That one," he said, gesturing in the direction Abigail had run off. "That one's trouble."

"You got them all back?"

"All except that last one. We can't get her to cooperate."

I took in the scene of the corral and remembered the egg I had found the night before. I scanned the sand near the fence and spied it resting against one of the posts. It had survived the chaos of the night.

Ignoring everyone and everything else, I ducked through the fence and hurried to retrieve it, tucking it into my sling to keep it close. Then I pulled the lever on the feed silo and bent low to peer through the legs of the approaching birds. In almost every nest, I saw the distinct white curve of an eggshell.

"You did it," I said to one of the females as she came close for her food. I thought how proud Grandma Helen would be, then corrected myself. They were my ostriches now. They had laid the eggs on my ranch, for me.

I left the corral to take in the charred footprint of my barn, acutely aware that Reuben, Matt, and his friends were watching me. The south side had fared better than the north. Blackened posts reached up from the cement floor and a few burnt boards remained in place, but the north side was gone.

"I'm so sorry," Matt said, following me up onto the cement block of the foundation. I could see his remorse. "I told you he wouldn't come back, and I was wrong. If I hadn't . . . if I had gotten here sooner . . ."

"It's not your fault." Bits of charcoal crunched under my feet as I meandered around the ruined barn. In the rubble, I found the remains of the metal frame that had held the photo of Grandma Helen. The glass was broken, the image burned away. A beam from the ceiling had fallen across the incubators, shattering the glass fronts. The eggs inside were burned to a crisp. It was a mess. But over in the corral, my birds ambled about as if nothing had happened. I went over to where Matt stood wringing his hands. "You came back," I said. "You didn't have to, but you did. And you brought your friends. And you fixed everything."

"Not everything," he said, kicking at a splinter of wood.

"You took care of my birds."

Matt opened his mouth to respond, but it was Aunt Christine's voice that called out.

"Tallulah!" She burst from the front door. She beelined through the small group of Matt's friends and wrapped me in one of her maternal hugs. I was barely able to lift my injured hand out of the way to avoid it being crushed by her embrace.

"I'm okay," I said, patting her back with my good hand.

"I was so worried," she said, holding me like I was one of her girls.

Behind her, I saw a red Dodge Ram taking shape in the shimmering heat of the desert. I wasn't surprised to see Joe Jared. He had no doubt heard about the fire and come to see for himself what the damage was.

Aunt Christine's arms remained strong around me, like if she let me go, I might lose another finger. "I'm okay, really," I said. But only when she heard the approaching truck did her arms loosen. "I've gotta talk to Joe Jared," I said, squeezing my aunt one more time with my good arm.

"Tallulah," Joe Jared said, his voice booming as he climbed down from his truck. "What a mess." He took in the remains of the barn and whistled. "I hope you're insured."

It was the first I'd thought of it, but of course Grandma Helen had kept insurance on the ranch. There hadn't been time for me to miss a payment. How had so much happened in so few days? I adjusted my sling and waited to hear Joe Jared's winded explanation of why the deal was off. Behind me, I heard Aunt Christine invite Matt and his friends for dinner, insisting it was no trouble, that she was just warming trays of food from the freezer. The whole group of them followed her into the house.

Joe Jared strode over to the sooty footprint of what had been the barn. "I've got a contractor out of Vegas," his voice thundered. "I was already talking with him about the demo work on the house. This . . . situation may be a blessing in disguise in terms of upgrading the facilities." He walked slowly around the rubble of the foundation and returned to where I was waiting. "We're going to need to renegotiate our price I'm afraid."

"You mean you're still interested?" I heard the shock in my voice.

"Hell yes, I am. We had a deal. You've got one hundred forty-two prime pieces of meat here." He indicated the ostriches.

I flinched at his calling them meat, like they were just a collection of parts waiting to be butchered. "One hundred thirty-nine now." Given the context, he probably thought I lost the three birds in the fire, but I didn't feel the need to clarify.

"You've been through a lot." He looked at my bandaged hand. "So, hey. There's no rush on my end. Just call me when you're ready and we'll go over everything with the lawyers . . ."

I nodded, astonished that he was willing to move forward. But it was just business to him. He hadn't been attacked and maimed, hadn't witnessed a murder, hadn't had his mother disappear into the night. My world had been pulled to pieces, but to Joe Jared, the sum total of loss amounted to three birds and a barn he had intended to rebuild anyway. Life carried on.

"Hell of a thing," he said shaking his head and climbing back into his truck.

Inside the house, the girls sat cross-legged playing Go Fish with Aunt Christine nearby on the couch nursing baby Grace, a thin baby blanket draped over her shoulder for privacy. The smell of tomato sauce filled the house. In the kitchen, Reuben opened the oven and pulled out a tinfoil tray far enough to decide that whatever was cooking wasn't quite done yet and pushed it back in. He stirred a pot on the stove.

"Tallulah. Come, sit," Matt said. He and his buddies were at the kitchen table. The four of them had enough tattoos to decorate a whale, but despite their tough exteriors, they had easy smiles. One pulled out a chair for me. "Explain to us why that one bird won't go into the corral?"

I settled in to tell them how Abigail was more of a pet than part of the flock. Each of the men had a glass of water in hand, even though I knew the fridge had beers to offer. They were sober, all of them. I wondered if any of them had counted Uncle Scott as a friend.

One of the girls shifted her position on the floor and little Julie howled, clutching her finger in her fist. "She stepped on me!" she cried.

"I did not!"

Aunt Christine shifted to come to her feet, but then hesitated. If not for the men in the room, she might have marched over there, breast exposed, to suss out the situation, but modesty had her pinned.

"Let me see," I said, beckoning Julie over to me.

My cousin rushed over and held the injury up to my face. Tears sparkled in her eyes and her bottom lip stuck out. She gave a sniff. I took her hand gently in mine and examined it. There wasn't a mark on her, but with a face like that, I figured I should play along. "Does it need a Band-Aid?"

She whimpered. I scooped her into my arm and carried her

to the mudroom, plopping her down on top of the dryer next to the crate of license plates. "Let's see here," I said, fumbling with my good hand to pull a bandage from the cabinet and wrap the supposed wound.

"Better?"

"Uh-huh," she said with a smile, then hopped down and rejoined her sisters.

I slid in next to Aunt Christine on the couch to report that all was well. "Thanks for that," she said. The baby fussed and Aunt Christine adjusted. I let the currents of activity in the house flow around me. The girls argued and the cat darted behind the couch. The guys at the kitchen table laughed as they continued a ridiculous debate over the merits of facial hair. A warm, contented feeling washed over me. These were my people, even the ones I barely knew. They were the family and friends who cared. I thought about my mom, alone in the world, always searching for this very feeling. How lucky I was to find it right there in my house, on my ranch. The deal with Joe Jared seemed like a ticking bomb about to scatter it all to the wind.

"Todd's moving in with Megan," Aunt Christine said. I could hear the tension in her voice. "He's giving me the house."

I could hear the steady, rhythmic catch in Grace's breathing as she nursed. One of the girls took a pair of cards from her sister. Reuben pulled plates from the cabinet. Matt and his buddies set the table.

"What if you and the girls moved in here, for good?" I asked.

"What about Montana?" she asked, skeptical.

So much had happened in the past few days that it was difficult to say what exactly had changed how I felt about leaving. There were just flashes: fighting Uncle Scott, my mom running away, the relief of ending things with Devon, the subtle joy of seeing my cousins every time I came in the door, the anguish at the death of my birds, and the responsibility I now felt to protect them. Montana had been my way of choosing a path for myself, of doing something not just because it was expected of me but because I wanted to, and the truth was, I wanted to stay. "I changed my mind," I said.

She adjusted her clothing and moved Grace to her shoulder, where she patted the infant's back with a solid and repeating thud. "If you really mean it, I could sell the house in Victorville. We could use the money to add a few rooms here."

"Absolutely," I said. Aunt Christine would make the house comfortable in a way I never could. She would be like one of my hens, arranging the sand around her to create a nest, but for my aunt, it would be new curtains and updated kitchen appliances.

I would happily hand over the house to her and focus on the work around the ranch. I would have my hands full through the off-season rebuilding the barn. In some ways, it was an opportunity to start fresh while staying put. We could remake our lives in whatever way we wanted. We would have the whole Jones family under one roof. Almost.

"Did my mom tell you she was leaving? Did she say goodbye?"

"No. I think she followed me into the house, but I was on the phone with 9-1-1, and then, well, the girls were pretty scared. I was just focused on them. I didn't notice until later that her things were gone."

I remembered the crash of Uncle Scott's truck, my screams, the chaos of the ostriches running free. It must have been pretty frightening for a mother with six little ones to protect. The silence drew out between us and I knew she was thinking about her brother.

"Do we have a funeral for him?" I asked.

She sighed. "It's important. It doesn't have to happen right away, but at some point, we have to mark his passing and ask God to accept him. I'll take care of it when the time comes."

Reuben announced that dinner was ready. We didn't all fit at the table, so Matt and his friends took their plates out to the wicker chairs on the porch, leaving the door open. The sun had set and the heat of the day was fading. Friendly voices filled the house. I let go of my fork and just sat there, reveling in the fact that all these people were here because of me. And I was staying. I was overwhelmed with satisfaction. I was also exhausted and the pain medicine was wearing off. My hand throbbed in its sling.

I took a few bites, chased them with a heavy dose of ibuprofen, and excused myself, insisting that they not end the evening on account of my going to bed but that I really needed to lie down. I hugged every one of them, despite only having one good arm. I even pressed my cheek to the baby's and gave her a kiss on her tiny nose.

Walking up the stairs, I thought of my mom. I pictured her hitchhiking her way north. She would be okay, I knew, because she was always okay, because she trusted in the fact that one thing would lead to another and deliver her to somewhere better. Her whiskey glass theory in action. It worked for her, I guessed.

Growing up with an alcoholic dad and a distant mom, Aunt Christine had embraced God and Uncle Scott had lost himself in drugs, but my mom learned to trust that moving forward would save her. One step leads to the next. One idea connects to another. There was nowhere she couldn't go.

But I was staying.

I marveled at that again as I struggled to brush my teeth with my left hand. I was staying. Grandma Helen had gotten what she wanted and so had I. I'd made a choice. The ranch was mine. I would have to tell Joe Jared the deal was off. And call the Forest Service to decline the position they'd offered me. And I would need to hire help, at least for the summer months, and whoever I hired, I would insist they stay for dinner once in a while.

Drifting off to sleep, I heard the sounds of people downstairs: chairs scraping against the kitchen floor, the faucet running, the clank of plates being washed, and the muffled voices of people who cared about me. The gentle noises wove themselves into a blanket around me and I drifted off to sleep.

SEVENTEEN

The throbbing in my hand woke me just after dawn. Opening my eyes, I noticed one of the license plates from Grandma Helen's collection propped against the wall next to the door. I had walked past it on my way in the night before, but from the vantage point of my bed it was hard to miss, all blue metal with yellow lettering: BCINGU. I picked it up and flipped it over, but there was nothing written on the back, no indication of how it came to be in my room. I set it on the dresser.

Downstairs, I found the ibuprofen where I'd left the bottle on top of the refrigerator, cap askew. I knew the prescription pills the doc had given me were stronger, but I felt the need to keep a clear head. I'd stick with the over-the-counter meds as long as the pain was manageable. The capsules rattled as I shook a few out.

BCINGU. *Be seeing you.* The phrase held such optimism. The yellow letters flashed before me again, a message from my mom. It was her way of saying goodbye. *Be seeing you.* I wouldn't hold my breath, but if she ever did come back, I'd be here. The ranch and the birds and Aunt Christine and the girls. We would all be here and she would always be welcome.

I crossed to the urn on the bookshelf. My right hand throbbed and I knew I should put the sling on to keep it elevated, but I needed to do something first.

Stepping outside, I was greeted by a wild bloom of desert marigolds. I'd never seen anything like it. I stopped in my tracks, amazed at the sight. The rains from the day of Grandma Helen's funeral had caused a thousand unseen seeds to germinate and given rise to as many tiny yellow flowers. They poured out across the land. Gold splashed along the crevices between the hills and flowed down the wide valley in the same path the water had taken during the storm. It looked like the earth itself was glowing.

I walked out past our property line into the surrounding desert, holding the urn with Grandma Helen's ashes close. I traced a winding path around the bushy plants, the flowers brushing up against my ankles. The sun was still low and its light hit the plants from the side, casting extended shadows that made the flowers appear even brighter by contrast. A gentle wind swept through and the petals fluttered. My feet were planted there among the wildflowers and the sun warmed my body. That was something I could trust. The sun would always rise and rainy days, no matter how dreary, would always bring the desert marigolds.

A shadow fell cool across my face. It was Abigail. "Morning, girl," I said, resting my free hand on her downy shoulder. We walked side by side toward the corral. The crunch of our footsteps carried over the sand. The latch of the gate clanked as I opened it. Normally, that was Abigail's cue to saunter off to somewhere else, but she stayed and followed me inside the fence. The rest of the flock stared at us, unusually calm. I passed a nest with an egg in it. Then another. Glancing around, I saw that every nest held an egg, bright and round against the sand.

I lifted the lid of the urn and tipped it. Gray flecks of ash fluttered to the ground. One of my birds came close to inspect the area and touched her downy cheek to where the ashes had fallen. I gave her some space and tipped the urn again.

I lost track of Abigail as one by one the birds gathered. I scattered Grandma Helen's remains bit by bit, and as I passed each bird, they lay down their heads, nuzzling the nearly imperceptible trail.

"Goodbye, Grandma Helen," I whispered to the sky. I stared up at the clear blue and let my heart ache.

I would never know the truth of what had happened that day on the highway—if she had chosen to leave or if it had truly been an accident. She was gone. That was all I could ever really know for sure.

One by one, my birds lifted their beaks to the sky. We rested together in a silent vigil, missing the woman who had brought us all together and made our lives worth saving. She had loved us as best she could.

"I miss you."

As my words floated away, a tall, male bird on my right let out a low whoop. Another joined him, and a chorus rose from the ostriches. It grew louder and louder until I could feel the deep vibrations of it rolling over the desert.

I fell to my knees in the fine sand. A few of the birds nestled there with me and lay their cheeks on the last stretch of land where I had spread the ashes. More came to rest, laying their necks across the backs of the first, as if consoling them. Soon the center of the corral was covered with intertwined ostriches. But one still reached her beak into the air, letting out the deepest of whoops, like the end of a sob. Finally, she too settled down. Quiet returned to the ranch. The sun rose higher and I felt the velvety rays on my cheek. My birds raised their heads. We sat together and watched a new day begin.

Thank you for reading *142 Ostriches.* Please consider leaving a review at amazon.com/author/aprildavila and visit http://aprildavila.com for updates on the author's upcoming second novel, an epic love story spanning two hundred years of California's history.

Acknowledgments

I am so grateful for the multitude of professionals who have brought this book into the world, but before a single page was read by any of them my husband, Daniel, was cheering me on.

Thank you, Daniel, my love, for ten years of encouragement with this story. Thank you for every 5 a.m. whisper of "write like the wind" as I trudged for the coffeepot. Thank you for taking care of the kids so I could attend writing conferences and for not minding when I missed our anniversary (twice) because I was at a writing retreat. Thank you for your thoughtful notes and insights. This book simply would not exist if not for you.

Many thanks to my agents, Joel Gotler and Murray Weiss. Your enthusiasm and expertise have not only seen this book through to print, but also encouraged me to keep writing.

And to the team at Kensington Books, thank you. I will never forget the experience of meeting you all at the New York office. An author really can never hear the phrase "we loved your book" too many times. You guys are awesome. Special thanks to my editor, John Scognamiglio, and the head of my marketing team, Vida Engstrand.

Thank you, Celeste, my ferocious reader, for reminding me every day what it means to truly love books. And to Sebastian, my writing buddy, for crawling into my lap every morning and insisting on helping. I love you both more than words can say.

Every struthious detail of this book owes a debt of gratitude to Doug Osborne, who quit his job as a stockbroker in 1992 to become an ostrich rancher without any experience or know-how. He was a kind man, who spent days sharing the details of his business with me. I regret that he died on July 23, 2012, long before I ever finished a draft.

To Amy Meyerson, Corey Madden, Lynn Elias, Alexandra D'Italia, and Erin La Rosa, thank you for your feedback on early drafts and for the many glasses of wine poured between us. I am honored to have you all in my corner.

To all the teachers who have guided me along the way: Gina Nahai, Janet Fitch, Mark Sarvas, Rita Williams, and Rick Moody. Thank you. Each of you, in your own way, helped shape me as a writer, and for that I am so appreciative.

Thank you to my extended family: Michele Collier, Summer Bradley, Bill Collier, Cassie Gruenstein, Juan Dávila, Liz Dávila, Cathy Parent, and Catherine Dávila. Each of you played a role by reading drafts, making space for my writing, and never letting me quit.

Thanks to Joel Page for his thoughts on the legal repercussions of accidentally shooting one's uncle.

For so many different reasons, additional thanks go out to Tessa White, Joy Johannessen, Katie Poole, Betty Sargent, Eric Brach, PT McNiff, Brian McGackin, Tom Barbash, Lisa See, Lindsey Lee Johnson, Edan Lepucki, and all the desert-loving Nappies.

The final draft of this book was completed during my time as a resident at the Dorland Arts Colony in Temecula. Thank you to Janice Cipriani-Willis and the whole team there for giving me the space to get this book across the finish line.

And finally, thank you to Mrs. Lehman, my AP English teacher at Montgomery High School, the best writing teacher I ever had, and from whom I stole the idea of the whiskey glass theory. She called it the Birthday Cake Theory. I hope she will forgive me for making it my own.

A READING GROUP GUIDE

142 OSTRICHES

April Dávila

ABOUT THIS GUIDE

The suggested questions are included to enhance your group's reading of April Dávila's *142 Ostriches*.

DISCUSSION QUESTIONS

1. Consider the men in this story. What role do they play in a family that is predominantly female? Are they, as Grandma Helen suggests, untrustworthy? Do you agree with Annie's assertion that we all need partners in life?

2. How has substance abuse affected each generation of the Jones family? Why do you think Aunt Christine has not turned to alcohol or drugs? What role, if any, do you think Aunt Christine's faith plays in her choices?

3. Aunt Christine suggests that the birds have stopped laying eggs because they miss Grandma Helen. Given the fact that there is nothing physically wrong with the ostriches, do you believe that their temporary barrenness is due to emotional upset? If so, what helps them deal with their grief and begin producing eggs again?

4. Is Tallulah an honest person? Honest with herself? Honest with others? After being arrested, Tallulah resolves to face her problems head-on, yet she struggles to be forthright in all of her interactions. What do you make of her tendency to hide from reality? Is it something you can relate to in your own life?

5. One of the main themes of the story is motherhood. Consider how Tallulah's mom, Aunt Christine, and Grandma Helen differ in their mothering styles. What is your opinion of Grandma Helen's assertion that you don't have to be close to someone to love them?

6. The judge at Tallulah's arraignment is easily convinced that she is an upstanding citizen. Why does this come as such a surprise to Tallulah? Is Tallulah a good person?

7. In what ways does the desert define Sombra? How is Sombra like other small towns? In what ways is it different? In what ways does the desert environment determine the outcome of this story?

8. How would the story change if it were set on a different type of ranch? A cattle ranch? Chickens?

9. How would the story be different if it were told from Uncle Scott's perspective? What about Aunt Christine's perspective? What if Matt were our narrator?

10. What is the difference between faith and trust in this story? How would Aunt Christine answer this question? Or Tallulah? How does Laura's whiskey glass theory distinguish between faith and trust? Is her theory useful?